Who Would Have Thought

Barbara Mostella

Visit the author's website at www.barbaraMO08.com.
Publisher: Stanton Publishing House
Library of Congress Registration Number: 2018955557
ISBN: 9781719828376 (KDP Amazon)
ISBN: 9781987021462 (Barnes & Noble)
Printed in the United States of America
Cover & Interior Design by Stanton Publishing House

DEDICATION

THIS BOOK IS IN DEDICATION TO MY PARENTS GRADY AND RUTHIE ELIZABETH MOSTELLA. THEY ARE NO LONGER WITH US. AS I HAVE KNOWN FOR MANY YEARS, THEY SACRIFICED A LOT FOR ME IN THE SMALL TOWN WHERE I GREW UP. THIS BOOK IS ONE OF MY TESTIMONIES, TO LET THEM KNOW ALL THEY SACRIFICED FOR ME GROWING UP WAS NOT IN VAIN. THE ADVICE THEY GAVE TO ME AT AN EARLY AGE, WAS THAT MANY OPPORTUNITIES WOULD BE OPEN TO ME, BUT NEVER WALK IN ANY DOOR, UNLESS I KNOW GOD HAS LED ME TO IT. WE DON'T ALWAYS CELEBRATE OUR PARENTS AS WE SHOULD, SO IF YOURS ARE LIVING TELL THEM HOW MUCH YOU LOVE THEM.

TABLE OF CONTENTS

ACKNOWLEDGMENTS

I give thanks, honor, and praise to God for the wisdom and knowledge to know when to complete this book.

A special thank you for the encouragement from my loving husband, James. He has been my number one supporter, and friend throughout this journey. You encouraged me to write no matter what was going on, even those times when I would have writer's block. You introduced me to Stanton Publishing House Book Boot Camp, and I will be forever grateful. The boot camp was my confirmation. This is my first manuscript, and you walked every step with me to completion. May God continue to bless you in every area of your life.

Thank you to all my family members, for just being family. Sometimes you just need family to be family.

To my best friends Minister Felicia Matthews and Terrie Welch, I thank God for both of you. You have been supportive of me for over 20 years. I hope in some small way, I have been as much a friend to you, as you have been to me.

God has positioned some wonderful people in my path, as I have gone through this spiritual journey, we call life. These people have encouraged me in many forms of communications. They have included prayers of confirmation, phone calls reaping with joy and jubilance, the promotion of excellence and leadership, texts just to say hello, unexpected emails and Facebook posts that give you that extra boost or smile. These reinforcements came from these wonderful and caring friends: David & Marian Hoskin, Ray & Dorothy Rankins, William & Yvonne Adams, Rev Eldridge & Patricia Lee, and Betty Jackson.

I was blessed to attend Stanton Publishing House Book Boot Camp. This was educational, enlightening and fun. This camp was confirmation and the final steps in this process to bring my dream to reality.

CHAPTER 1

FAMILY, DEATH, AND FRIENDS

IT had been three years since the mysterious death of Violet's husband Daniel, with no real evidence or suspects from the Washington DC. police department. The only conclusion they gave was he had committed suicide. His wife Violet came to the realization she would never know what happen to him, and with little hope, she accepted that.

Daniel was a good husband, father, and provider. Violet and their children always had what they needed. She and Daniel were both native Alaskans from a small unincorporated town called Delta Junction. Violet continued to live in the Delta after Daniels death because it is where they shared history and family memories.

Before his death, they discussed moving to Fairbanks or closer to their children in Atlanta or Washington DC. Fairbanks was only a hundred miles away from Delta Junction, but they both seemed to really like it. Fairbanks was a lot like Atlanta and DC. They have public transportation, shopping centers. They also had plenty of entertainment and a variety of restaurants.

We used to travel as a family to Fairbanks every two months, get a hotel and stay overnight. It was a mini vacation for the children. For me, it was like a honeymoon with Daniel, because he traveled so much without the family for his company Q'UP that he was employed by. The other reason we travel to Fairbanks was to go to a foods store called Whole Foods. They carried unique health foods and other products we could not find in the Delta.

The last stop for us while in Fairbanks, was the Mall. My daughter Kathleen and I would go in one direction, Daniel and Landon in another. I would buy myself a new pair of jeans each time. My daughter Kathleen called me jeans junky. Since Daniel was not at home that often, I did not do a lot of dressing up, so jeans were my favorite choice of clothing no matter what the occasion. I could dress them up and be a diva or dress them down and still turn heads as my husband would say. On our way back home from Fairbanks, we would also drive by this condominium community called The Hillside View. Daniel and I thought this would be the perfect retirement place for us.

Both of our parents were born, raised, became entrepreneurs, and died in the Delta. Daniel loved traveling quite the opposite of his father, John. He owned J&C painting with three employees and was home each day by three p.m. to have dinner with his family in the evening. John's wife Cora had a successful home-based baking business before they married. Almost all weddings in the Delta contracted with her for wedding cakes.

My parents Rodney and Jessica were owners of RJ Construction for building and selling single-family homes, apartments, and condominiums. Both of our families were close. My father contracted with Daniel's father to paint the inside of his building structures.

I fell in love with Daniel at one of my father's New Year's Eve dinner parties. He was a meticulous dresser, had a pleasant smile, and seem to have such a caring disposition that everyone wanted to talk to him to include me. I kept looking at him throughout the dinner party until he noticed and finally came over to speak to me. At first, I could not get any words out, but he made me feel comfortable. Then we started an excellent dialogue. Daniel asked for my phone number that same evening. After a year and a half of dating and getting to know each other, he and I got married. We had two beautiful children that I am so proud of.

My father passed within six months after our wedding of prostate cancer. Shortly after my father died, my mother had a massive heart attack and died. I am so thankful I had Daniel to help me get through the loss of my parents because I was an only child. We were able to find a buyer for my dad's construction company fairly quickly. Not long after we finished with my parents' estate, Daniel's parents were in a fatal car accident hit by a drunk driver and killed them both.

So here we are both suffering and hurting together over the loss of our parents. Daniel stayed home for a month after our parents died so he and his brother Johnny could take care of their parent's affairs. Like my parents, they had laid things out in their will, what they wished, so it made it easy for Daniel and his brother to handle things. Daniel was employed as a Quality Control Specialist with a company named Q'UP that shipped, inspected, and evaluated products international. He did not usually talk about his work when he was home. I did overhear one of his conversations with someone at the Pentagon. They were referencing a company called AllTuck and some type of bad software. It sounded like someone was doing something wrong on a military installation.

For more years than I can count, Daniel did a lot of traveling, and I stayed at home with the children. I missed our Friday date night out at Pizza Bella even though the kids were with us. The kids loved pizza, and Daniel loved the deer burgers. Since Landon and Kathleen moved away, I only go there maybe twice a year now. Over the past couple of years, I have developed a taste for Asian food, so my Friday nights are spent at Hard Wok Café in the Delta. Since Daniels Death, I have become best friends with a Cheechako to Delta Junction named Madison. Cheechako is the name given to someone who is new to Alaska. Everyone knows when there is a newcomer in town. Madison does not talk much about her past life before moving to the Delta. It makes you wonder if she has something to hide. I guess even close friends don't always tell everything.

Madison is a beautiful lady with long brown hair and a body that is so shapely it makes you stop and take a second look whether you were a man or woman if you passed by her. One of the things she and I have in common is jeans. You could tell over the years that she has been doing some smart things like exercising and eating healthy. I wonder why she does not have a man in her life, being as smart and beautiful as she is.

Madison's lives with her mother whose name is Jamel in the Delta. Her second husband Cooper died of pancreatic cancer around the same time my husband died. Don't know anything about her mother's first husband Sam, who is Madison biological father. I just know that Madison wished she had a closer relationship with him. Jamel had multiple strokes, and the last one was so devastating that she did not recover enough to walk after rehabilitation.

There is limited long-term and in-home care facilities and services in Delta Junction. Madison moved from Atlanta to take care of her. Parents and seniors are living a lot longer today, and so children must either bring their parents to their homes or go live with the parent to keep them in familiar surroundings. I hope never to be a burden on my children. Parents don't want payback for raising their children. They just want them to grow up and be responsible adults. Madison's mother is also a good-looking woman at her age of eighty-five. She is a petite size six. Before the stroke, Jamel kept her nails manicured and feet pedicured and made frequent visits to her favorite beautician Lisa. Since Jamel has become ill, Lisa always made time for her. She comes to her home and does her hair every two weeks at no charge.

Lisa's salon is called You Decide, and she has a clientele of about 60 women. It is a diverse salon and anything you wanted to know about the community just go to You Decide. It is the news capital for gossip in the city. The salon is very upscale in the décor and the way the beauticians dressed and greeted you. No client waited more than 30 minutes for their service. Lisa felt like everyone's time is valuable and is very reasonable in her pricing.

Before now, Madison had not visited her mother often since her second marriage to Cooper. Cooper loved her mother as much or more as her biological father Sam according to Madison and was a good stepfather. Her mother can only be left alone for a short length of time. This is the time Madison would go to a local restaurant called Nooks that she had found since moving to the Delta for breakfast. This is also the place where Violet and I met.

I know what it is like having your children live far away. My son Landon resides in Washington DC and my daughter Kathleen lives in Atlanta. Violet thought it time to visit them and start traveling some herself.

Violet and Madison were scheduled to meet this morning for breakfast at Nooks. This place has a southern and northern mix of food. Anyone could be satisfied when they dined there. It was on the list of small towns well-known restaurants to visit as a tourist in Alaska. "Mother I am getting ready to go meet Violet for breakfast at Nooks. I should be back to start with your exercise within two hours.

That should give you enough time to take a short nap and digest your breakfast. Your cell phone is lying on the pillow beside you. If you should need anything, please call," said Madison.

"Madison honey, you go and enjoy your time with Violet. Tell her I said hello," said Jamel.

Nooks breakfast is the main meal of the day, and it closes at two p.m. Their breakfast gets you started in the morning and wakes up anyone that tries to sleep later than seven-thirty. I believe most great decisions are made in the morning and most people that are trying to interpret them do not fully understand them because they are looking at decisions made in the morning at night.

"Violet I woke up at five a.m. this morning to bathe mother, then I dressed her, and fixed her breakfast. She likes breakfast at six-thirty and then she sleeps until around nine-thirty a.m. So around ten a.m. she and I start a little exercise routine." Madison said proudly. "Mother said to tell you hello."

"That's great. You have a wonderful mother. Cherish every moment. Let's eat so I can make some great mind decisions today." Violet responded with a warm smile. "Guess what Madison, I am going to Washington DC and Atlanta Georgia for a two-week trip to spend time with my children."

"That is good news, Violet. It is time you get out of this small town and start to live your life. I know your husband Daniel would want you to."

"I've always wanted to see the Washington Monument and walk inside the White House where the president and his family lives. I also want to see the United State Capitol in person. Where the US Congress make the laws that affect us all, whether they are good or bad." Violet rambled on and on. "Going to hot Atlanta has always been a dream of mine, home of the braves and the land of the free. The home of civil rights leader and noble peace prize recipient Rev. Dr. Martin Luther King, Jr. to see Stone Mountain and go to The Varsity and eat a hotdog."

"So many movie actors and actresses, musicians, and all types of professional people live there. According to some of my research, many producers have built movie studios and are now making and producing movies at a much lower cost in the area as compared to other states such as California and New York."

"I cannot wait to eat at some of those well-known restaurants, go to malls and do some real shopping. Who knows I may come back with a makeover from head to toe, and you won't even be able to recognize me! Having lived in this small town all my life, I am ready to venture out and see what else the world has to offer."

Madison appeared to be in a daze for a moment and was thinking to herself that it might be good for her to go back to DC. I need to ensure that no loose ends have come up about Violet's husband's death and to contact Elliott to see if he is still in Atlanta. I have not talked to him for over a year now. Violet was also thinking to herself. Why did Madison say she knew what my husband wanted me to do as for as traveling?

"Are you okay Madison? You seem to be in somewhat of a cloud this morning. Is everything okay with your mother?" Violet asked out of concern.

"Yes, everything is okay. I am envious of you but glad you have decided to adventure out from the Delta. You know I spent a lot of time in both cities. I could probably give you some good tourist information about the best places to shop and eat. But your son and daughter live in those places, so I am sure they have an excellent knowledge of where to take you. If my mother did not require twenty-four hour seven days a week in home care, my bags would be packed, and I would travel along with you," said Madison.

Before they could finish their conversation, Rowena, the waitress who knows both very well called them by name when she came to take their order. "Good morning Madison and Violet. Two of my favorite customers whom I can always count on to leave a good tip and the latest gossip. Can I serve you your usual or are you ladies going to surprise me and order something different today?" Asked Rowena.

"I'll just have my usual. Don't know about Violet, she is talking about going east and finding a man. She may be having something different today," Madison said jokingly. Since Madison is from back east, she had not been in Alaska long enough to get used to eating the deer sausage. So, she ordered her usual grilled vegetables, tomato, basil & goat cheese frittata with Alaskan seasonal fruit and coffee.

"We both look forward to coming here every week because of the special treatment we get from you Rowena," Violet told her with a warm smile. "You just be quiet Madison, I am only going to visit my children. Just taking a break and getting away from these dark, cold, snowy days. Being adventurous has been on my radar today, so I am going to order something different."

Violet usually ordered deer sausage, one soft scrambled egg, and a short stack of blueberry pancakes, cappuccino, and water. So many people who are not native Alaskan often think that reindeer originated in Alaska, but they were brought to Alaska from Siberia in 1800. Today I am ordering more of an eastern style breakfast. "Rowena, I will have the rise and shine breakfast." The rise and shine which consisted of smoked Alaskan salmon, cream cheese, sweet onion, capers, & tomato on a toasted bagel with a latte, and water.

Rowena took their orders, and they were both ready in about fifteen minutes. Rowena's day was a great one to serve them because they always left a generous tip, unlike some of the other customers that frequented the Nooks. They finished their breakfast and departed their separate ways by walking back home.

Delta Junction population is less than a thousand people. Therefore, you can almost walk everywhere, except on those days when it is exceptionally cold or dark. Currently, no local public transportation is in place for the residents. Today was a sunny day with just a little chill in the air, good for walking and just clearing your head of whatever had been clouding it all week. The seasons are so different in Alaska as compared to the rest of the country.

The summer months from June to August are called solstice where you have daylight for twenty-four hours a day. September is normally the Fall month and a lot of tourist visit. Spring is when the snow starts to melt down from March to May. November to January are the usual months that you would get twenty-hours of darkness. December to February are winter months.

The overall crime rate here is low, so you feel safe walking or driving to your destinations. Everyone in the Delta knew Violet and Daniel. As she walked home from Nooks, she passed many of the local store owners and was greeted by them all. When Violet arrived home, she phoned both her children and they let her know dates for her visit had been coordinated. She called the local travel office in the town and confirmed that her reservation tickets with Delta Airlines had been completed. It was called in by her son.

"Hello Briana, this is Violet, just checking on my reservations."
"Everything is ready for you to pick up, come in anytime," said Briana.

"Okay, I will be their around four p.m. this afternoon." "We will be waiting for you," Briana confirmed.

Violet decided to cook a little dinner before going into the travel office. It will be ready and waiting upon her return.

Violet got into her Toyota and drove to the travel office. She walked in fifteen minutes early, and they had two other customers waiting to be seen. "Hello Ms. Violet, it is so good to see you. We will be with you in a few minutes. We are running a little behind today," said Briana.

"I am okay, take your time," said Violet.

The travel office was a small office with only two employees Elizabeth and Briana. They were two locals from the Delta Junction area. Their business name and logo were "Travel Your Way." The office was decorated with the logo colors two shades of blue and silver. Live green plants were strategically placed throughout the office. You felt the energy and ready to travel when you walked in the door.

My husband used to coordinate his travel plans with them. Except for the last trip he made before his death. It was organized by someone else, and I did not understand it. As I am starting to complete my travel plans many things are beginning to resurface in my mind about my husband's death. This office did not provide transportation to and from the airport but would start to have shuttle service two months after my dates of travel. I will have to rely on my own transportation for this trip.

"Ms. Violet you can come on into my office," said Briana. "Just need you to sign your name that you received the tickets and you will be out of here."

"Thank you, Briana. You ladies are getting a lot of business," said Violet.

"Yes, we are, thanks to some additional advertising we have been doing and good customers like you and your deceased husband." "We do miss him, and I am sure that you do as well. How long were the two of you married?"

"We were happily married for thirty-five years." Violet expressed with a smile on her face.

"Here are your tickets. We have enclosed our office contact information in case you have any problems. You have a wonderful trip, and I look forward to meeting your children someday."

"They are both busy with their jobs and do not get a chance to come home often. I will not continue chatting because you have customers waiting. Thank you and Elizabeth for making this so easy for me."

"Come to visit us when you return, we would love to hear about your trip."

Violet-headed back home in her Toyota Camry. I guess I need to start thinking about some new transportation. I have had this Toyota for over ten years. It is starting to cost me a lot for maintenance. This was a birthday present from Daniel.

Violet had made a fire in the fireplace before leaving for the travel office, so it was nice and cozy when she walked into the house. It was now five p.m., so she had an early dinner and decided to sit near the fireplace and enjoy it for a while. For a moment while sitting by the fire, she thought about her husband. Daniel's brother Johnny always suspected that the family was not told the truth about what happened to him. I suspect he was having an affair.

During his last year of travel, he always had problems with his cell phone and contacting me while in his hotel. I suggested that he purchase a new one, and he did not think that would solve the problem.

Statistics and surveys show that women are the last to know, but I beg the difference. I say the wives and significant others are the first to know. Because we know their daily routines and habits more than anyone else. Men typically change their routines without realizing it when having an affair.

I have wondered several times if Madison met my husband while she was living in DC and working at the Pentagon. Maybe not, otherwise she would have said something by now. Sometimes she makes comments, that makes me think she knew him well. However,

I am not going to let that speculation ruin my thoughts about seeing my children, and the excitement of traveling.

CHAPTER 2

THE CASE REOPENED

THE law firm of Soco & Soco has offices in Alaska, Washington DC. and Atlanta, started by four brothers to investigate mostly high crimes and government-related cases. Jason and Jermaine run the Alaska office, Darnell the Washington DC office, and Jacoby runs the Atlanta office. Whenever the four brothers are together, they are known as the striking four, because every case they defend they attack them with extraordinary evidence to win. Neither one has ever lost a case.

Alphonso is their best investigator in the Alaska Office and has been called in for a meeting with Jason and Jermaine on a Sunday afternoon concerning a three-year-old Washington DC case. This case was brought to the firm by Johnny, the brother of a deceased native Alaskan named Daniel who lived in Delta Junction.

Alphonso did not get much time to socialize with the opposite sex because he devoted an enormous number of hours to the firm. He is a very serious, dedicated investigator and the best among the five other investigators in the firm. Not only is he paid the highest salary of the other five but is also well known throughout the USA. "Alphonso, we need you to take a trip to our Washington DC and Atlanta offices of Soco & Soco for a high-profile government case that has not been solved. It is a cold case file, but new evidence has been brought forward. It involves the death of a native Alaskan from Delta Junction who was a quality control specialist/investigator. He worked for a company called Q'UP. This case will require several investigators, with you as the lead," said Jason.

"It turns out that Daniel was an investigator for the legal department of Q'UP instead of a quality control manager. We also need you to visit the Pentagon and contact special agent Narvell, to get some detail information on this case. You will need to travel on Monday, and Mr. Narvell is expecting you at eight a.m., on Tuesday morning," explained Jason.

"The firm's office manager Joan has made airline and hotel arrangements for you. All you have to do is pack a bag," Jermaine said laughing.

"What am I looking for in this case? Are their contacts?" Asked Alphonso.

"All this will be revealed to you on your visit to the Pentagon. I have also left some background information with Joan for you. This case is three years old, and the victim's brother Johnny never believed the authorities gave them the truth. This was and still is a high-profile case. Some important people could lose their jobs and big money because of it."

"The death of this native Alaskan was very mysterious. The initial cause of death listed by the Washington DC Police department was suicide with a gun. New information has been brought forward involving a woman Daniel was having an affair with. We suspect she now lives in Alaska," stated Jason.

"If she lives in Alaska, why am I going to Washington DC?" Asked Alphonso.

"You will be talking to her past and present supervisors. Narvell was her supervisor at the Pentagon and Matthew is her supervisor in Atlanta. The historical records concerning this case reside with an investigator in Washington. The details will be revealed to you on your visit to the Pentagon. The deceased was an investigator like yourself." Jason explained further.

"You have to also go to Atlanta because the last two locations that the deceased were seen was Washington and Atlanta."

"If I find that special lady on this trip, I may be gone more than two weeks," said Alphonso.

"How many times before have you said that. We hope you get lucky this time. You are getting to be an old man," said Jason, while he and Jermaine were laughing.

"I will see you when I get back," said Alphonso.

Alphonso left the meeting and stopped by Joan's office. She makes the job administratively very easy because of her proficiency and organizational skills. I believe her husband Aaron and her two sons, Amiel and Asa are thrilled to be in her life. Whatever the firm is paying her I think they need to pay her a lot more. "Good afternoon, Joan, how are you doing on this wonderful Sunday?"

"Hi, Alphonso I am doing great. It seems as though you are headed for another long trip."

"Yes, you are right. This time I am going to get lucky and find that special lady on my own since you will not introduce me to any of your friends."

"I do not have any friends that you would be interested in." "How do you know?"

"I have been working with you for over ten years now. I believe I have a good idea of the type of person you are looking for."

"Am I that easy to read?"

"No, you are not. It took me a while to understand you because you are always out of the office. I do believe that from what I have learned of your personality, you would make a good husband and a great father."

"I am glad you think so. Tell those brothers we work for what you believe. They say I am getting too old."

22

"You have to ignore those two. No one gets too old for love."
"We will have to take this conversation up when I return."

"I stop by to pick up my tickets and information for my trip."

"I have everything ready for you right here. Have a good trip, and I will be waiting for your good news when you get back."

"Ok, Joan. Have a good rest of the day with your family." Joan is the glue that keeps us all together as a family here at this firm. You don't want to make her mad. Most of the time she is justified when she gets upset. Because some of us have done just the opposite of what she has told us.

Alphonso went home to pack his bags, coordinated arrangements for his mail and newspaper to be stopped. He lives in an affluent condominium community named The Hillside View. One of the first residents to move into the new condo community and was now thinking about purchasing a house. The residents he knew called him Al. He loved to socialize and would be attending the social tonight at seven p.m. at the clubhouse.

Lorraine the manager of the condos, planned a welcome social for new owners of the remaining unoccupied condos. Alphonso would have to make it an early night because of his flight the next day. Alphonso parents had five children of which he is the youngest. All of them have spouses and children except him. He was going to work on this when he finished this case. Maybe he would meet someone special on this trip, or he could possibly meet someone at the social this evening.

Lorraine is a very organized person, and every time she plans an event at the clubhouse everyone enjoys themselves. For this event, there is karaoke and a tasting fair with different dishes catered by a restaurant called 'Keep Coming Back' furnished by the developer. After the entertainment, Lorraine introduced the new owners and asked them to comment on why they chose this community.

The new owners consisted of three single ladies, two single men, and two married couples. Glancing and checking out the single ladies, neither one struck Alphonso as a potential mate. As they were introducing themselves one of the single men introduced himself.

"My name is Elliot, and I am a retired police officer from Atlanta. A friend of mine name Madison recommended Alaska as a place to settle down. In my research, I found this place with all the amenities you could ever want. Located in a city much like the one I came from. I look forward to meeting everyone and making some new friends," said Elliott. Alphonso said to himself he knew most of the singles and there is no owner name Madison.

After meeting and greeting the new owners, and having some refreshments, and flirting with the manager, Alphonso headed back to his condo. He needed to get some rest and ensure he had packed enough clothing and toiletry for the two weeks. Every time I travel, I forget something and end up going shopping at my final destinations.

This is not going to happen on this trip. If I should meet that special lady, I want everything perfect even down to the fingernails.

CHAPTER 3

PREPARING TO TRAVEL

ALPHONSO could not believe the alarm from his phone was beeping so loud. He said to himself I guess the quicker I can get started, the quicker I can begin to find that special lady and work at the same time. He jumped out of bed, headed to the bathroom for a shave and shower. Looking in the mirror while shaving he mumbled how dare Jason say I am getting too old. I look more handsome and younger than him. What does he know? He has no clue what women want today because he has been out of circulation too long.

After finishing his shower, Alphonso dressed in a brown and rust color cashmere sweater, brown slacks, and brown shoes. It will not be as cold in DC and Atlanta as it is in Alaska. I will carry my wool blend brown coat. Everything must be in place today from head to toe. After taking one last look in the mirror, he headed out the door with his luggage and briefcase in hand.

Alphonso owned two cars, one an antique blue 1947 Mercedes, handed down to him from his father, and a white 2017 Toyota Camry he purchased himself. Today I will drive the Toyota to the airport because it is cheaper on gas than the Mercedes. It has every technical gadget and more than anyone could ask for in a vehicle.

From my condo, it will take me forty minutes to get to Fairbanks International (FI) airport. I like using FI because everyone is helpful and friendly. I will rack up on frequent flyer miles for my honeymoon travel. Wow, I like how that sounds.

Alphonso pulled into the long-term parking area at the airport. He noticed Sam was there to give him his long-term parking ticket. Sam is eighty-seven, and his ex-wife Jamel left him for another man after twenty years of marriage. She moved to a small town called Delta Junction. Jamel was his first and only love.

After Sam retired from working as a secondary education school teacher, he took this job as a parking attendant. This gives him something to do and get him out of the house each day. He has one daughter who never visits because of the demand of her job. His son was killed in the military.

"Hi, Sam how are things going with you today?"

"Hello, Alphonso. I am doing great. If I were doing any better, I would not be able to live with myself. Where are you off to this time?"

"I am headed to the Capitol City, Washington DC., where all laws are passed whether they are good or bad, and then to hot Atlanta." "Hopefully one day I can take a trip to Washington DC to see my daughter, she works at the Pentagon."

"What is her name? I just might run into her, and if I see her, I would like to let her know what a wonderful person you are."

"Her name is Madison."

"That's a beautiful name. I guess I'd better get out of here so you can harass the other people that are behind me. See you upon my return, said Al."

"Have a good trip, Mr. Al."

That is the second time I have heard that name Madison in the last two days. She recommended one of my neighbors move to Alaska. I may be talking to my future father-in-law. On the other hand, she must be a traveling lady because her father says she is in Washington DC. Elliott the man I met at my Condo yesterday says he met her in Atlanta. Alphonso found a good parking space near the terminal area check-in for Delta. He would have to thank Joan upon his return for ensuring that he fly Delta Airline. This airline fly's to Atlanta and Washington DC twice a day. The two places I travel to most often. As he arrived at the ticket counter for check-in, he found his favorite ticket agent Jocelyn.

She is single, beautiful, and knowledgeable. I can picture her working in the corporate world as a CEO or higher. She is everything I believe a man could want. I always flirt with her, and she manages to tease back a little. Could she be the one? Two possibilities of mates and I have not even left Alaska yet.

28

"Good morning, Mr. Al. Where are you taking me today?"

"I am going to boring Washington DC. If I were traveling with you Ms. Jocelyn, we would be going to Paris, France, where there is nothing but love in the air," said Alphonso.

She smiles at him blushing and says, "let me see your ID so I can make sure you don't have a double. I could not handle two of you coming up in here." Alphonso hands her his ID.

"How is it a fine specimen of a man like you is still single?" Asked Jocelyn.

"I have been seeing you in this airport for three years now, and the fine specimen of a woman like you has not said yes."

She continues to smile and blushes. "Mr. Alphonso, you so crazy." "You have driven me to that point, so you need to bring me back. Wait, I don't know if I want to come back, because I like it."

"Mr. Alphonso, how many bags are you checking today?"

"I am checking two bags because I don't know exactly how long I will be gone. I will be missing you the entire time I am away."

"Mr. Alphonso, I have two bags checked first class seat 2A Gate A09 leaving at eleven-thirty a.m. Have a safe and enjoyable trip. We do thank you for continuing to fly Delta. I will be here when you get back." "Thank you for the individual attention and excellent customer service during check-in, and I will continue to fly Delta, so I can see you." "You are welcome." He headed for the security check-in and off to gate A09 to board for Washington DC.

Hmm, what a good-looking man. What I would do to fly away with him to a remote site, where there are no more women. He is about six feet tall, one hundred and eighty pounds of muscle. He dresses nice, clean shaven, low cut brownish hair, beautiful white teeth, charming personality, and has money, I think. I will flirt a little more the next time he comes through. This could lead to a beautiful relationship, especially if he is single. You never know what type of drama or secrets people are carrying when they come through this airport.

CHAPTER 4

ENCOUNTERS AT THE AIRPORT

VIOLET was so excited about getting out of Delta Junction, she almost overslept. She did not want to fall asleep driving to the Fairbanks airport, so she had a light breakfast. A bagel with cream cheese and a cup of coffee with no cream. It is about one hour and fifty-eight minutes from the Delta to Fairbanks. It takes most people about one hour and thirty minutes to get there via interstate AK-2, AK-3 and AK-4. I drive the speed limit or slower, it will probably take me two and a half hours.

Don't want to miss my flight after my son had so carefully made the arrangements. He had to change his work schedule just for my arrival. I am so looking forward to seeing him. Violet decided to call her friend Madison at seven a.m. for they both are early risers.

"Good morning Madison. I am getting ready to leave for the airport. I had my mail and newspaper stopped until I return. Just double checking to ensure I did leave the house key with you to check things while I am away. I will miss our weekly breakfast, but I am excited about seeing my children."

"I will miss you as well, but please do enjoy yourself while you are there. You might even find a DC or Georgia man to bring home with you."

"I am only going to visit my children and hopefully see some of the tourist attractions I see on the TV and in the newspapers. No man is part of this trip. I will call you when I get there, to let you know I arrived safely."

"I will be awaiting your call, Violet." "Goodbye Madison."

Ever since I let Madison know I was going to DC, she has been asking me a lot of unusual questions. She is acting like I should not go for some reason. Madison worked in DC before moving to the Delta, but not sure exactly what type of work she did or who was her employer. Madison and my husband use to travel to some of the same locations at about the same time. I wonder if she has any knowledge of his death or knows someone who does. We will have to have a long talk upon my return home.

The possibility is high that Violet will meet my father at the airport if she parks in long-term parking. On this trip, she could also learn of the affair I had with her husband. If she finds out about my past and the knowledge I have about her husband's death, she may no longer be my friend.

The drive-up Richardson highway is such a pleasant drive from the Delta, when there is no snow, even if you are driving alone. This highway is named for an explorer and geographer of Alaska, U.S. Army General Wilds P. Richardson. Many accidents have occurred, on this highway, so I must be extra careful. It stretches about 368 miles. When you are driving on it, the road is so narrow it's like it closes in on you on both sides. It gives you a view of the mountains that is so breathtaking as though you are driving straight into the hills.

Traffic is light today. Therefore, I should make good time driving at a moderate speed, my children would say slow. They are living in those fast cities like Atlanta and DC., so the traffic is always moving at a rapid pace. My husband Daniel did not want me to drive on these trips that we made down this road when he was living. He said I could cause an accident at the slow speed I drive.

This drive also gives me time to reminisce and to remember the good times we had making this trip with and without the children to Fairbanks. We would always pack a light snack. The kids would have their favorite computer games on their iPads so they would not get bored on these trips.

I never understood why they got so much enjoyment out of those games. I am not a computer literate person who stays abreast of the latest technology, but my husband did. He wanted the children to keep abreast of technology because we didn't know what careers they would choose.

Children must start early with their education today. Otherwise, they will be behind all the other children when they start school. After our children became teenagers, they wanted to stay with their friends instead of traveling with us. Their interest and focus changed drastically, what seemed like overnight.

However, I guess that happens with all children. It's interesting how kids change when they are thirteen and fourteen. They don't want to be seen with their parents, even though it is the parents who make life enjoyable for them. I arrived at the airport one hour early and drove up to the long-term parking attendant.

"Good morning, my name is Sam." "Hello, Sam. My name is Violet."

"How long will you be leaving your car?"

"About two weeks. I am going to visit my children in Washington DC and Atlanta."

"I wish that I could go there and see my daughter. She works at the Pentagon. Have not seen her in a few years."

"I have not seen my children in a couple of years as well. That's why I am going to visit them. My husband died about three years ago, and this is my first trip out of the state since his death."

"What city in Alaska do you live?"

"I have lived in Delta Junction my entire life. I like the small-town atmosphere."

"I like the small-town atmosphere also. But I was born and raised in Fairbanks. My wife and I divorced after twenty years of marriage. Upon retiring from the school system, I decided, to take this job, to have something to do."

"You favor a friend of mine who lives in the Delta. Do you have relatives that live there?"

"No, but my ex-wife lives there. Guess I have talked enough, let me go in and get checked-in, don't want to miss my flight. It was nice talking to you." That man's facial features remind me of someone. I can't remember at this moment. Maybe it will come to me when I get checked in and settled at the gate for my flight.

I wonder if she knows my ex-wife Jamel, who also lives in Delta Junction. I have not had any contact with Jamel since we divorced. I wonder how she and her husband are doing. My daughter does not speak of her mother to me, because she does not know exactly why we broke up. She knows my life has not been the same since her mother married a man named Cooper. There will always be a place in my heart for her, for she was my first love, and we had a beautiful daughter and son from our union.

Ms. Violet is a gorgeous woman and by her appearance has taken good care of herself. Have not met a lovely lady like her in a long time. Of course, I have not been looking either. Alphonso and Violet have made me want to see my daughter. When I get home this evening,

I am going to look at my vacation time and plan a trip to see her in DC. It would be even better if I could get her to visit me.

I don't know why my daughter never got married. Would be great to have some grandchildren, especially a grandson. She works long hours at her job, so maybe she must focus on work and don't have time for a relationship or marriage. Marriage and grandchildren are something we need to talk about the next time I speak with her. Here comes another traveler, better focus my mind on work.

As I walked up to the Delta ticket counter, the ticket attendant who is waiting on me was named Jocelyn from her name tag.

"Hello, my name is Jocelyn, how may I help you?"

"My name is Violet, and I have an eleven-thirty flight reservation for Washington DC."

"How many bags will you be checking, and may I see your ID?

This ID is a beautiful picture of you. So many times, when you get your driver's license, they don't take a good view of you."

"Thank you, I have two bags."

"Ms. Violet, I have two bags checked for non-stop to Washington, DC. Your seat assignment is first class seat 2B. Your flight will be departing out of Gate A09 leaving at eleven-thirty a.m."

"We had some flight cancellations so, please listen in case your flight is late. Have a safe and enjoyable trip, and we do thank you for flying Delta Airlines Ms. Violet," said Jocelyn.

"Thank you, Jocelyn, for being so kind and patient, and you have a beautiful day as well."

I hope she does not get too friendly with Alphonso since she is sitting next to him on the plane to Washington. I will have to look up Alphonso's phone number from his ticket information. Give him a quick call while he is traveling and try to hook up with him on his return trip home. I will find out if he is flirting or is, he serious.

Violet proceeded to the security check-in at gate A09, for it was now ten-forty-five a.m. security check-in was quick and easy. I was thankful for that. As I was walking in the gate area, I noticed a man staring at me. His face was not familiar to me, but he was very handsome. I sat in a chair with my back facing him, because I am not used to men staring at me. No one had stared at me like that since before my husband died.

As soon as I sat down, the airline attendant came on the intercom system and said the flight coming from Washington DC is delayed four hours due to the weather. The same flight leaving out of Alaska would be late also. Approximate departure time was three-thirty p.m. The plane being late will delay the time my son would pick me up at the airport in DC.

BARBARA MOSTELLA

Violet proceeded to call her son from the cell phone he had purchased for her. I am old fashion when it comes to electronics, but I am quickly learning, and I like it. My son bought me an android phone from Samsung, and he is paying the contract on it. Never thought my son or daughter would one day be making purchases for me. I thank God for how successful they are with each of their careers and looking out for their mother.

"Landon, don't rush to the airport to pick me up, my flight has been delayed and will be arriving in Washington at seven-thirty p.m."

"No problem Mom, I will be able to run out and pick up a few things, that I did not get on yesterday. I'm anxious to see you after my one visit to Delta Junction last Christmas."

"Talk to you later Pee Wee." "Goodbye, Mom."

Landon was small throughout his adolescent, so we nicknamed him Pee Wee. He hates it when I call him that. So, I try only to say it, when we are around family or the two of us and his sister.

Landon is thirty years of age and very smart. He graduated from the University of Alaska in Anchorage, with a Law degree in criminology.

He passed the bar shortly after graduation.

After moving to the DC area, he had to retake the bar for that area and passed it. I think it is silly you must take the bar exam in every state in which you plan to practice law. However, I guess every state has different requirements.

Landon has become well known for cases he has tried in the DC. area. He works for a firm called Soco & Soco. An odd name for a law firm. Having worked there for five years, he was hoping to make partner soon. As a mother, I am ready for grandchildren. However, he has not found that young lady he says would be his soul mate.

My husband Daniel and I raised him to be a very respectable young man and always to be respectful of women where he worked. He has not disappointed us yet. I wish his father could be here to see how successful he and his sister Kathleen have become. Kathleen is a Dentist in Atlanta and has her own practice. We never made them feel like they had to stay in the Alaska area when they finished college. We wanted them to be a success no matter where they chose to live

As I was sitting there thinking about what a great son Landon has turned out to be. The man that was staring at me earlier when I walked up to gate is now stepping in front of me and looking at me again. I guess maybe he was either going to the restroom or maybe to get a snack. This man made me feel uncomfortable. He was talking on his cell phone as he was passing by. He had the same type of cell phone I have, so it must be a popular phone.

Alphonso was calling the Soco & Soco firm in DC. He had a very close relationship with all the Soco brothers. Anytime he was in the DC. or Atlanta area, they would have a gathering at their home or some local restaurant, put together by one or the other wives. "Darnell, my flight, has been delayed by four hours so I will be arriving around seven-thirty p.m. It will be too late to drop by the house. Let's get together tomorrow night.

"You are not going to believe it, but I think I have found my soul mate in the Fairbanks Airport," said Alphonso.

"How can you tell she is your soul mate?" Said Darnell.

"Because she is the most stunningly beautiful woman I have ever seen in my life. She seems so innocent, yet very sure of who she is. I have never been afraid to go up to a woman and speak, but this time I am fearful that I may say the wrong thing or come on to strong."

"Just be yourself."

"I am going to get me a bottle of cranberry juice and a sandwich, so I can relax because I did not eat any breakfast this morning. Maybe after that, I will get the courage to say something to her, and my stomach will not be speaking to her before I do. I will chat at you when I arrive at the hotel in DC."

After about thirty minutes of reading the Fairbanks News. Violet thought about the parking attendant Sam and finally realized that he favored or had some of the same features as Madison. I wonder if that was her father. It can't be her brother because she told me she was an only child. Madison did not say her father worked at the airport.

However, I did realize that she had been acting a little withdrawn since I told her about my trip. Violet decided to get up and go to the restroom and hoped that she would not run into that guy who was staring at her. As she reached the bathroom, she found a long line. It is always a long line in the women's restroom. I can't ever recall seeing a long line coming out of the men's bathroom. I guess the reason for that is women have more clothing to pull down and back up than men.

We usually check our makeup and give our hair another combing. Whereas I think men go in, zip down, let it out, pull it in, and zip it back up. Wash their hands and run their fingers through their hair, and for those who have decided to be bold and go bald, take a quick look, and they are ready to go.

All freshened up and ready to board the flight to DC. Violet heads to the gate for they are now calling all zones to board.

CHAPTER 5

WHO IS HE

FEELING sad that he did not see his soul mate when he returned to the gate for boarding. Alphonso settles in his first-class seat 2A. He was hoping whoever sat next to him, for this long flight, likes to talk. "Mr. Alphonso, how are you today. Would you like a glass of wine, soda, juice, or water while we are waiting for the rest of the passengers to board?" Asked flight attendant Jonelle.

"I am doing fine. Yes, I would like a glass of wine."

"We only have red wine today. Is that ok and would you like chips or peanuts to go with it?"

"The red wine will be fine, and I will take the peanuts with it. Thank you." "You are welcome. I will be right back."

The flight attendant makes you feel special in first class because they know every passenger's name. While waiting for the wine, Alphonso recognized the young lady come on the plan that he thought would be his soul mate. Sweat started popping across his forehead and in his hands. Where will she sit, and how was he going to connect with her?

Such a stunning lady, all he could do was just stare. Her long hair was brown, and skin looked smooth. Her physical body maybe a size eight. I only know that because, I have four sisters. Her jeans and blouse fit in all the right places. Just enough jewelry to accent her clothing. Pretty grayish brown eyes, cute nose, and small luscious lips. I wish I were kissing them now. Where is that wine, I had requested? I need something to relax my nerves.

Violet began to feel panicky when she notices her seat 2B. It is next to the man that was staring at her in the terminal. It was too late to ask for another seat, or even to get on another flight. She hoped he was not a talkative person. While on this flight she just wanted to read her book, and take a nap.

Maybe this guy was one of those Marshals they talk about being on each plane since 9/11 terrorist attacks. So that could be a plus. She was grateful her son purchased a first-class ticket because it was going to be a long flight otherwise. Violet noticed this man staring at her was very handsome. His brownish color hair was cut low and almost the same color as mine. He has small brown eyes, with a big cute nose.

Why am I noticing and thinking about these things? I have not had any thoughts about a man since my husband died. I wish these people in front of me would hurry and get to their seats. I am not anxious to get to mine, but I just don't want to think or wonder any more things about this man.

If my friend Madison knew I was analyzing a man I knew nothing about, she would say I told you so. I'm just going to prove her wrong and get to my seat and just concentrate on the wonderful time I am going to have with my son in DC.

Violet quietly as possible sat in her aisle seat. As she was sitting down the stewardess Jonelle came right behind her and stood next to her with a glass of wine in her hand.

"Here you are Mr. Alphonso, can I get you anything else?" "No that will be all for right now, thank you."

"You are welcome."

"Good afternoon Ms. Violet, can I get you something to drink before we start our take off?"

"Yes, I would like a cranberry juice, if you have it," said Violet.

"Will cranapple be okay and would you like some peanuts or chips with it?"

"The cranapple juice will be fine, and the peanuts." "Will bring it to you shortly."

"While you are waiting, here are menus for each of you to select from. We will be serving a light lunch as soon as we are at a cruising

44

altitude." Alphonso took a few sips of his wine to calm his nerves before he said anything.

I knew I should have purchased those breath mints in the bookstore in the airport. No need of worrying about it now.

"Hi, I am Alphonso, some people take my first name to be the last name." "Nice to meet you, I am Violet. The stewardess knows everyone name I guess?"

"Only the first-class passengers."

While they were getting acquainted, the stewardess came with her drink request and peanuts.

"Here is your cranapple along with your peanuts you requested Ms. Violet."

"Thank you." Violet picked up her book to start reading because she really did not want to have a lot of conversation with Alphonso. The pilot came on and said that we were next in line for takeoff and instructed the crew to finish up their safety presentation and to get to their seats for takeoff. It is funny how everyone is quiet on the plane when it first takes off.

Once the pilot had the aircraft in the air, there is chatter all over the place. The same thing happens when the plane is getting ready to land. "We will be reaching an altitude of 35,000 feet and then level off.

It is sunny and 65 degrees in Washington, DC. We will have a smooth ride all the way.

After we are at a cruising altitude, the stewardess will be serving lunch. There will be a movie after the meal for those who want to watch it. Everyone can sit back, relax and enjoy the ride, and thank you for flying Delta." said the pilot. Alphonso is now relaxed. "What are you reading?" Asked Alphonso.

With a nervous smile on her face. "I am reading a tourist guide to Washington DC. This is my first visit there. I want to ensure I visit the recommended tourist attractions."

"You are going to love DC because there is so much to do. It is one of the most sought-after cities to have dinner or lunch because of the variety of restaurants."

"I am visiting my son, so he will know all the places to take me." "Excuse me, Mr. Alphonso and Ms. Violet, have each of you made your selections from the menu?" Asked Jonelle.

Alphonso knew what he wanted, so he allowed Violet to go first.

"I will have the rosemary baked chicken, with broccoli, rice, and the spinach salad, with another cranapple juice," said Violet.

"I will have the lemon baked chicken with the same vegetables and a tossed salad, with a cranapple juice as well," said Alphonso.

"We will have it ready for you shortly."

We have similar taste in food and drink, Alphonso mumbles to himself. She is not very talkative, only answers questions, so how do I get her to talk?

"I noticed that you ordered the chicken versus the beef. Is beef not in your diet? "

"Yes, you are right. The only red meat I eat is lamb. How about you?" "I do eat beef as a treat to myself but not any pork."

After Alphonso and Violet finished their entrees, the stewardess brought them both coffee at their request.

"Ms. Violet and Mr. Alphonso, would you like headphones to watch the movie? It will start in fifteen minutes," said Jonelle. They both said yes. The name of the movie was 'The Bucket List' with Morgan Freeman and Jack Nicholson.

"These two actors are my favorite. I have seen every movie they've had a role in," said Violet.

"I have watched reviews of this movie, but never seen it. With my busy schedule, I don't get to the movies often."

"I don't get out much to the movies either. But I have seen this one. The town I live in is so small that we only get movies after they have been in every other theater in the state."

"What city are you from?"

"I am from Delta Junction. As I recall you said you were from Alaska as well."

"Yes, I am from Fairbanks. Born, raised, went to school and now work there."

Over the intercom, the stewardess announced the movie is now showing for your viewing. Violet and Alphonso put the headphones on in preparation for the movie. The movie was about one and a half hours long. Made the time go by while in the air. Violet hated that the film was over because she did not want to talk any more to Alphonso. She got up from her seat and went to the bathroom.

Alphonso watched her every move as she headed for the bathroom and mumbled to himself, I think I am in love. How do I get information from her to see her again after this flight? She lives about two and a half hours away from my condominium. How will a long-distance relationship work? If this is my soul mate, it is worth it.

Violet returned back to her seat from the bathroom and was thinking that as soon as she sits down, she is going to sleep. Before she sat down, she opened the overhead compartment and removed a blanket and pillow. This will let Alphonso know I do not want to talk. She quickly sat down and covered up. "Are you cold?" Asked Alphonso.

"No, I just want to take a nap. It has been a long day for me."

"Okay. Do you mind letting me out to go to the restroom before you start your nap, and then I won't disturb you anymore?"

"Sure." Alphonso got up and walked to the restroom. He was thinking all the while he was heading to the bathroom. What did I do to make her not want to talk? Maybe I was too bold in asking her personal questions. What am I to do? Because I believe my mind is made up about her.

Alphonso quickly came back to his seat. "I am going to be bold if I can and ask you one question. I am attracted to you, and I'm single. Are you married? Can we get together and have lunch while we are here in Washington? I will be there for a week maybe two."

"My husband is deceased, and I am not interested in seeing anyone right now. That was two questions." They both laughed.

"Is there a way I can make contact with you somehow once this flight lands in Washington?"

"No, just not interested."

After she answered the last question, she turned her head to take a nap. The next thing she heard was from the stewardess.

"We will be landing at Washington Reagan International in ten minutes. All tray tables up, and seats pulled to an upright position. All electronic equipment, including cell phones, must be put away.

Everyone must have their seat belt fasten for landing until the captain has turned the seat belt sign off.

If you have connecting flights at the Washington International airport, there will be an attendant waiting to assist you once you have deplaned. Thank you again for flying Delta and keep us in mind for your future flying needs," said the stewardess. The plane landed a few minutes earlier than expected.

I hope my son Landon is on time to pick me up in baggage claim.

Alphonso had to stop at the restroom once he deplaned. Still thinking about Violet, and how he will ever see her again. But he could not see her if she did not want to see him. When Alphonso approached the baggage area, he was surprised not to see Violet. She deplaned before he did. So, he just grabbed his luggage and headed for the rental car pickup.

CHAPTER **6**

MOTHER AND SON REUNION

AS Violet approached the baggage claim area, to her surprise, she did not see Alphonso. She removed her bags from the conveyor belt. Just as she turned around to exit, there stood her son. "Landon you look so much like your father, I thought I had seen a ghost. Seeing you brought back so many memories of how your father looked when he was your age," said Violet. Landon just hugged her the same as when he was a kid.

"Good evening, Mother you look stunning. I may need to get my gun out while you are here, to keep the men from hounding you." "Hello to you son, and you are just a sight for sore eyes. I am thankful you are here on time, and I did not have to wander around. This is the first time I have been out of Alaska since the passing of your father. I only had two pieces of luggage, so I am ready to go. I am a little tired, for it has been a long day for me."

"Did you meet any interesting people either on the plane or in the airport?" Asked Landon.

"No, not really."

"We will talk later, let's get to the car because we have a forty-five minute drive to the house. I fixed a light dinner because I did not know if you would be hungry when you arrived."

"I had a snack on the plane, not really hungry, but since you've cooked, I'm interested in seeing how well you for cooking with all the options you have for restaurants in the area?"

"Mother, sometimes I work long hours and all I want to do at the end of the day, is come home and fix a sandwich or quick salad then relax."

" I won't get grandchildren if you are not out being social and looking for a wife."

"Mother, I don't have a lot of time for a meaningful relationship right now. I have some goals I want to accomplish at the firm. I do have a friend that I have dinner with occasionally, but it is not serious."

"Could it get serious? You are not getting any younger."

"I don't know that mother. She is a doctor at Washington University Hospital and works long hours like me," replied Landon.

"What is her name?" "Her name is Connie,"

"That is a beautiful name."

"What does her parents do for a living?" "They own Rest in Peace Funeral Home."

"They are keeping it all in the family. The patient gets sick Connie treats them. The patient dies, Connie sends them to her parents' funeral home."

"Mother, you have become a comedian since the last time I saw you. You should take your show on the road. I believe you would make lots of money. Okay, Mother, enough about me let's talk about you."

"Don't try to get off the subject Son. Sometimes men are a little slow and don't realize women are just waiting to be asked."

"That's the way it was with your father and me. I knew the first time I met him, that he was the one for me. But it took him about a year and a half to realize that I was the one and only one for him. Because of that special union of love came you and your sister. You will know when that special young lady comes your way. Keep your eyes open and be ready because it is a joy to have someone to share your life with."

"Mother if you decide that you want to have a relationship with someone, it will be okay with me. I don't like it that you are alone in that cold Alaska town without Kathleen and me. I know that neither of us will come back there to live. You should consider coming to live with one of us. Kathleen talks about it all the time that she wishes you were near. We both have ample room to accommodate you in our homes."

"Landon that is sweet of you and your sister. I know you both have your own lives to live, and I am used to living in Delta Junction. I have friends there and lots of family memories. Right now, I am okay. So, let's get off that subject. How much farther do we have to go to get to your house? I need to use the bathroom."

"We are only two miles away from the house Mother."

Violet got quiet for a moment and started thinking about Alphonso. He was nice and seems to have a good sense of humor. There would never be another man like my Daniel. I guess I could have given him my phone number. It was good to know that a man had noticed me.

I think no matter how old you get, no one really likes to be alone. If our paths cross again, I will be friendlier.

"Mother, what are you smiling about?" Asked Landon. "Oh, nothing son."

I wonder if mother is okay, that is twice she has given me an indirect answer. "We are here Mother."

"Landon, what a beautiful home, can you afford this?" "Yes, mother, I can afford it, unless you want to contribute." "I can't wait to get inside to see how you have decorated."

"Well, I did not do any decorating. I hired an interior decorator and told her what I wanted, and you will see the results. Hope you will like it."

"I know I will." Landon pulls into the two-car garage, and we got out and went into the house through the laundry room. He has one of those front loader washer and dryer set. I guess that means he washes his own clothes. Next to the laundry room is the kitchen.

"Landon, what a big beautiful kitchen. My small little kitchen would fit inside your kitchen. You have lots of cabinet space and an island in the middle. Granite top cabinets. I see why you like to come home and fix your meals."

"Mother lets go to your room and put your things away, so you can use the restroom and then we can take a tour if you like." "Okay. Landon." As she was walking to her room, she was thinking to herself, my son has really done well, and I am so proud of him. His father would be happy to know we did a good job.

"This bedroom is beautiful and spacious. It is even decorated with my favorite color red."

"Mother, I am glad you like it. The bathroom is just on the right side of the bed. So, you don't have to get up at night and go out of your room. You get settled in, and I will warm up the food."

"Pee Wee, I just want a small amount of whatever you have cooked. I don't like to eat a lot and then go to bed."

"Take your time. You have not called me Pee Wee in a long time. I thought I had grown out of that name?"

"You will always be Pee Wee to me, but I won't say it around other people unless it is your sister."

"I am calling Kathleen now and let her know you are here. Mother, it is great having you here. I love you."

"I love you son."

CHAPTER 7

THE VICTIM'S ROOM

ALPHONSO was thinking, Joan always does her research when booking travel arrangements for the staff and me at Soco and Soco. The DoubleTree hotel she booked for me is perfect. It is only minutes from the airport and the Pentagon. I can either walk to the Pentagon or catch the shuttle. No need for driving and getting a headache trying to find a parking space. Once checked in and unpacked at the hotel Alphonso called Darnell at home.

"Good evening, Darnell, this is Alphonso. I hope I am not calling too late. Just wanted to let you know I arrived at the hotel without any problems. I'm going to make it an early night, because I have an eight a.m. meeting at the Pentagon. I want to be refreshed and sharp when meeting with Mr. Narvell. I will also be meeting at the firm with you tomorrow at two-thirty to give you an update on what I get from my meeting. What do you know about this case I am working on?"

"Not a whole lot, except the victim, was from Delta Junction. He was found dead with a single gunshot wound to the head by one of the staff in the hotel you are staying in. The weapon was never found, and neither was any suspect arrested. It was ruled a suicide. That is the extent of my knowledge. I hope you can solve this one because it is a three-year-old case," said Darnell.

"Hopefully, my contact at the Pentagon can share some additional information concerning the case."

"Good luck. My wife Juanita and I look forward to seeing you tomorrow night for dinner at the house. We will leave from the firm if it is late. If we get finished early, our driver will pick you up at the hotel."

"Sounds good," replied Alphonso.

"Have a good night sleep, and don't let the bedbugs bite you," said Darnell.

"How corny is that, you are still that starving comedian Darnell." "Goodnight Alphonso."

Alphonso was glad the hotel provided 24-hour room service. It had been almost six hours since the last time he had eaten. He ordered the smoked turkey sandwich, with a cranapple juice. It would take thirty minutes for delivery. While waiting, he jumped in the shower, got into his pajamas and found a good movie to watch on TV.

He was able to find the same movie he and Violet watched on the plane. This is no coincidence, I was meant to meet that beautiful woman.

WHO WOULD HAVE THOUGHT

As Joshua was making his way to deliver room service to room 305-A. He started to get a funny feeling in his stomach. This would be the first time he entered this room in over three years since he had found that guy Daniel from Alaska dead. I am thankful that the hotel staff and the police did not suspect that I had anything to do with the murder.

My friend Elliott who was a police officer was supposed to have a meeting in this room that same night with Daniel. He told me that he had gotten held up at a conference and did not make it. I lost contact with Elliott after that night, and I don't know why. Some other friends of mine said he was a dirty cop and had moved to Atlanta. I probably should have left right after that incident, but I did not have any other job prospects at the time.

As Alphonso was now relaxed and sitting waiting for his room service, he started fantasying and thinking about Violet. What is she doing right now? Is she in bed, or up talking with her son, or was she just thinking about me? I did not get her sons name. But she appeared to be very proud of him when talking about visiting him. There has got to be a way to see her somehow.

Room service arrived and interrupted his thoughts.

"Good evening, Mr. Alphonso. Hope that you are comfortable in your room, here is your dinner. Please do enjoy," said Joshua.

"I will, here is your tip."

"Thank you, sir, and have a good night." "You the same," Alphonso replied.

That guy seemed nervous that brought my food to the room, as a matter of fact, his hands were sweating. I wonder if this was his first day on the job. Whatever was going on with him is not my problem, he is a hotel employee. He brought my food on time that's all that matters. The sandwich was good, and it was just what I needed, before closing my eyes.

The cranapple juice was sweet and cold, another reminder of Violet. I can't get this woman out of my head. Alphonso has been plucked by the mother hen, without even a chase. It was now two-a.m. when Alphonso finally relaxed and laid down for the night to sleep.

CHAPTER **8**

LIFES CONCERNS, LOVE, AND CHOICES

MADISON arose early Monday morning. She dressed and had breakfast before her mother Jamel was awake. She required 100% of her time. I know this is not a good thing to say, but mother having a stroke saved my life. Madison heard her mother calling out for her in the bedroom.

"Good morning Mother. How did you rest last night?"

"Madison, I slept better last night than I have slept in a long time. It is such a blessing and comfort that you are here with me. Don't know what I would do at this point if you were not."

"Well mother, you don't have to worry. I am so happy that I can be here. Being able to take care of you has been a joy. What would you prefer for breakfast this morning?"

"I think I would just like some oatmeal, a boiled egg and a cup of coffee. Have you already eating?"

"Yes, mother, I wanted to devote all my attention to you and whatever you needed this morning. I am going to fix your breakfast first, and we will take a bath afterward. Would that be okay?"

"That will be fine, and I'm a little hungry this morning." "Would you like to eat in your bedroom or in the kitchen?"

"I would like to eat in the kitchen."

"Okay, lets head to the bathroom to wash your face and brush your teeth, then you can have breakfast." When I was working at the Pentagon, I was a special agent with no chance for advancement or salary increase. I worked long hours most of the time seven days a week. Before my last supervisor Jim retired, I really enjoyed my job. He made sure everyone had at least a weekend off every month, so you could have some time to yourself.

The big difference between Jim and my supervisor Narvell is that Jim had a wife and children. He tried to spend as much time as possible with them. He also encouraged everyone that worked for him to do the same. Narvell did not have any immediate family that we were aware of, so his job was his life.

What kind of name is Narvell? Narvell came in as though he had to prove something to his boss above him. Everything we did was secretive. We had to be ready to travel anywhere within an hour's notice sometimes. I took a leave of absence to take care of my mother. And while I was on vacation, I resigned my job at the Pentagon and accepted another position with AllTuck in Atlanta, Georgia.

This job with AllTuck is a software engineering manager, which I had minimum experience. It pays more than the Pentagon job. We dealt with software on a small scale in the office I worked at the Pentagon. So, I had a learning curve at AllTuck. My supervisor Michael took me under his wings and taught me everything he knew and then some. I was grateful.

Michael was nothing like Narvell at the Pentagon. The job came with regular working hours where you had weekends off. There was some overtime not much, no last-minute travel, just minimum. I really liked AllTuck, because they had such a diverse workforce and various age groups. Everyone could learn something from each other. If you needed help people did not mind taking time to help you.

This job is not perfect, it came with some challenges because most of their contracts were with the military exchange stores in every state in the United States. So, a lot of things was different in ways you would not imagine.

There was also an opportunity for advancement in the company if you wanted it. It was because of this job at AllTuck that I can spend time with my mother. I'm thankful for being able to take care of her. She and my father Sam worked hard to ensure me, and my brother Scott had a good life, education, and a lot of fun times at home when we were together as a family. I miss those days.

"Mother you did really good with your breakfast this morning. I do believe you were hungry."

"Food always tastes better when someone else cooks it for you." expressed Jamel.

"So, we will now head back to the bathroom for your bath." "Have you heard from Violet since she left to visit her children?"

"No, mother I was waiting for her to call me. But I will let her know you asked about her when she does call."

Madison was just finishing up bathing her mother and putting her in her favorite chair in the living room. This chair had a perfect view out the window. From the window, she could see the trees, the birds flying from limb to limb, and squirrels sniffing on the ground looking for crumbs of food and acorns. Sometimes she would have me throw out food to the birds and squirrel, so she could see how fast they grabbed it up. This made her really laugh. She could also see the tree leaves changing colors for the different seasons when it was not cold, but most of all she loved to see the snow falling and how it accumulated on the ground.

"Madison this is my favorite place in the house. I come here and see all the beautiful things God has created with help from no one. It helps me to accept the loss of Cooper, and to deal with my current physical limitations. Many people have more restrictions than I do, and they are living productive lives. It is why I don't allow myself to drown in self-pity."

"This is why I love you so much mother because you have not allowed these restrictions to get you down. Your strength has made me stronger as a person. I am going to clean up the kitchen while you are enjoying the view."

I don't know why my mom and biological father got a divorce. Neither of them will talk about it. I am going to put forth an effort to see what really happen one of these days. The last I knew before their separation, they were happy together. But when she married Cooper, she was just as happy. So, the only children she had were me and my brother Scott by my father.

I am happy that both my parents live in the same state, even though my father does not know I am in Alaska. My mother did not want my father to know she was sick. My father has not remarried. He said there was no other woman for him but my mother, Jamel.

I did not understand what that meant at the time my father told me, but since I met Daniel, I have a grasp of what he was telling me. There had been other men in my life in the past, but I was always trying to get someone to make me happy, and I never was. I finally figured out you must do whatever is necessary to make yourself happy.

Daniel and I met at a conference for new managers, and I was impressed with him the first time I heard him speak. We had a breakout session at the meeting, and he and I ended up in the same group. Each person in the breakout session had to give their view of what a good manager should do or how they should treat the people they supervise. I will never forget what Daniel said.

He stated to be a good manager, you must first have self-respect, second think about how you want to be treated as an individual, and third understand that everyone has something to offer and everyone has different talents. When you can follow those three principles, then you will be the best manager anyone would want to work for.

After his explanation, the facilitator for our session made a joke and said, this session is over because Daniel has told you everything, I was going to emphasize in three minutes that was going to take me forty-five minutes. Everyone in the meeting just laughed to include me. After that, I said to myself Daniel is not only handsome, he is smart and caring. A kind of man I would want.

During our lunch break, I made it over to Daniel to talk, and he wanted to converse as well. While he was holding his soda to his mouth, I noticed he did not have a ring on. I was thinking, he is good looking, smart, not married and he is talking to me. Did I hit the jackpot or what?

This conference was a two-day conference, and they had a happy hour with food and drinks for all the participants that evening. Both Daniel and I attended the event. That evening was the start of our relationship because we exchanged phone numbers. I miss him so much.

Before Daniel was found dead, he told me he had accidentally found out something about the death of a soldier who knew something about the case he was working on. At the time I did not realize it was my brother he was referring to. The military said , he accidentally killed himself handling his military-issued gun. He was monitoring a contract for the military that involved AllTuck. Scott loved being in the military.

I miss both Daniel and my brother. My relationship with my brother was not as close as I would have liked it, but we did occasionally talk on the phone. There will never be another man for me like Daniel. Violet doesn't know how lucky she is to have had a husband like him. She gets lonely sometimes, but has no thoughts of being with another man. Hopefully, she will meet someone on this two-week trip. Violet is very proud of their two children.

Just thinking back over good times Daniel and I had. The trips we travel together to Florida, Colorado and other places, brings tears to my eyes, knowing that I will never see him again.

Since I am now friends with his wife, and she does not realize that Daniel and I had an affair. I don't know how I am going to explain this to her. Most people don't have a relationship with their friend's husband, but I did not realize at the time who she was.

She has been that one friend to me that everyone wants to have. You can talk about anything, they know you better than anyone else, sometimes even better than your parents. That's the kind of friend Violet is. I hope she can find happiness again.

CHAPTER 9

GATHERING CASE INFORMATION

ALPHONSO was awakened by a five forty-five a.m. wakeup call from the front desk which he had forgotten he requested. The hotels today have these complicated wakeup calls on the phones. I did not have my smart hat on when I arrived in my room last night to try and figure it out. All I could think about last night was Violet and sleep. I must get focus on this case today and think about Violet later.

The order of business is taking a quick shower, get some breakfast, and catch the shuttle from my hotel to the Pentagon to meet with Mr. Narvell at eight a.m. There were a lot of people involved in this case, who assumed it had been closed. Therefore, Soco and Soco had to go through some high-level connections to make this meeting happen, so I don't want to be late. When I arrived at the Pentagon security entrance at seven forty- five, Narvell was waiting. He completed the necessary paperwork for my access.

"Good morning Mr. Alphonso. It was a great idea to have the red sticker on your lapel for me to easily identify you. Please call me Narvell. Security requires a picture id to get a visitor pass. After you do that we can head to my office," said Narvell.

The guard verified my id with the paperwork he had been provided and then gave me a preprinted badge with my name and expiration date.

Narvell had made this process a lot easier than I thought it would be for entrance into the Pentagon.

"Greetings to you this morning Narvell, and please call me Alphonso. Thank you for taking care of the security access for me."

"No problem. It is a short walk to my office, lets head that way."

Upon reaching his office, Alphonso was looking around and made a quick observation of how beautiful it was.

"This is a nice office you have here in the Pentagon, no comparison to the little cubby hole I have in Alaska."

"Thank you. The building is old, so the government makes up for it by designing nice offices to work in. Have a seat and make yourself comfortable." Narvell closed his door after they both entered. "I closed the door, so we won't be interrupted. Would you like some coffee?"

"No, I am fine. I had my limit for the day with breakfast at the hotel." "How are your accommodations at the DoubleTree?"

"Could not ask for anything better. I slept like a baby because I got in so late last night. I'm rested and ready to work."

"Let me explain why my office wanted me to make my first contact with you Narvell. We were told that the hotel thought Daniel was a federal employee, so they contacted the police and this office."

"Your office was the first on the scene with the police, and you worked together with them to solve the case. Daniel's company provided some information concerning some other cases involving the government that he was involved with," said Alphonso.

"All that you have said is correct. Not sure how much you know about the case, but it is a shocker for us that it has been reopened."

"Who requested that it be reopened?"

"The brother of the deceased came to our Alaska law office and requested it. He felt the family was not told the truth and the circumstances by which the police department reported his brother's death were not believable. He thinks that his brother was murdered. You know there is no statute of limitation on a murder case?" Said Alphonso.

"Yes, I do," replied Narvell.

"We understand that this case was ruled as a suicide initially. The deceased was found with a single gunshot wound to the head at the DoubleTree hotel where I am staying. There was no evidence of foul play. The gun was never found that he was shot with. Daniel was licensed to carry a gun, but his gun was not found either. No one heard or saw anything," said Alphonso.

"You are correct Alphonso." "Who found the body?"

" A staff worker by the name of Joshua employed by the DoubleTree." "I wonder if that is the same Joshua that brought room service to me last night?"

"I believe he is the same person because he still works there.

He is an ex-con. The hotel has a program called Help-One. It is an intern type program where they help ex-cons to start there life over when they leave prison. I have heard that everyone who has gone through it for the last five years has been successful. These ex-cons are either working at the DoubleTree or some other business that is in partnership with the hotel," said Narvell.

"Had anyone visited Daniel's room while he was in the hotel?"

"Through our initial investigation, it appeared, no one had visited him that day. The only fingerprints in the room other than the deceased were housekeeping. Housekeeping prints were expected because they clean the rooms every day, but they were released from any suspicion," noted Narvell.

"There was no gun found on the scene, but we did find bullet fragments in the wall beside the bed. The only other bullet found was in Daniel's forehead from a .45 ACP (Automatic Colt Pistol). Even though we ruled his death a suicide, we had some doubt that he was shot with his own gun." Narvell said.

"Would that not be reasonable doubt that he did not shoot himself accidentally if you have not located the actual gun that was fired?"

"Yes, I guess you are right. We were not allowed to autopsy the body, so we went with the evidence we had."

"I would like to get a copy of the ballistics report that would give information about the gun. Why was Daniel at the DoubleTree?"

"Daniel worked for an investigative firm name Q'UP. They are headquartered in Atlanta and a small office here in the DC area. He was investigating a high-profile case here in Washington and had been at the hotel for several weeks."

"There could have been multiple people wanting him dead because of the case he was working at the time. Based on registration found, he was authorized to carry a .45 ACP gun. The case Daniel was investigating has been solved. It involved kickbacks from a contracting firm that the government hired. These kickbacks were given to assure one contractor was awarded over another contractor who was more qualified. The charges proved not to be true." stated Narvell. "What was the name of this company?"

"The company was named AllTuck Incorporated. They supply various government agencies in 20 states with telephone services, software applications, and internet services."

"Do you have a point of contact for the company?"

"Yes, I have prepared a folder for you. It has a list of contact information, transcript testimony, and a complete investigative report."

"Is there anything in the report that might indicate that AllTuck company might have been involved in the death of Daniel?"

"We did not find any evidence of such, but it is possible."

"Don't you think it was strange the bullet found in the wall next to the bed was different from the one found in his forehead? That should have been the clue that he did not kill himself," stated Alphonso.

"At this point, I agree, but we had limited evidence three years ago. The Pentagon got involved because an agent name Madison was a long- time friend of the victim and an employee in this office. She retired and moved to Alaska after all this went down," replied Narvell.

"The death of Daniel being such a high-profile case at the time, I am surprised the FBI did not request an autopsy. Since we have taken on the case, the brother of the deceased has gotten permission from the widow and has asked that his body is exhumed, and an autopsy performed."

"Was there any reason to think that Joshua at the hotel could have been involved in this case or had any evidence concerning the death?" "No evidence was found that he knew anything or had any involvement." "Was he questioned at any time?"

"Yes, we have his transcript testimony. He was found innocent."

"So, whoever committed this crime was a professional and possibly knew something about forensic since no evidence was found at the crime scene," said Alphonso.

"Tell me more about Ms. Madison."

"We know she and Daniel were having an affair, and it had been going on for about a year."

"According to Madison at the time, Daniel was in the process of getting a divorce."

"Was she a suspect?"

"Madison had an alibi and was in Atlanta when the incident occurred. We have a transcript of her testimony."

"How well did you know Madison?"

"Madison worked for me before she took early retirement."
"What type of employee was she?" Asked Alphonso.

"I must admit she was a hard worker, but a lot of the other employees said they did not like her. They stated, she acted as though she was above everyone."

"What do you mean?"

"Madison was a higher grade than most of the other employees. She treated anyone with a grade below her like a second-class citizen. She wanted my job, but knew there was no path to promotion except my job." "Were there any suspects that could not be found that needed to be questioned?"

"No. The finding of suicide negated the reason to suspect anyone." "Were the children's whereabouts question at the time of the incident?"

"Yes, Daniel has two children, Landon and Kathleen. Landon lives here in DC., and Kathleen lives in Atlanta. The daughter who is a dentist was with clients at the time. The son who I believe works for your law firm here in DC and is one of their best lawyers. He visited the father the same day he was found dead, and there was a trace of his prints in the room. We were able to account for the son's whereabouts except for a thirty-minute window, he said he was stuck in traffic."

"We all know that is possible because of the traffic problem here in the city."

"Landon was aware of the affair his father was having with Madison. When we looked at the deceased calendar, he had penciled in lunch with his son and daughter for Saturday. He was killed on Wednesday before that Saturday. He also had penciled in his schedule vacation the prior month with Madison in Florida."

"What about his wife, Violet?"

"The wife at the time of his death was at home where she lives in Delta Junction. We have not kept up with her whereabouts since the case was ruled suicide. We have provided her last known address. There were no pictures of her, in the criminal database because she has never committed any type of crime, not even a jaywalking ticket if there is such a thing anymore."

"What about Daniel's financial status at the time of death?"

"He had some debt but nothing that would bring about any suspicion." "Were you provided a copy of his financial records and taxes?"

"Yes, we were."

"I would like to question some of his creditors can you provide contact information for me?"

"That information is in the folder I have put together for you." "Where is AllTuck located?"

"They are located USA wide, with a headquarters in Atlanta."

"Looks like I am going to have a little work to do when I get to Atlanta on Friday. Thanks for all your help and taking time out this morning to answer my questions. I had many questions for the Washington Police, but you have answered most of those."

"No need to contact them right away. I would like to leave the lines of communication open in case I have additional questions," said Alphonso. "All my contact information has been provided," said Narvell.

"You have given me a lot of information to get started on this case, and I really do appreciate it. You will be notified of the outcome before it is publicized. Now if you would lead me out of this maze, I won't take up any more of your time. Have a good rest of the day," said Alphonso.

While waiting for the shuttle, Alphonso was thinking, that was a lot of invaluable information provided by Narvell. I wonder why Soco & Soco did not relay to me that Daniel's son works for our firm. Maybe that was an oversite, or to make sure I had no bias for him being an employee. Once back at the hotel, I will put together notes for my meeting with Darnell this afternoon. Next, I would like to question Joshua and find out why he was nervous and sweating when he brought room service last night. As the shuttle was approaching, Alphonso thoughts changed to thinking about Violet. Since her son works for our firm, I may get another opportunity to talk with her. To impress her, I must be careful how I handle the son.

CHAPTER 10

LIFE HAS ITS MOMENTS

VIOLET arose to the smell of bacon and coffee. I wonder how long my son has been up. I slept longer than I had planned. I will get me a shower and get my clothes on because no one likes to eat leftover or warmed up breakfast. My son does not have to work today. We are hanging out and going to some sightseeing places I wanted to visit. I can't believe he took this whole week off to spend time with his mother.

"Good morning Landon. How did you sleep last night?" Violet asked.

"I slept, great mother. It gave me a sense of comfort and protection knowing that you were here."

"How did you sleep?" I slept like a baby. I felt protected and safe here in this lovely home of yours."

"I miss you and wish that you would reconsider moving to Washington or Atlanta. You don't have to live in the same homes with Kathleen or me. Both states have retirement community for seniors, and mother I don't think you should continue to live alone in Alaska when you can be near your kids. Moreover, you are in such good health, and you are only fifty- eight years old. I would feel so much better knowing that you are much closer than where you are now."

"Son, I can say that being here the one day has made me want to be closer. What would I do with my house?"

"You can sell it or rent it, Mom."

"Baby this is a lot to think about, let's eat this wonderful breakfast you have cooked and stopped talking about moving for right now. I promise we will talk about it tomorrow after I have had another good night of sleep. I would love to be near you and your sister. I know neither of you will move back home."

"Let's eat up Mom. We are having dinner this evening at Darnell's. "Are you taking that special lady you are dating?"

"No, you are my date for tonight."

"When do I get to meet her? What's her name and what does she do for a living?"

"Remember I told you her name was Connie, and she is a doctor at Washington Medical Center here in Washington. Maybe on Friday, the three of us can go out to dinner."

"I would like that."

"You must promise me you will behave, and not ask too many questions." "Okay, Landon."

"Let's get ready to head down to Pennsylvania Ave and downtown. It will take us about four hours today to see some of the main attractions. Our focus will be on the National Mall and tourist sites within proximity to the mall. The first stop will be the Washington Monument. I hope you are not afraid of heights because we are going to the top of the monument."

"They say it only takes seventy seconds to go all the way up. It is five hundred and fifty-five feet up in the air. We will check our time and see if they are right."

"Son how could I be afraid of heights when I just got off an airplane yesterday."

"Mother, you are funny, but you are right. We will also tour Martin Luther King Jr, Jefferson and Lincoln Memorials."

"After which we will have lunch and head back to the house to take a nap or sit and chat until it is time to go to dinner."

"Sounds like a plan Landon. Oh, your phone is ringing, I bet you that is Connie."

"Mother how do you know." "It is that motherly instinct."

"Hello Connie, are you at the hospital already this morning?"

"No, but I am in-route. Just checking with you before you, and your mother get busy today."

"I was up around six-thirty fixing breakfast, and now we are in the car headed to the Washington Monument and more places around the National Mall."

"Well, some people have to work, and others are out having fun," Connie said jokingly.

"Your patients would not have it any other way. I have enjoyed spending time with my mother so far."

"I look forward to meeting her."

"She is excited about meeting you. Would you have dinner with us on Friday evening? By then we will be finished with sightseeing and probably be rested."

"That sounds good, see you then. Talk to you later Landon," "Goodbye Connie, have a good day."

"See I told you that was Connie, and that conversation was too casual. You did not tell her that you loved her."

"Mother I did not say that I was in love."

"We will discuss it later. We have arrived at our destination, and I am so excited to be here with you," said Violet.

Connie parked her car in the designated space at the hospital. I don't know if I will be nervous around Landon's mother or not. I have not told him how I feel about him. We have dated for three years, and neither one of us has talked about a commitment.

He is such a workaholic trying to make partner at Soco & Soco. I classify myself a workaholic to.

Landon has told me on numerous occasions how much he and his sister Kathleen missed their mother. They would love for her to move near one or the other. Maybe this trip to visit them will help make up her mind.

I wish my parents had more children so that I would have a sibling to talk to, visit, or hang out with. But, they chose to have one child, and they are happy today with how I have turned out.

I have done some terrible things in the past, that I know would not make them proud. I hope they never find out because it would break their hearts. If my patients knew about my past, they would not want me to be their doctor. I am going to be thankful today, go in and do my job. I will look forward to Friday evening with Landon. There is one of the patients I do look forward to seeing every day. I call her my adopted grandmother; her name is Lucy. I hate she has been in the hospital so long and alone. She has a brain tumor and is terrified to have surgery.

Her surgeon and I don't want her alone at home after surgery. She does not have family in the area. Her husband died about five years ago. She has a daughter named Louise who lives in California and will be here in the next couple of days. Her daughter is just like me, she is an only child and is going through the same thing. For three years, Louise has been trying to get her mother to move to California with her and her husband.

However, her mother is like Violet she feels like she will be intruding. After surgery, she is going to need some help and won't be able to take care of herself for a while. Connie walks into Grandma Lucy's room. "Good morning grandmother how are you doing this morning?" "Granddaughter Connie, I am doing better now that you are here."

"I am so glad you are feeling well. Did Louise call last night?"

"Yes, she is still bugging me about California. I don't want to leave my home."

"Grandmother, do you not want your daughter to take care of you?" "Yes, I guess so, but I don't want to be a burden to her and her husband."

"I don't believe they think you would be a burden. You know after you have this surgery, you are going to need help, so you can get well faster."

"There you go, you talk just like my daughter."

"It is because we love you. Has the doctor been in to see you this morning?"

"No, not yet. The nurse said he would be in at nine-thirty."

"Grandmother, I would love to spend all day with you, but I have other patients I have to see. I will come back in and see you when I get a break. While I am gone, you think about all the fun you can have in California. No cold weather or snow like we have in DC every year," remarked Connie.

"I'm going to think about it, and that's all. If you are thinking about it, then there is hope for your daughter. I will see you later."

"Okay, Connie. See you later."

CHAPTER 11

PUTTING TOGETHER THE STRATEGY

ALPHONSO was in his hotel room finishing up notes for his two- thirty meeting with Darnell at Soco & Soco. The meeting with Narvell this morning gave me a foundation to develop a strategy for this investigation.

From that meeting, I know Daniel was found dead in the room that I am staying. That is sort of creepy, but it was three years ago. I understand why Joshua was nervous when he brought me room service last night. He was the one who found Daniel dead. Joshua was cleared of any wrongdoings, but right now he would be my number one suspect until I can interview him. I will need to get the okay from DoubleTree management to interview Joshua onsite and other staff who were on duty that night.

The cameras for the hallways of the DoubleTree were not working that day for about six hours, so no one was captured going in or out of Daniels room. That is a problem. Will need to talk to hotel security.

Daniel had an affair with a lady name Madison who now possibly lives in Alaska, but lived in Atlanta at some point in time. She recommended a man name Elliott move to Alaska. Elliott lives in my

Condominium community and is a retired police officer. I may have to get Jason, Jermaine or one of the other investigators in the Alaska office to interview Elliott. I need to get more information about him.

Daniel's son Landon works for Soco & Soco. He was aware his father was having an affair with Madison. Don't know if he was aware that his father was planning on getting a divorce. I don't believe the daughter was aware of the affair. I had this feeling while talking to Narvell he had a crush on Madison, but she was not interested. I got the impression he was jealous she was having an affair with a married man and could have had a relationship with him a single man.

Landon could be a suspect because Narvell stated he could not account for thirty minutes he was stuck in traffic the same day his father died. I will set up an interview with him after I talk with Darnell.

I need to contact Q'UP the company where Daniel worked, and DoubleTree management for two separate meetings on Wednesday. Soco & Soco identified Peter as the contact at Q'UP and Jennifer at the DoubleTree. Darnell can give me a time to talk to Landon on Thursday at our meeting today. Mr. Daniels body will be exhumed before Wednesday and readied for an autopsy at the request of the brother and okayed by his widow Violet. I will have the results of that on Friday.

It looks like I have a plan and information for my report to Darnell this afternoon. I will now make some phone calls. Peter had told Susan his executive assistant he was expecting a phone call from Soco & Soco law firm investigator and to contact him as soon as he called. Peter phone rang, and it was Susan. "Peter, Alphonso from Soco & Soco is on the line."

"Okay Susan, I will pick up," said Peter.

"Greetings Alphonso, I have been expecting your call. What can I do for you?"

"Hello Peter, how are you? I know that Soco & Soco had contacted you before my call. I am following up to schedule an appointment for Wednesday."

"That will be fine."

"What about ten a.m?" Stated Peter. "That will be great," replied Alphonso.

"Do you have the address? If not, I will transfer you back to Susan to get it."

"No, I have it and will see you at ten tomorrow. Is there any security I must go through for the appointment? Asked Alphonso.

"No, Susan will meet you at the receptionist desk and bring you to my office. I look forward to meeting with you."

"See you, tomorrow. Goodbye."

Jennifer the DoubleTree hotel manager phone was ringing. "Hello, this is Jennifer."

"Hi, this is Alphonso one of your hotel guests and an investigator for Soco & Soco law firm. How are you?" Asked Alphonso.

"I am doing fine," said Jennifer.

"The case of a deceased guest of the DoubleTree named Daniel who died here three years ago has been reopened. I am the investigator from Soco and Soco and would like to question some of your staff while they are at work. The people I am most interested in are Joshua and your security personnel. They were working here at the same time during Mr.

Daniels stay before his death. I understand I am staying in the same room as the deceased."

"You are correct about the room, and I was expecting your call. I received a call from the corporate office letting me know the case has been reopened, and to expect a visit from your firm."

"I will contact Paul who is our hotel security manager and Joshua, then give you a call back about fifteen minutes."

"If possible, would like to talk to both after one p.m. on tomorrow." "How have your accommodations been since your arrival at the hotel?"

"Everything has been excellent, and I appreciate you asking."

"If you have any problems or if I can assist you further feel free to contact me directly."

"Thank you very much, Jennifer." "Goodbye."

I will make a quick call to Darnell while waiting for Jennifer to call back, to see if our meeting is still on for today. If so, I will have a quick lunch at the hotel and then head over to the firm.

Bethany just finished talking to Darnell and getting the conference room set up for a meeting with Alphonso when her phone started ringing. "Hello, this is Soco & Soco law firm, Bethany speaking, how can I help you?"

"Good afternoon Bethany, this is Alphonso. Just calling to confirm that my meeting with Darnell is still on for today."

"Yes, Alphonso, it is still on. It has been a while since we have seen you, Darnell is excited about your visit. We have changed our security procedures for entrance into the building so I will meet you at the front desk when you arrive on site. Just buzz me as soon as you get her. I will make sure you do not have to wait," said Bethany.

"I look forward to seeing everyone as well and thank you."

"I have another call coming in will see you later Bethany," As soon as Alphonso hung up with Bethany, he had another call. "Hello, again Alphonso. This is Jennifer the DoubleTree manager." "I recognized your voice."

"Paul will see you at two p.m. on Wednesday and Joshua at three- thirty p.m. Each will meet you on the third floor in our hotel conference room so that you will have privacy."

"Thank you, Jennifer, for getting back to me so quickly." "You are welcome. Goodbye."

One more phone call to AllTuck in Atlanta for an interview on Friday then I will have lunch.

Alphonso dialed AllTuck, and a man answered on the fourth ring. "Hello this is AllTuck, Matthew speaking, how can I help you?"

"Matthew, this is Alphonso from Soco & Soco law firm." "Yes, I was contacted by your firm last week,"

"I am calling to coordinate a meeting with you on Friday afternoon if that is possible?"

"Will two p.m. be okay?" Asked Matthew.

"Yes, that will be great, my flight gets in at ten a.m. That will give me time to get a rental car and check in at the hotel and possibly have lunch before we meet," said Alphonso.

"I will be awaiting your visit," said Matthew.

"I will have the executive assistant Joseph to bring you to my office, so I will see you on Friday."

"Thank you,"

"Goodbye," said Matthew.

Things are going better than I expected. Don't know how the interviews are going to go, but at least everyone has agreed to talk. I am going to head to the hotel restaurant, and hopefully, they have a good salad. I want to be alert when I speak to Darnell and not be sleepy. If I remember correctly, Darnell is a high energy person. I must always be on my A- game with him.

When Alphonso walked up to the door of the restaurant, the sign said, The Blue Room. I thought that was an odd name. The waitress seated me right away. I looked around the room to see the landscape, but there was nothing in the place that was blue. However, I did notice that about three tables across from me eating lunch was Joshua. I just nodded my head toward him to let him know I recognized him.

He glanced at me in a sort of nervous form. I wonder what that was. There is something suspicious about this guy and if there is, why has he hung around working at the hotel these past three years. Hopefully, I will get all my answers tomorrow in the interview. The waitress came back and took my order for a salad and bottled of water, but she seemed a little preoccupied with something.

She said, "I will bring your order shortly." Within five minutes I was eating my salad. After I had finished, the waitress came back.

She said "how was your meal sir, my name is Gina?"

"My meal was delicious. It was all I needed before my meeting this afternoon."

"I am glad you enjoyed it," said Gina. "Are you ready for your check?"

" Yes, but I would like to ask you something first."

"Why is the restaurant named The Blue Room, when nothing in the room is blue?"

"When this hotel first opened, there was a couple by the last name of Blue. They were the first guest here and had planned to stay for two weeks. They were celebrating fifteen years of marriage."

"On their second week here, Mr. Blue had a stroke and passed away. So, in honor of the first couple that stayed here as a guest, they named the restaurant after them. His wife still visits the hotel at least once a year with her family."

"That is a beautiful story and a great tribute to that family. I bet you get asked that question a lot."

"Someone asked almost every day." "I will take my check now."

"I have it with me."

"I will pay cash." He paid the check, left a good tip and headed back.

CHAPTER 12

WHO ARE YOUR FRIENDS

ELLIOTT was just getting settled into his Condo but needed some decorations to make the place look and feel like home. Lorraine, the condo manager, recommended a company by the name of CN&Y to hire as a decorator. Cindy is the owner, so I called her.

"Cindy this is Elliott at The Hillside View condominium. I was provided with your contact information from Lorraine, the condo manager."

"Hi, Elliott. Glad you contacted me. Lorraine is a great manager. What can I do for you, and do you have a specific timeframe in mind?"

"No, just soon as you can get me on your schedule."

"Mr. Elliott it depends on what you want. Let's start with what you had in mind. Are there any specific colors you like in any room? Is there a preference for wall items such as pictures? Do you like antique furniture pieces?"

"As for as colors, in the Master bedroom and bath, I would like black and gold. I know you are familiar with the layout of the condos. In my condo, there is a living room, master bedroom and bath, kitchen, guest bathroom, and an office. You can decide the other color schemes and any furniture that is needed for the other rooms if they are masculine. I don't have anything on the walls. So, whatever you come up with, I believe it will be great."

"The description of your condo, and just having a masculine look, makes it easy to come up with something you will like. First, I would like to come over today if possible and do a walkthrough. I can have everything ready to decorate by this Friday at 10 a.m. Is that good for your schedule?"

"My fee is $1500 per room, but I am giving you a 10% discount because of the referral. Your total is $8,000. We take cash, check, and any form of credit card, that is due upon completion of the job. If you have an email, I will send you a contract agreement for the work requested and the fee. You can sign electronically and email it back to me."

"That sounds great. I will send my email via text to your phone. Thank you for getting me on your schedule so quickly. Will see you later today Cindy."

"Thank you for your business, Mr. Elliott."

I told Cindy what I wanted over the phone. She came over the same day, did a walk-through of my condo, asked me a few questions, and told me everything would be in on Friday. She just needed to know what time I would be home.

Cindy asked me if I knew Alphonso because she had just finished decorating his condo. She suggested I look at his condo, to see what type of work they do. Cindy's company has done the interior decoration of at least twenty of the condos to include the Clubhouse. I told her I did not know him, but I had met him briefly at the new resident's party last Sunday. I said to her she came highly recommended, so I did not need to see any of the other condos. I can finally settle in a place where no one knows me.

I have been retired now for six months, and I must find a hobby or something to keep me occupied. Being a police officer for twenty-five years and then retiring has been a significant change for me.

Elliott's phone is ringing interrupting his thoughts. "Hello, this is Elliott."

"Hi Elliott, this is Madison. I was thinking and wondering about how you are doing. Where are you located now?"

"Madison you told me you were taking care of your mother in Alaska, but you did not say what city."

"I am in Delta Junction. Where are you?"

"I am in Fairbanks and only been here for a week. I decided to take your advice and move to Alaska."

"I don't know if that is such a great idea right now. This call is not a social one. Have you heard, Daniels' case has been reopened at the insistence of his brother Johnny? They supposedly have new evidence."

"Some hotshot investigator is on the case from a law firm called Soco & Soco located in Fairbanks. He is in Washington DC as we speak. That is all I know right now. I don't know if he will interview Daniels company Q'UP in Washington and AllTuck in Atlanta. How did you leave things in Atlanta?"

"I buried the gun where it will not be found," said Elliott. "Are you sure you did not leave behind any evidence?"

"I did not hear anything before I left, because you know I still have friends in the police department."

"I don't want to know where you hid it. That makes me feel a little better."

"Do you know the name of this investigator?" "No, I was not able to find out his name."

"Daniel's wife lives here in Delta Junction, and I have become her best friend. She is currently in Washington DC visiting her son and going to Atlanta to visit her daughter."

"Do you think that was a good idea for you to become friends with the wife."

"Our meeting happened by accident. Violet and I go to the same place for breakfast at least once a week. She introduced herself to me. So, the friendship started from there. I know it's probably not a good idea. I don't know what she will think of me if she finds out. One thing I am pretty sure of if she does find out, I won't be her best friend anymore. Keep your eyes and ears open. Don't call me unless you must, and I will do the same. Talk to you later Elliott."

After getting off the phone with Madison, Elliott started thinking to himself. Right when I thought things were beginning to turn out well, I get a shocking news call from Madison. I do believe whoever is investigating this case will come to the same conclusion as the police department and the DA's office did three years ago in Washington DC.

There was one thing about Daniel that I did not understand three years ago and that was he did not make a sound when I entered his room.

One other thing as I was walking down the hall in the hotel that same day, a guy was coming toward me with room service on the same floor. I will never forget him because he had a unique tattoo on his arm, that may have meant he had been in prison. Maybe I did leave some loose ends. Madison does not know the entire story of what happened to Daniel.

I was not able to talk to Daniel as I thought I would, but I was able to get his only hard copy of that AllTuck report.

I deleted the electronic copy from his laptop, and that's all Madison knows. At least we are both in the same state. She was so abrupt with me on the phone, I did not get a chance to ask about her mother or let her know how much I had missed her.

Was it a mistake coming to Alaska, hoping she and I would get together? I will give it some time because I have only been here a week. When I get my condo decorated, I will invite her and her mother for a visit.

As soon as Madison got off the phone with Elliott, she started wondering. I believe I can trust Elliott, after all, he was a police officer for twenty-five years. However, I have known some cops to turn dirty after being on the force for a long time. I don't believe Elliott gave me all the details of what happened at the hotel three years ago, except for what was in the news.

I had to vindicate my brother Scott somehow because him being in the military, he found out some of the same information that Daniel had found out about AllTuck. My brother's death was ruled accidental, but I believe he was murdered. He was one of the best soldiers, and I knew he was always careful. They told me his gun went off accidentally while he was cleaning it.

The two people I loved the most Daniel and Scott were taken away from me the same year. It was more than any one person should have to handle. My mother became ill the same year. So, it was almost like losing three people.

Daniel and I had planned to get married and he was going to inform his wife and children after he finished his last assignment. However, things did not work out.

I did not think anyone could love me as much as my father did, but I felt like Daniel loved me just as much. I do miss all the trips we went on and the long talks we had. He was my true best friend. A friend like I had never had before. I am friends with his wife, but that is a different friendship. I will call her tomorrow to see how her trip is going. Violet is that one of a kind individual like her husband. She loves and respects everyone and has no enemies.

Meeting people, she does not know for the first time you would think she has known them all her life. Sometimes I think she is too trusting of people. She and Daniel raised two beautiful children. I was hoping someday that Daniel and I would have at least one child. He told me Violet also wanted another boy. Just as Madison was finishing her thoughts, her phone starts to ring.

"Hello Madison, this is Violet."

"Oh, hello Violet. I did not recognize your voice. I was thinking about you and, I planned to call you tomorrow. You sound so relax and cheerful. Did you meet that special guy yet?" Asked Madison.

"I met someone on the plane, and I told him I was not interested," "You did what. You are not going to meet that special man by telling him you are not interested."

"Well, it did feel good that a man noticed me. I had not felt that way since my husband died."

"What was his name and how did he look? Was he tall and handsome?"

"His name was Alphonso, and he was handsome, tall, and had a body that you only see in the movies. I can't believe I am talking this way. He did ask me for my phone number so that we could have lunch while I was in the area, but I did not give it to him. I told him I came to DC to spend time with my son."

"I call to see how you and your mother are doing and to let you know I miss our morning breakfast. My son and I are having a great time." "Mother and I are doing fine. She asked if I had heard from you. I am glad you called. It is great you are having a good time. I miss our morning breakfast as well," said Madison.

"My son Landon and I were taking a break from sightseeing and having some lunch. I am going to my daughter on Saturday in

Atlanta, can't wait to see her. I will call later in the week or when I get to my daughter's." "Goodbye Violet and thank you for calling."

After Violet got off the phone, she thought Madison sounded happy to hear from her at first, and once I mentioned Alphonso, she paused for a long time before she said something. So glad her mother is doing well. I have become attached to her like she is my mother. Madison takes good care of her. I wonder if Madison knows this Alphonso guy I mention in our conversation.

She never talks about a man in her life. Maybe this guy Alphonso was the one, and something happened between the two of them. Perhaps he broke her heart, but he did not seem to be that type of guy. I will not worry about her personal life on my vacation. Landon and I are going to finish up our lunch and go to our last tourist site the Jefferson Memorial. I may have to reconsider this thing about moving near my children.

CHAPTER **13**

SOCO & SOCO LAW FIRM UPDATE

ALPHONSO was thinking about his lunch at the DoubleTree as he was driving to meet Darnell. The salad he had was healthy, enjoyable, and one of the best he had in a long time. It was a mixture of some of his favorite vegetables and fruits with a house dressing that made it taste even more better. I must continue to eat like this if I plan on attracting that special lady.

Soco & Soco is only a forty-five-minute drive from the hotel and lucky for me there is not much traffic today. I will call Bethany right now since I am only five minutes away from the office. Bethany phone is ringing. "Hello Bethany, this is Alphonso. I am now pulling into the parking lot will see you in five minutes."

"Okay, Alphonso. I am on my way to the receptionist desk."

Alphonso parked his car and walked swiftly to the building. As he was coming up the steps, he saw Bethany. "Hi, again Alphonso. Darnell had a quick office meeting. He will be a few minutes late. We are going directly to the conference room, and he will join you there. Have you had lunch yet?"

"I had a wonderful lunch at my hotel restaurant."

"They have an awesome deli on the first floor of this building, and I highly recommend it. So just get settled in the conference room, and Darnell will be in as soon as he finishes. Should be no more than fifteen minutes." "Thank you," said Alphonso.

In about twenty minutes Darnell walks into the conference room and greets Alphonso with a hello, and a hug. "Sorry had to keep you waiting. I will be in court on Friday, so I had to get some updates from my client. Man, it is good to see you. My other brothers and I feel like you have not only been good for our firm, but you are just like our other brother that mother never told us about," stated Darnell. Alphonso and Darnell both had a big laugh from his comment.

"If I am a brother, why don't I have ownership in this firm?" They both started laughing again.

"You are still the comedian in the family, and we need more investigators like you."

"That is some greeting and compliment. I feel honored and blessed," said Alphonso.

"Since our firm has reopened Daniels case I know you will get to the bottom of it. Let's talk and see where I can be of help."

"I had a meeting with Narvell at the Pentagon yesterday and man that guy had a wealth of information. I feel like I have a running start already. I have coordinated interviews for tomorrow with two of DoubleTree employees Joshua and Paul and with Peter at Daniel's company Q'UP. On Thursday I would like to meet with Landon, the deceased son who works here for Soco & Soco.

On Friday the autopsy results will be out in Fairbanks, and I am flying down to Atlanta to talk to Matthew at AllTuck the company that

Daniel was investigating. I have not been able to contact Landon's sister in Atlanta, but I plan on talking to her on Saturday, and visiting the last residence of Madison who was having an affair with Daniel."

"Can you give me a little information concerning each one of these interviews and why you think you need to interview these people and companies."

"As for as the DoubleTree employees, Joshua was the last person to see Daniel in his room because Daniel had ordered room service. When Joshua reached Daniel room, his door was open, and he found him dead and notified the hotel security manager Paul. On the day Daniel died the security cameras on Daniel's floor were not working. The meeting with Paul will deal with cameras. Security did not capture anything that day." "It could have been a planned downtime for the cameras," noted Darnell. "Daniel had completed his investigation of AllTuck and provided that information to his company at Q'UP. Hopefully, they will share that information with me, if not this is where I might need your help to get the report as discovery information."

"That would be an easy one, just let me know when."

"I received some information about Daniels creditors from Narvell, so I may need you to make the legal request for that information."

"Was he in financial trouble?"

"Don't think so, but when you start searching, you may find something unexpected."

"I want to speak with Attorney Landon for obvious reasons. He is the deceased son, and to see what he knew about the affair his father was having."

"Is Landon a suspect?"

"Not at this time. The only way I can eliminate him is by questioning him. I want to talk with Matthew at AllTuck because he was aware of Daniels findings, and how those findings would affect the company and its customers."

"Was that report electronically transmitted or hard-copied?"
"That I do not know yet."

"The gun that killed Daniel has not been found. Maybe the autopsy report will give us some clues. The wife of the deceased consented to the exhumation of his body. With all the new forensic information and tools, they have today, I believe we will find something because there was not an autopsy three years ago."

"The FBI should have insisted there be one, due to the high-profile cases Daniels were investigating at the time."

"Hopefully, I can make contact with Kathleen the daughter of the deceased while in Atlanta."

"There was a residence that the mistress Madison lived in a while in Atlanta and is now occupied by new residents. I hope they can shed some light on how anxious Madison was to sell the house."

"That should be interesting and probably scary for the current residents," said Darnell.

"Narvell provided me copies of all the transcript testimony, so there is no need to talk to the Washington police department right away. I will review this information sometime today or tomorrow. I will also meet with the Atlanta police department on Monday to see what they can contribute. The last person I would like to talk to when I travel back to Washington on Wednesday is Connie, Landon's girlfriend. She is not a suspect. I would like to know if she knew what type of gun Landon's father owned. Now you know as much as I do," said Alphonso.

"Alphonso, you have got your work cut out for you man. You have gathered a lot in just one day. From what you already know, do you suspect anyone?"

"I think Joshua, the company AllTuck, and the mistress of Daniel may have had something to do with his death but did not commit the act themselves. There are a lot of unanswered questions at this point. Of course, you know from your experience as a lawyer, it is not always the one you suspect committed the crime, but the one you don't suspect," expressed Alphonso.

"I will coordinate with Landon to come in the office on Thursday morning around ten a.m. He is on leave this week because his mother is visiting. Enough talk about work, let's talk about socializing this evening. Since we have a company car, I am going to have the driver pick you up at the hotel around five p.m. Dinner is at six. I am going to get Bethany to escort you out of the building. We look forward to seeing you at dinner tonight."

CHAPTER **14**

DINNER IS SERVED

DARNELL'S wife Juanita was so excited and taking a final look around the house for the dinner party this evening. Most people say I am a perfectionist, but I disagree. I just want to make sure everyone is comfortable when they visit our home. She did the last-minute check with the caterer for the food. We will have cocktails at five-thirty p.m. and dinner at six.

Darnell will be home at four. Our daughter is having a sleepover this evening at her friend's home, so I don't have to listen to her complain about how bored she is. I don't understand teenagers today. They have everything at their fingertips, and more, such as the latest computer technology, the most current cell phone that is out and yet they are still bored. I'm anxious to see Alphonso this evening. He is like a brother to Darnell. Alphonso does a lot for the firm of Soco & Soco overall. A great guy who is liked by everyone. I wish that I could find someone for him.

He deserves someone who is as unique as he is. The only single person I know coming this evening is Landon's mother.

I suspect she is not his type, but she does live in Alaska. Oh, enough matchmaking talk, let me get dressed so I can great everyone this evening looking my best.

While Landon was in his room getting dressed for the dinner at Darnell's, he was thinking to himself. What else must I do to become a partner at Soco & Soco? I have had a great relationship with Darnell the past five years. I have brought in more clients than any other lawyer over the past six months and have maintained those clients. My reputation for volunteering in the community is excellent and in line with the firm's vision. My personal relationships do not interfere with my work. After this vacation with my mother, I will have a talk with Darnell.

In the middle of his thoughts, Landon's mother walked in. "Landon, I have not been to a dinner party in years, so I hope I don't embarrass you with my old fashion social skills."

"First of all, mother you look stunning in that black dress. You have really taken good care of yourself. You will be fine just be yourself."

"Thank you, son. My friend back in Delta Junction helped me pick out this dress. She said I would probably go to a dinner party while in Washington, and you can never go wrong with black."

"Your friend was right. Why don't I take a picture of you, and you can send it to her this evening when we return or when you get a chance tomorrow."

"That would be great. Madison will be happy to know that I'm going out and having a good time. Are we ready to go?"

"Yes, I will turn all the lights out except the hallway light, so we don't walk into a completely dark house when we return this evening."

"Do you always turn the alarm on when you are away from home?" "Yes, except for when I'm running late for work and forget. We had several break-ins in the community the past six months, so I do my best to remember to turn it on."

"I downloaded an app to my phone that allows me to turn my alarm on away from home if I forget."

"I will never be able to do all those things that everyone does with their smartphones."

"I will give you some free lessons while you are here, and you can always search YouTube videos for anything you want to do."

"I have been doing some of that, but as I said, I am not technically savvy as you are. I can maneuver and do the things I need to do, and I am satisfied."

"Mother I will open the car door for you."

"You are a gentleman like your father, which tells me you were watching some of the things he was doing for me growing up. That also demonstrates that you are a gentleman with Connie."

Landon mumble to himself. Father was a gentleman with others as well. "What did you say about your father, Landon?"

"Nothing Mother, I was just mumbling to myself." "Are we still having dinner with Connie on Friday?"

"Yes, we are. Connie is looking forward to meeting you." "I am looking forward to meeting her as well."

"It should only take us about thirty minutes to get to Attorney Darnell's home." Landon was silent for most of the ride to Darnell. Violet was thinking to herself, why did Landon make that statement about his father opening doors for other women. I guess he thought I did not hear him.

Alphonso had just finished putting on his jacket when he received the call from Darnell's driver. He is parked in front of the hotel in a black limousine with Soco & Soco name on it. I feel special that Darnell has sent a car for me. That means I can have more than one cocktail, and I don't have to drive back to the hotel. It does not get any better than this.

Now if I could just meet a lovely lady at the party. It would be nice if I were taking Violet to the party. She probably has not had a second thought about me, but I have been thinking about her. There was something special about her, and I can't put my finger on it. I am going to put her out of my mind for right now and concentrate on enjoying the party.

I was able to get a quick phone call into captain Royster at the Washington police department before getting dressed. He clarified information for me concerning the bullet in the wall beside Daniel's bed, and the bullet shot to Daniel's forehead. He mentioned that there maybe be a connection of Daniels death to the death of a military sergeant locally at the military base. Narvell failed to mention that little piece of information. Alphonso arrived at Darnell's home at five-fifteen. Darnell and Juanita greeted him at the door. Darnell shook his hand, and Juanita gave him a big hug.

"It is so good to see you, Alphonso. You are just as handsome as the last time I saw you. We are going to have to find you a Washington lady and get you out of cold Alaska." Juanita said smiling.

"You are very kind, but I would love to find a lady who would move to Alaska. I could be persuaded if the right one comes along to pack my bags for Washington. How is my favorite niece Shanta?"

"She is going to hate she missed you, but she is at a sleepover at one of her friends. I get a break from parenting tonight, and I am going to enjoy it. She is doing good and growing up too fast."

"How old is she?"

"She is thirteen going on forty-nine."

"Come on Alphonso let's get a cocktail before we have dinner," suggested Darnell.

"I must go in the kitchen and check on things."

"Darnell thank you for sending a ride for me. You and your family have made me feel special and a part of the family."

"You are a part of the family, and all family members get treated the same. We have a bartender for the evening, so what are you having?"

"I'll have a Mojito to start." "Give me the same."

I will ask Landon this evening to come into the office on Thursday so you can interview him. Is that ok?"

"Yes, that will be fine."

"You know Landon is one of our best lawyers at this location of Soco & Soco. As a matter of fact, my brothers and I have mentioned making him partner this year."

"We need him cleared of any wrongdoing in his father's death." "Darnell, I don't think he is guilty. I just need some things clarified about his testimony he gave three years ago. The missing thirty minutes he testified to being in traffic getting to his father hotel the day he died, and when did he learn about his father's affair?"

"All those are great questions. Landon's mother is visiting this week so she will be here for dinner tonight. So, let's not alarm his mother of anything."

"Excuse me, Alphonso, I hear the doorbell ringing." Darnell goes to open the door. "Hello, Landon." Hello Attorney Darnell."

"No formal names tonight, just first names. This must be your beautiful mother."

"Yes, this is my mother, Violet."

"Welcome to our home, and it is nice to meet you."

"I see where this young man gets his good looks. He is one of the hardest working attorneys we have in the firm."

"It is nice to meet you as well. I have heard nothing but good things about Soco & Soco law firm and especially great things about you Darnell," "Thank you for those kind words. Here is my wife, Juanita."

"Hello Violet, welcome to our home." Juanita hugged Violet, and it made Violet feel a little more comfortable meeting them for the first time. "Landon has told us so much about how great a mother you are, and I can say that you have raised a great son and we are glad to have him in the family,"

"Landon, I need to speak with you a minute, Juanita can you take Violet into the parlor and see if she would like a cocktail?"

"Let's head to my office Landon, this will only take five minutes." Darnell opens the door to his office. "Come on in Landon. I don't know if you know, but your uncle Johnny came to Soco & Soco in Alaska to request us to reopen the case of your father. He brought new evidence. I don't have knowledge of what the new evidence is. We have an investigator name Alphonso from the Alaska office here tonight who is doing the investigation for the case."

"He would like to interview you on Thursday morning at the Soco & Soco office at ten a.m. I hope this time does not interfere with any plans you and your mother may have. He just wants to ask a few questions about your testimony you gave from the transcripts at the time of the initial investigation."

"No that will be fine. My mother and I have plans, but it was not a specific time. So, I will be there."

"Your mother is a beautiful lady, so I hope she enjoys her dinner tonight as well as the rest of the time she is spending with you."

"Landon let's get back to the parlor and have a drink. The drinks are on me tonight."

"I would hope so." Both just laughed as they walked back to the other guest.

On the way to the parlor, Juanita told Violet they were having drinks until the other guest arrives.

"You have a lovely home."

"Thank you. It is sometimes in chaos when my teenage daughter is here. She is at a sleepover with friends of hers tonight, so we have a little breather while she is away."

"I remember those days when my children were going through those teen years as well. So, I understand that you just need a break occasionally." Expressed Violet.

As they walked in the room where drinks were being served, Alphonso was seated in one of the chairs, and to his surprise there was Violet. He starts sweating and thought he was going to faint. Juanita walked over to Alphonso and began to introduce Violet, and he interrupted.

Alphonso nervously said, "I met Violet on the plane coming from Alaska to Washington. It is good to see you again Violet."

"Good to see you again as well."

"That is great you two have already met. Violet would you like something from the bar?" Asked Juanita.

"Yes, I would like a glass of white wine." The bartender poured the wine and Juanita handed it to Violet.

"Thank you," said Violet.

"Oh, I hear the doorbell, can you two excuse me for a moment. Violet have a seat, please. I will be right back."

"I never would have thought I would see you again. And please forgive me if I was so forward in asking to see you again and wanting your phone number on the airplane. You look beautiful this evening." expressed Alphonso with a smile.

"Thank you. I am sorry if I was rude in any way on the plane as well. I was guilty of watching too much news and seeing how women are being approached by strangers. I was just being cautious."

"You were right in being cautious. How is your wine?"

"It is good, help me to relax a little around people I have never met before."

"I have that same problem." "Would you like another wine?"

"No this is good for right now. Maybe I will have another with dinner." "Landon is your son that you were coming to visit here in Washington."

"Yes, he is my only son. I have a daughter in Atlanta. They are both doing well, and I am proud of them."

Juanita entered the room with the rest of her guest and made introductions.

After the introductions, Darnell and Landon walked in. "Dinner will be served in fifteen minutes."

"Everyone, get acquainted, have as many cocktails as you want, and I will be right back. Darnell will finish the introductions."

In about fifteen minutes Juanita came in to announce dinner is served and asked everyone to follow her. As they entered the dining room, Juanita stated, "there is no special seating arrangement, everyone should just sit where they feel comfortable."

After Landon and Violet were seated, Alphonso made it his business to sit next to Violet. Darnell and his wife sat at the head of the table on each end. There were three other guests, and they sat opposite of Landon and his mother. There was a total of eight people at the table to include the host. "We want to welcome Landon's mother from Alaska, and to thank her for dining with us this evening as well as Alphonso the best investigator in the country from our headquarters firm in Alaska." "Landon one of best lawyers in the firm and the son of Violet. Thank Ben and Julie for dining with us this evening. Ben is Darnell golfing buddy, and Carol is Juanita's bridge partner."

"Juanita and I are so happy that each of you could dine with us this evening, and we hope we can do this again soon. My wife has done a fantastic job, as usual, to make everyone comfortable and what a great meal we have for this evening."

Darnell blessed the food, and the caterers proceeded to bring in the first-course cucumber salad, then an appetizer of small vegetable egg rolls and cheddar bacon loaf. Next was the main course of glazed salmon, spinach, and parsley mashed potato with a roll and a beverage of Pinot Noir wine. After the main course, everyone was served coffee and a desert of deep-dish apple pie.

Violet commented Juanita on how beautiful the table was decorated, and Juanita thanked her. The meal was enjoyed by everyone. There was no legal talk at the dinner table, it is something that Darnell and Juanita had established when they first got married. So, the table talk was about family, current events and how to save the world. Landon seemed nervous all through the meal and did not say much the entire time except when he was asked a question. Alphonso and Violet had some active conversation going on, and Violet really enjoyed herself and thought that her son worked for a great firm. Darnell and Juanita thanked everyone for coming, and everyone departed at eight-thirty p.m.

CHAPTER 15

EVIDENCE REVEALED

ALPHONSO rolled over in the bed Wednesday morning thinking about Violet. What a great dinner party last night at Darnell and Juanita's, and especially sense Violet was there. Man, how beautiful she looked. I got a chance to sit next to her at dinner, and I can't believe I got her phone number. Getting that number was the highlight of the night.

Violet's son Landon was not very happy at dinner and did not talk much. He could have been upset because I was sitting next to his mother. I don't know what Darnell told him about the interview on Thursday. I have a long day with meetings this morning and afternoon, so I have to put thinking about Violet on hold.

First, I must get out of this comfortable bed, get a shower, and go down to the Blue room restaurant for a light breakfast. It would be nice if I had the Soco & Soco limousine to chauffeur me to Q'UP for my interview this morning.

Landon arose at six a.m. thinking about the interview he would have on Thursday with Alphonso. What new evidence could they possibly have when it was such a thorough investigation of my father's death. I don't understand why uncle Johnny would have the case reopen without talking to Kathleen and me. Mother and I will discuss this when she gets up this morning.

There is a soft knock on Landon's bedroom door, "yes mother I am awake." Violet opens the door.

"Landon, I got up to get some water from the kitchen and saw your light on. Is everything okay? Why are you up so early?"

"Mother lets go into the kitchen and make some coffee." "Landon, I will fix breakfast while you make the coffee," "Mother, did you know that father's case has been reopened?"

"Yes, Landon. I was going to discuss that with you at an appropriate time."

"Don't you think now would be an appropriate time?"

"Your uncle Johnny called me several weeks ago and wanted my approval to have your father's body exhumed so it could be autopsied. Your uncle never believed Daniel committed suicide, and neither did I. Johnny thinks the investigators missed something and he has not told me what new evidence was available to reopen the case. Landon, I hope this is okay with you and Kathleen because I want to know what happened to your father as well."

"Well, you did not seem to be concerned last night when you gave Alphonso your phone number."

"Is that why you are up so early this morning? Why were you unsociable last night? The people you work for appear to be terrific. They were kind to all their guests to include me."

"Landon, your father, was my first love, and will always be special in my heart."

"Your father is no longer with us, and I'm sure he would want me to have some happiness. It felt good someone noticed me because I haven't travel or had the attention of another man in three years. Truthfully, when I met Alphonso on the plane, I was rude to him. After arriving at your home, I felt terrible about how I treated him. Just because I gave him my phone number does not mean we are getting married tomorrow."

"It might be nice to have a male friend to talk to. You notice I said friend and not husband. Don't you have a female friend namely Connie that you talk to sometime and have dinner with?" Violet was a little upset. "Yes, Mother. I am sorry for my actions last night and not trusting your judgment. I want you to be happy and hopefully decide to live near me, or Kathleen."

"Mother while we are on this subject, I must go into the office on Thursday morning at ten a.m. for an interview with Alphonso concerning my father's death. It should only delay our sightseeing to the wax museum for about two hours. We won't have much time together, because Saturday you will be flying down to Atlanta to see Kathleen."

"Yes, it will be okay. You were not involved with your father's death, why are you being interviewed?"

"Mother, I won't know until Thursday. Let's take our focus off the investigation and eat this delicious vegetable omelet and toast you have prepared. After we finish, we can go sightseeing."

Alphonso arrived thirty minutes early for his appointment with Peter at Q'UP and gave the receptionist his name.

"Mr. Alphonso if you will just be seated, Susan will be with you shortly." Susan came in about fifteen minutes later. "Hello Mr. Alphonso, I am Susan. Will you follow me, Peter is waiting for you in the conference room. Did you have any problems finding the office?

"No problems at all, just a lot of DC traffic."

"Unfortunately, traffic is the norm seven days a week. Here we are the conference room. Peter this is Alphonso." Peter shakes Alphonso's hand. "How are you doing Alphonso?"

"Doing great. Thank you, Peter, for taking the time to talk with me today. I won't take too much of your time."

"Thank you, Susan. Will you close the door, so we can have some privacy?"

"Peter I am here because Daniel's brother requested the firm of Soco & Soco reopen his case. There was no absolute evidence that he committed suicide. My questions for you will focus on the final report that Daniel submitted to Q'UP. Can I get a copy of that report?"

"Absolutely, I will buzz Susan now, so she can have it ready when we are finished."

Peter rang Susan. "Susan, can you make a copy of the last report Daniel submitted concerning AllTuck, for Alphonso? He will need it before he leaves. Thank you."

"I want to know what happened to Daniel, a dedicated employee. He was not a quality control engineer as some people thought. He was an investigator like yourself who was investigating AllTuck because of a software barcoding problem. AllTuck contractors developed software for the barcoding system for the military exchange stores and it was overpricing all items when the customers checked out at the register."

"For example, if a bag of chips cost $2.99, and the cashier swiped the barcode for those chips, it would show up as $3.99, a minimum of one dollar more. The customers were not noticing this at first, because the software was doing this on every other item. This went on about six months until a young Sergeant by the name of Scott reported this to his Supervisor who was Sergeant Major Rick. Rick was responsible for ensuring this software was implemented and working correctly. He did not believe Scott when he reported this to him. Daniel and Scott found out that Sergeant Major Rick was getting money under the table from this company."

"This contract was more than a billion dollars. AllTuck was in jeopardy for losing this and all future military contracts as well as going out of business."

"Daniel believed that Scott was silenced by his death. The military investigated and ruled it accidental from cleaning his military issued weapon. Daniel had to end this investigation because he was having an affair with Scott sister Madison who coincidently worked for AllTuck."

"Daniel did not find out about Madison and Scott until he was almost finished with the investigation and Madison never mentioned her brother to him. Even though Daniel suspected Madison had some involvement with the AllTuck contract, he and Madison still planned on getting married before he died. That is the rest of the final report."

"Tell me what kind of person was Daniel?"

"Daniel was the type of employee everyone wanted to work for. When he first came to work here, he was the best investigator the company had. Cold cases that had been closed for years, Daniel solved them."

"A dedicated husband and father until he met Madison."

"I don't think Violet knew Daniel was an investigator. I think she thought he was a quality control officer. Daniel's job could get dangerous at times, so he did not want Violet to know. His children Landon and Kathleen adored him. He was detail oriented, people person, who got along with everyone here at the office. Daniel was very considerate of others, and compassionate when it came to families with problems in the office. So, I would say he was an ideal employee."

"Did his wife ever visit him here in DC while he was working on a case?"

"Not that I am aware of. Violet was sort of a homebody. She stayed home and raised the children while he was away, and never complained. There were times when Daniel travel for long periods for the company, and I found out later he was spending some of that time with Madison."

"Did the other employees know he was having an affair?"

"I think maybe some of them did, but I don't believe anyone said anything about it."

"Did he have any enemies in the office?"

"If he did, I saw no evidence," replied Peter. "Did Daniel own a gun?"

"Yes, the company required him to have one, and he was bonded. It was purchased by our company, but it was never found during the investigation."

"What type of gun was it?"

"I believe it was a Springfield XD .45 ACP. We did turn in a lost report to the police department for that gun."

"Well, I guess that wraps up things for me. Thank you so much for being so cooperative and answering all my questions Peter."

"I will have Susan to bring you a copy of the report, and she will escort you back to the reception area."

"It was nice talking to you, and if there is anything else, I can do to help you bring closure to this case, feel free to call," said Peter.

"When this case is solved, I will ensure that you are notified before it goes to the media." Peter went back to his office and Susan came in.

"Here is your report Alphonso. We will head back to the reception area so you can get on with the rest of your day," said Susan.

"Thank you for everything."

That interview went well with Peter and did not last but an hour. I will drive back to the DoubleTree before the traffic gets bad and grab a salad for lunch at the hotel before interviewing DoubleTree employees. I am puzzled as to why Madison did not tell Daniel about her brother. Maybe she did not tell him when they first started the affair and told him later after the relationship progressed.

After meeting, Violet, can't imagine why Daniel would get involved with Madison. Of course, I have not met Madison, so I have no comparison. Alphonso finished his lunch in the blue room and then caught the elevator up to the third floor of the Doubletree for his interview with Paul, the security manager. As soon as he reached the conference room, the door was already open, and Paul was waiting.

"Hello, you must be Alphonso," Paul gestured to shake his hand. "Yes Paul, I am Alphonso and glad to meet you. Thank you for responding. I won't keep you long. I work for the law firm of Soco & Soco as an investigator. I am here because the case of Daniel has been reopened."

As you know, he was a guest here three years ago and was found dead in his room. I understand that you were the security manager on duty the night of his death."

"Yes, I was here."

"Why were the video surveillance cameras off that night in the hallway on Daniel's floor?"

"The cameras had a planned outage of four hours that night for an upgrade to the software. It ended up being six hours due to some compatibility issue the software and the hardware. The update was performed remotely from DoubleTree headquarters, and all DoubleTree hotels were getting the same update during that week. Security at this hotel location had no control of the update. We received a phone call from DoubleTree headquarters right after the upgrade was completed and we were instructed to restart the cameras," explained Paul.

"While the cameras were down, we were not able to capture any activity on the floor where Daniel the deceased was found, but this upgrade affected the entire hotel."

"Was this upgrade publicized to the public or the guests in each of the hotels?" Asked Alphonso.

"It was publicized in general to the public, but no details or dates were given," answered Paul.

"When was this hotel notified?"

"All DoubleTree hotel and security managers were given a schedule." "Could someone in the hotel have gotten access to those schedules?"

"No, I don't think so. This is a huge hotel, and we have a lot of guests all the time as well as a lot of DoubleTree staff and contracted workers that keep this hotel operational daily."

"Who has access to the operations center or control room for security besides you?"

"Operation center is the correct name. We have three shifts and three people on each shift, for a total of nine people who would have access. Two people monitor all the time, and one person manages each shift." "When one of the monitors goes to lunch or to the bathroom what happens?"

"The Manager for the shift steps in, as I said before, there is always two people monitoring,"

"Who notified you of what happened that night?"

"Joshua was delivering room service and found Daniel dead. He called me right away. I then notified the hotel manager Jennifer. She called 911." "How much time will you say went by before 911 was called, and how long did it take the police and the coroner to arrive?"

"I was notified within a couple of minutes of the discovery of the body. I went to the room to verify guest was deceased. I called Jennifer, and she met me in Daniel's room. It took the staff about ten minutes for notification, and the police and coroner arrived within twenty minutes of the 911 call for a total of thirty minutes. That is great timing for this area because of the traffic."

"When and who notified the deceased family?"

"The city police notified the son Landon here in DC, then the son notified the sister Kathleen in Atlanta, and the brother Johnny notified the wife Violet in Alaska."

"You seem to know all the details for notification of family members." "The hotel has a standard plan for notifying guest family if an incident or emergency happens and we do all we can to assist a family."

"What did the police say was the initial cause of death?"

"They ruled it suicide based on what the coroner found."

"Did you know the deceased, or anyone that may have been associated with him?"

"No, but I did see the deceased have dinner here at the hotel frequently with a woman. I know now she was not his wife. He also had dinner here with his son on several occasions."

"That wraps it up for me. Thank you for your cooperation, time, and honesty. I don't feel that I will need to get any further information from you, but if I do, I will notify the hotel manager."

"Here is my business card you can contact me directly," said Paul.

"No, I think it best I go through proper channels by notifying the hotel manager."

"I am going to just wait here in the conference room for Joshua if that is okay? Thank you again," said Alphonso.

"I'm glad I was able to be of assistance."

Alphonso was thinking to himself after Paul left. He seems to have a lot of knowledge concerning this case and was eager for me to contact him directly.

The transcript that I was given by Narvell did not mention anything about a software upgrade for the surveillance cameras. Why was that important detail left out of Paul's statement at the time of Daniel's death? As Paul was walking back to his office, he remembered that he talked to his retired police officer friend Elliott about the schedule and when the cameras would be down. I also mentioned to Elliott the hotel would have no surveillance for four hours the same day Daniel was found dead.

Paul and Elliott frequently had drinks on the weekend when he was still living in the DC area. Elliott was familiar with surveillance equipment, because of the nature of his job. Elliott's home was in DC, but he also had a rental in Atlanta. He kept the house in DC after his wife died from cancer. They did not have any children. The last time they talked was six months ago at our favorite bar Joe's place. He told me he was moving to Alaska. I will have to give him a call this evening or tomorrow.

Within twenty minutes after my interview with Paul, in walks Joshua to the conference room, and he was nervous.

"Come on in, I take it that you are Joshua, and I am Alphonso, have a seat."

"I am an investigator with the law firm of Soco & Soco. My reason for this interview is the case for Daniel has been reopened. I understand he was the guest you found dead in his room three years ago. I am a guest now in that same room."

I noticed Joshua was sweating badly. "Yes, you are right." "Relax Joshua you don't have any reason to be nervous."

"I am still on probation, and I can't get in trouble here at the DoubleTree. They have been good to me."

"I am only here to ask questions and get some clarifications. Is it correct that you have worked here at this hotel since the incident occurred?" "Yes, that is correct. Because of my troubles and background with law enforcement, my family and I thought it best to stay here."

"The DoubleTree has given me an opportunity that no other employer would. So, I am both thankful and grateful."

"Joshua, what time was it when you brought room service to the deceased?"

"If I remember it was around eight p.m. not much later. I remember that time because I work the same hours today as I did that night."

"And what were those hours and why did you choose to work them?" "My hours are from two till ten p.m. I have two kids, and my wife works from eleven p.m. to seven a.m. This time works out for both of us to ensure one of us can attend school activities. It also ensures someone to be at home with our children at night," stated Joshua.

"Joshua I am happy for you that the hotel worked that schedule out for you and your family. Now when you arrived at Daniel's door what happens next?"

"The door was slightly open. I was almost afraid to go in because the hotel management teaches us not to enter a guest room if it is open. I had a funny feeling, so I opened the door and called out for Mr. Daniel, but he did not answer. I walked into the room and what I saw was Mr. Daniel lying on the bed with blood coming from his forehead. I dropped the tray of food and immediately stepped out of the room and called Paul the security manager."

"Did you touch anything?"

"Only the door, which I pushed open with my left hand." "What happened next?"

"Paul asked me to stay outside the room, within five minutes he arrived and entered the room. After calling Daniel's name several times, he did not answer."

"We both assumed he was dead. Paul called Jennifer the hotel manager. She came to the room within minutes. She walked into the room where Paul and the deceased were. Jennifer asked Paul if he was sure Mr. Daniel was dead and Paul said absolutely. There was a single gunshot wound to the head. Shortly after Jennifer called 911. She asked Paul and me to stand outside the room and wait for the police."

"Jennifer went back to her office to call corporate DoubleTree CEO. Jennifer arrived back at the room with the ambulance service and the coroner."

"I know that you were questioned by the police that same day. Can you recant some of the things they asked?"

"They asked when I arrived at the room, did I touch anything?" "Was anyone in the room when I arrived beside the deceased?" "Did I go to any other room beside the bedroom?"

"Was anyone in the hallway when I came in the room and when I came out? They asked me the same questions you asked me today?"

"I am going to ask you one more of the same questions that the police asked you. When you got off the elevator and were walking down the hallway to Daniels room that evening, was their anyone else in the hallway or waiting to get on the elevator?"

Joshua thought for a minute. "A man was waiting to get on the elevator. He had on a hat and a badly wrinkled jacket, with a funny looking mustache. He also had his head down when he walked passed me going toward the elevator. He was actually built like someone I know, but if it was that person why would he not speak to me?"

"Who do you think that person might have been?"

"I think it could have been my neighbor Elliott or someone of his same build. I did not see his face so I cannot say for sure it was him."

"Did you notice anything unusual in Daniel's room?"

"I would not say it was unusual, but I believe there was a bottle of wine on the nightstand, with one glass sitting beside it."

"Did you know the deceased, or anyone connected with him?"
"No, I did not."

"Thank you for your cooperation, time, and patience with my discovery for this case. If I have additional questions, I will contact the hotel manager," said Alphonso.

"I am glad I was able to assist, and I hope this case is brought to closure once and for all," commented Joshua.

"I will lock the room on my way out if you are finished."

"Yes, I am finished. Let me just gather up my laptop. Thank you again, Joshua."

Alphonso realized it was going to be a long night analyzing all this information from these interviews that he had conducted today. He decided he would order room service for dinner. It appears a lot of information was missed by the police in the initial investigation. I'd like to reference some of this information when I interview Landon tomorrow. I believe the key to this entire case is the surveillance system not being operational in the hotel.

I now understand why Joshua was so nervous. He is a good man, looking out for his family even though at some point in his life he made a mistake. The key to him being able to take care of his family was this job at the DoubleTree. Narvell had mentioned how successful this program had been for the DoubleTree, and how they were making a difference in this Help-One program, by giving inmates a second chance.

CHAPTER 16

IS HE A SUSPECT

ELLIOTT was just returning home from a sightseeing tour of Fairbanks and was happy he had moved to the area. Even though his condo looked a little bare at this time, Cindy would be coming on Friday to decorate and make it look more like home. Fairbanks was a lot like Atlanta, just not hot. Elliott cell phone was ringing as he walked to the kitchen to get a soda. He recognized the area code as Washington DC, but not the number. "Hello, this is Elliott."

"How is it going Elliott, this is Paul?" "Hi, Paul, I did not recognize your number."

"This is my work cell number. What have you been doing since you retired?"

"Absolutely nothing. Love it, should have retired sooner. I do miss the job, but not the headaches that came with it. Instead of moving back to Washington to my home where there are lots of memories of my wife, I purchased a condo in Fairbanks, Alaska."

"I was also able to find someone to rent my house in DC."

"I got a recommendation from a longtime friend, who stated Fairbanks is a great place to live if you don't mind the cold and some days of complete darkness. What do I owe the pleasure of your call?"

"Did you know that the case of Daniel has been reopened due to new evidence? He was the guy that was found dead in the DoubleTree hotel three years ago."

"A law firm out of Alaska, by the name of Soco & Soco, has assigned their well-known investigator Alphonso, to handle the case. I was questioned by him today,"

"Why would he want to talk to you?"

"He wanted to talk for the same reason I called you. Do you recall about three years ago you and I had a drink at our favorite bar? I told you about the software upgrade for the surveillance cameras for all DoubleTree hotels. I also mention the hotel would be unsecured for a four-hour timeframe. Alphonso asked me if anyone could have gotten the schedule and the specific time for our hotel location?"

"I told him I didn't think so. Then I remembered I had mentioned it to you."

Elliott asked Paul in a concerned voice, "is that what you told the investigator? I don't recall you relaying that information to me."

"No, I did not tell Alphonso I talk to you. At the conclusion of my interview, the investigator stated he would not have any further questions for me."

"Did the investigator interview anyone else besides you?"

"Joshua an ex-con who works in the restaurant and does room service is the only other person I know Alphonso interviewed."

"Did you say Joshua works there?" Elliott seemed surprised.

"Yes, he has been working here for three years. He is an outstanding employee according to the manager."

"Have you heard anything from the police department since you retired?" Paul inquired.

"I have not contacted anyone since I left. Is that all?"

"Yes, I just thought I would give you a quick call since you were a police officer on the case for a short period."

"Thank you, Paul, for the information. If you hear anything else feel free to give me a call,"

"I will do that. Goodbye, Elliott." "Goodbye, Paul."

I was not expecting that phone call. I thought the DC police department did a very comprehensive investigation. What could they have missed?

The aroma of coffee coming from the kitchen woke Landon up on Thursday morning. He walked into the kitchen to find his mother drinking a cup of coffee and holding her head down. "Good morning mother how are you doing?"

"Landon I am okay just concerned about your interview with Alphonso today."

"Mother did you not get the memo, not to worry?"

"What did you say about the memo Landon," Violet asked.

"Don't worry about what I said, it was just a joke we use around the office. Mother no need to worry, you are forgetting, I'm the best lawyer in the Washington area. I know my rights and how to handle myself. I had nothing to do with my father's death don't you believe me?"

"Of course, son. I'm just concerned about them wanting to question you again after all this time has gone by."

"Mother, do you want to know the truth about what happened to father?"

"Yes, I do, but I don't want our family to go through this all over again. I am partly the blame for this because I allowed your uncle to reopen the case. For right now I must get my mind off all this. I am going to fix you my special one egg omelet and toast, so you don't go into your interview with an empty stomach,"

"That will be great. I will take a quick shower while you are doing that."

"Are you going to be okay here until Connie arrives?"

"Yes, I will be fine. I look forward to meeting Connie. We will have a lot to talk about."

"Mother can I trust you not to tell Connie all my childhood secrets."

"Who's going to talk about childhood, we will be busy talking about you and her future."

"I knew this was not a good idea, but I did not want to leave you here alone."

"Connie should arrive about the same time I will be leaving for the office. She has a patient consultation at seven-thirty a.m. at the hospital and then she will be here."

As Landon and his mother were finishing eating their breakfast, the doorbell rang. "That must be Connie. I will get the door mother, please behave for a few hours."

"Good morning Connie," Landon gave her a quick kiss on the lips. "Good morning Landon," with a smile on her face.

"Come on in and thank you so much for staying with mother for a couple of hours. I know this was last minute."

"Glad I could help. We will have a great time while you are gone."

"We just finished breakfast, so she is in the kitchen cleaning up the dishes."

Connie and Landon walk to the kitchen where his mother was waiting. "Well hello, Connie."

"Hello, Ms. Violet how are you this morning?"

"I am doing just fine. Glad we finally meet and get a chance to hang out. Have a seat. Would you like some coffee or tea?"

"Yes, coffee would be great. I was up early with my patient this morning, so I did not get a chance to have my early morning cup of joe."

"My briefcase is in the car, so I am going to head to the office. Should be back around noon."

"Okay, son, see you then, be careful."

"I am blessed to have a son like Landon. No mother could ask for any better."

"He is a great guy. A woman like me with such a busy life is lucky to have met him."

"Tell me about Connie. How did you decide you wanted to be a doctor?"

"It started with my grandfather, my mother's father. When I was ten years old, he got colon cancer and had to be hospitalized for a long time. His doctor tried some experimental medicine on him that helped him to live two years longer than they had predicted. After he passed, I told my parents I wanted to become a doctor when I grow up, so I can help people to live longer. So here I am saving lives one day at a time."

"If we only had more doctors like you, people like me would not mind going to the doctor."

"Connie lets go into the living room and get more comfortable." They sat on the sofa next to each other.

"Did you meet Landon's father before he passed?"

"Yes, I did. The first time I met Daniel I thought I was being interrogated. Landon and I had dinner with him. He asked many questions about my background. The second time I met him, he was a little bit more relaxed, but I was still nervous."

"Oh, I'm sure he did not mean you any harm. He was protective of Landon throughout his entire childhood, from the first day he was born till he left home for college."

"That explains why they had such a close father and son relationship. But I did learn a couple of things about him. He loved you, his job, and he enjoyed drinking California Sonoma Coast Pinot noir wine."

Connie paused for a few minutes and stopped talking. She was thinking to herself if Daniel loved Violet so much, why did I see him all hugged up kissing another woman on several occasions? If I keep talking about him, I'm going to tell her what I know. I don't think she knows the truth. They say like father, like son, but I hope that Landon will not be that way. I am more into Landon than he is into me, but he did ask me to sit with his mother that has to mean something.

"Connie you got very quiet and seemed nervous for a moment, are you okay?"

"Yes, I'm okay, just a little concerned about Landon. I wonder why he is being questioned again about his father's death? He had nothing to do with it."

"You seem pretty sure. Is there something you know that could help with this investigation?"

"No, I did not mean to insinuate or upset you, but Landon has been gone for three hours. I hope everything is okay."

"I am concerned too. Let's try not to worry," expressed Violet with concern in her voice.

"How did you and Landon meet?"

"We met at a restaurant called Le Diplomate, a favorite of local politicians. As a matter of fact, I think the three of us are having dinner their Friday evening."

"I was sitting at the bar having a glass of wine waiting for a table, and Landon came in and sat at the bar next to me. He ordered a glass of wine. This restaurant is always crowded, so it is best to make a reservation, and neither one of us had done so."

"We introduced ourselves, and for about twenty minutes we talked about each other's jobs. I was bold and asked him if he would like to share a table for dinner?"

"He was hesitant, then he said how harmful can it be to have dinner with a doctor. When the waitress came to seat us, we told her we would share a table. Before dinner was over, we both shared each other's cell phone numbers. And can I say the rest is history."

"What a beautiful beginning for you and my son and I am so glad he met you. Every time I talk to him on the phone, he is working and not doing much of anything else. I think he is still grieving over the loss of his father. He never mentions him unless I bring it up, so It appears he has some sort of guilty feeling about his death, and I don't know why? Connie, I have just about talked your head off. Let us watch TV. It will take both of our minds off what is going on with Landon. He should be here shortly."

Landon arrived at Soco & Soco at nine forty-five a.m. for his appointment with Alphonso. He went directly to his office to put his briefcase down. Logged into his computer to take a quick look at his email. As he was accessing his email, Alphonso tapped on the door. "Good morning. Hope I am not interrupting anything,"

"Good morning to you Alphonso. I was just making sure I did not have any emails that needed my immediate attention. I have not been in the office since my mother came to visit. Why don't we meet in the conference room, so we don't have any interruptions?"

"I will see you there," said Alphonso. "I will join you shortly."

Landon finished looking at his emails, then left his office to join Alphonso in the conference room. "Come on in Landon, this won't take long." Alphonso noticed that Landon appeared to be nervous. I must make him comfortable; otherwise, I won't get my questions answered.

"Landon you are not under any suspicion, about your father's death. I must interview everyone that may have known your father or anyone that was interviewed three years ago. I am sure Darnell mention to you, or you probably know by now that your uncle Johnny hired this firm to reopen your father's case and that your mother authorized exhumation for an autopsy."

"Yes, I am aware."

"Before we get started, I will need you to sign a consent form agreeing to my recording our conversation."

"That sounds like you suspect me of some wrongdoing. Are you trying to ruin my career here at the firm? I have worked hard here since day one, and I was hoping to make partner this year."

"I was not trying to upset you, Landon. We are getting off to a bad start. Would you feel more comfortable if Darnell was in the room while I ask questions?"

"No, I don't need him here thinking the same thing you are. I don't have anything to hide so I will sign the form."

"Landon, I work for this firm as well, and I have to answer to them for this case. I just have some verification questions that were asked of you by the police department at the time of your father's death. If you are ready, we will get started. What kind of relationship did you have with your father?"

"He and I were very close, and we could talk about anything."
"What kind of relationship did he have with your mother?"

"As for as I knew at the time, they had a loving relationship. My father was away from home a lot, and I think it might have put a strain on their marriage."

"Were you aware that your father was having an affair with a lady by the name of Madison?"

Landon paused for a second and had a surprised look on his face. "Yes, I was aware."

"You seemed surprised."

"I did not know how many people knew about the affair."

"Were you aware your father and Madison were planning on getting married?"

Landon had an angry reaction to this question and said in an angry voice. "No, I did not know that!"

"How did you find out about the affair?"

"I saw them together a couple of times here in the city."

"Did you confront your father about the relationship and how did he react?"

"I did confront him, and he apologized and told me it just happened and that he loved my mother very much."

"How did that make you feel?"

"I could not understand how he could love my mother and then have an affair with another woman. A woman that you now tell me he was going to marry."

"Did you discuss the affair with your mother or anyone else?"
"No, I did not want to hurt my Mother."

"On the day of your father's death, did you visit him in his room at the DoubleTree hotel?"

"Yes, I went there to talk about the affair and hoped, he would end it, but I was unsuccessful. He said he loved Madison and my mother."

"In the police testimony you gave during the initial investigation, it stated that you were stuck in traffic for thirty minutes before getting to your father's hotel, can you explain that?"

"Yes, the traffic is always bad in DC; therefore, you can never give someone the exact time that you will arrive at a particular location." "Do you recall anything that was going on specific that day?"

"I don't recall, but it might have been an accident."

"Did you tell anyone what time you were meeting with your father?" "I don't think so."

"We have been here over an hour; would you like to take a ten-minute break?" Asked Alphonso.

"Yes, I need to use the bathroom." As Landon was leaving the bathroom, he said to himself, why can't I remember what was going on in traffic that day I was visiting my father.

Alphonso and Landon returned to the conference room about the same time.

"I feel better now that I have emptied my bladder. I had two cups of coffee this morning for breakfast, and I could not hold it any longer," stated Alphonso.

"Before we start with new questions, I did remember something when I went to the bathroom. I told my friend Connie the night before I was going to see my father and what time I was meeting him."

"Thank you for your honesty."

"Do you own a gun and when was the last time you fired it?"

"Yes, I do. About every six months, I go to the rifle range that is not far from my home."

"Do you have a license to carry and what type of gun is it?"

"Yes, I have had a license for about four years now. The gun I own is a Springfield 45."

"That is a very expensive gun. Is there any particular reason why you purchased that specific gun?"

"My father recommended I buy that type because he had the same one. There have been several break-ins in my subdivision and several others in the surrounding area. My community has security, but not 24-hour coverage. Having the gun was a way of protecting myself."

"Did you have the gun in your possession the night of your father's death?"

"I don't remember. Are you trying to say I had something to do with my father's death because I own a gun?"

"No, I am just going through my list of questions I need to ask. Did your father have his gun on this trip?"

"I assume so, because he is bonded, and his gun was purchased by his company."

"Let's go to a different topic. How long have you and Connie been dating?"

"We've been seeing each other about three years."

"Are their immediate plans for you and Connie to get married."

"Not at this moment. The both of us have hectic schedules, so we don't get to spend a lot of time together."

"How does she feel about you?" "I think she is more serious than I am," "Why do you say that?"

"She talks about having more children than her parents because she did not have siblings growing up, and she would not want that to be the case for her children."

"Did she meet your father and how did your father feel about her?"

"Yes, she did. My father has always been protective of me, so the first time he met her, he asked a lot of questions. He actually made both of us feel uncomfortable."

"Did she know about the affair your father was having?" "I did not tell her, so I don't think so."

"Does Connie own a firearm?"

"She has never talked to me about one, but that does not mean she doesn't have one. So now you think that Connie had something to do with my father's death. She did not even know him that well." Landon answered in a frustrated tone.

"No, again I am just asking the questions I had on my list."

"Did the police question Connie, because I did not see any testimony in the transcript?"

"No, they did not have a reason to talk to her."

"Did you know they had surveillance cameras at the DoubleTree hotel?"

"I did not, but I do know most hotels do have them for the safety of the guest."

"Were you aware of your father's occupation at Q'UP?" "Yes, he was an investigator."

"Did you know the nature of the last case he was working on before his death?"

"No, I did not. My father did not discuss his cases with me, and neither did I discuss mine with him."

"Do you know of a Washington police officer name Elliott?"

"I don't know him personally, but he worked on my father's case initially, but was taken off the case and transferred to Atlanta to work on another case."

"There was a bottle of wine in your father's room when he was found, did you take him that wine and if not, did you notice if the wine was open?"

"No, but I did notice the wine. Not sure if it was open," "Was there anything special about the wine?"

"Yes, it was his favorite, California pinot noir. I do remember there was one glass sitting beside the bottle."

"How did your father feel when you left his room?"

"He was upset that I had confronted him about the affair, but he was also concerned about a report he had to submit to his company about a case he had been working on. He did not give me any details about the report. But, did tell me he was going home to see my mother after he submitted the report to his company."

"You have answered all my questions, and I did not plan to keep you for three hours."

"Can you recall or think of anything else that might be relevant to this case, that we did not cover in this interview?"

"No, I don't."

"I do have a question for you concerning my mother. I noticed at the Dinner party at Darnell's that my mother gave you her cell number. What if any intentions do you have?"

"Well at this point I can't say I have any intentions, except to solve this case."

"I met your mother on the plane on the flight coming from Alaska to Washington on Monday. I did not know at the time you were her son. I wanted her number in case I have questions concerning your father's investigation."

"I would appreciate you coordinating with me when it comes to father's case."

"I will do that. Again, thank you for your cooperation," "Did I have a choice?"

"At this point, no. Keep your head up about the partner with Soco & Soco. I've heard nothing but good things about your work. The Soco brothers are fair and awesome people to work for."

As Alphonso and Landon were leaving the conference room, Darnell approached them at the door.

"You guys had a long meeting."

"Little longer than we expected," said Alphonso.

"I am headed home, I left Connie with my mother while I was here." "Okay, Landon see you in the office on Monday."

"Alphonso, can I have a word with you in the conference room?" "How did the interview go with Landon?"

"It went well. I was able to get all my questions answered. Landon was angry at first and sometimes nervous during the interview. He made me think he knows something about the case he is not telling."

"I know you will get to the bottom of this case."

"Alphonso, I just got a call from the police department in Atlanta, and they have found the gun that may have been used in the shooting of Daniel. Interestingly the gun was a Springfield XD.45."

"That's the same type of gun that Landon owns. Is that a coincident or was that a very popular gun during the time Daniel died?"

"I did make contact with my brother Jacoby in Atlanta, he may have the information concerning the gun by the time you get there."

"They have sent it to the forensic lab for fingerprints. I know you are scheduled to go to Atlanta tomorrow, so you need to reach out to them as soon as you arrive there," stated Darnell.

"My flight leaves tomorrow morning at ten a.m. I plan to talk with AllTuck contracting company, visit the home where supposedly Madison lived, interview Daniel's daughter and possibly his wife, Violet. Madison seems to be the key to this investigation."

"We need to get your brothers in Fairbanks to find Madison and interview her and Elliott. I will email you and them a summary of what I have so far."

"I have some doubts about some of the questions that I asked Landon."

"I look forward to reading your report."

"I am headed to the hotel, to get ready for my trip to Atlanta."

As Landon was driving home, he called Connie to let her know he was on his way. After about a forty-five-minutes he arrived back at home. He parked his car in the garage and walked inside through the laundry room. Connie and his mother were in the kitchen preparing lunch.

WHO WOULD HAVE THOUGHT

"I am just in time, what are we having?" Asked Landon.

"Tomato basil soup and roasted turkey on wheat bread. I was worried about you Landon," said Violet.

"There was no need, the interview just went longer than we expected. Connie thank you so much for staying here with mother."

"No problem, I had cleared my schedule for the day. I don't have to be back at work until eight a.m. tomorrow."

"Let's eat this wonderful lunch you ladies have prepared." "Okay," said Violet and Connie in unison.

"Landon, I need to leave about three p.m. to pick up some laundry from the cleaners before it closes at four-thirty."

CHAPTER **17**

FAMILY AND AUTOPSY

"HELLO Daddy, this is Madison."

"Hi, honey I was just thinking about you, and your mother."

"Mother and I were talking about you as well. Daddy, I am in Delta Junction with mother, and I have been here about a year."

"Why have you not called me before now? I thought you were still in Washington. I was thinking about taking a trip to visit you. It is a good thing I did not plan that trip."

"Daddy, it has been over three years since I lived in Washington DC." "Is your mother okay?"

"No daddy, mother has had two strokes. The second one she did not recover completely. She now uses a wheelchair to get around."

"How is she handling being confined? Your mother has always been so physically active. This must be devastating?"

"She has gotten used to it. At first, she did not want to get out of bed because she felt the wheelchair limited her. She had one stroke right after Cooper died. Not long before I got here, she had another. I took a year leave from my job in Atlanta to be with her. I may have to go back there eventually."

"Since Scott died, she only has me."

"I really do miss Scott. Not a day goes by, I don't think about him. I just don't believe he accidentally shot himself while cleaning his gun. He was cautious with his army-issued weapon. I have had thoughts about getting his case reopened," said Sam.

"Daddy, there is no need of you wasting your retirement money. I don't think the military would lie about what happened to Scott."

"I am not so sure, but If you insist and believe that the military performed a thorough investigation, I will leave it alone."

"If I have to go back to Atlanta, would you be able to look after mother for a while?"

"I would be more than happy to assist her. She was my first and only love."

"You have told me that a million times Daddy." "Is your mother okay with me coming to assist?"

"Yes, we have already discussed it, and mother is looking forward to seeing you. Are you still working at the Airport?"

163

"Yes, I am, but It is only part-time. I do it just to have something to do."

"Madison is this a good number for you that I see on my caller ID. I tried to call you several times, and I got a busy signal, or out of service message?"

"Yes, this is a good number to reach me. Daddy, it was good talking to you. I must get to mother and get her daily routine started. I will keep in touch. Will talk to you soon."

"Love you honey and goodbye."

I feel so much better after talking to daddy. He assured me, he would take care of mother if I needed his help. I will call Elliott to see if he knows anything new before I get busy with mother.

Elliott was just sitting in the kitchen having a cup of Starbucks coffee. He had purchased a pound from the grocery store on yesterday. Nothing like a good cup of coffee in the morning to wake you up. When he worked at the police department, they always had some cheap coffee that someone always made to strong. Now I can sit back and enjoy a real cup of coffee.

He heard his cell phone ringing which he had left in the bedroom. When he picked it up, he recognized the number was Madison. All he could think was what has happened now. "Hello, Madison."

"Hello, Elliott, just calling to see if you had heard anything about the case."

"I was going to call you later today to give you an update about

Daniel's case being reopened. Have you heard anything," "No, I have not. What is your update?"

"I received a call yesterday from Paul, the security manager at the DoubleTree. He told me that he and one other person had been interviewed by that hotshot investigator Alphonso from Soco & Soco firm headquartered in Alaska."

"Why were they interviewed and why did this guy Paul think he needed to call you?"

"He was questioned about the surveillance cameras being out the night of Daniels death. Paul thought he remembered telling me about the timing of the outage over a drink at a bar downtown DC. I convinced him he did not tell me, even though he did. That's why it was so easy to get in and out of Daniel's room."

"Did he relay this bit of evidence to the investigator?"

"Actually, he did not remember until after the interview with Alphonso."

"Who's to say he won't be interviewed again, and this Paul guy tells the truth about the software upgrade. I thought you did not leave any loose ends?"

"There is nothing to worry about. Paul can't prove he told me about the surveillance cameras."

"Who was the other person that was interviewed?"

"It was an ex-con by the name of Joshua. Paul does not know what was discussed in their interview."

"Maybe you need to find out."

"Don't you think that would make me suspicious?"

"I guess you are right. This investigator will probably interview Q'UP and AllTuck. It may just be a matter of time that I get interviewed because Daniel and I were going to get married."

"Do you think Daniel was going to leave his wife for you?" "I don't think so, I know he was going to leave her."

"At the time of his death, the police said he had a good relationship with his wife. He could have been using you to get information about AllTuck."

"I don't want to hear any more of that kind of talk from you. I will talk to you later." Madison was upset at Elliott's remarks. She hung up without saying goodbye.

No one can connect any dots that would lead to Madison involvement in this case, and hopefully me either expressed Elliott. I will cook me some breakfast, have another cup of coffee and relax for the rest of the day.

It is finally Friday, and I have an early flight to Atlanta this morning. As he was drying off from his shower in the bathroom, he heard his cell phone ringing. I wonder who that could be. The only person I want to talk to this early would be Violet. I know her son Landon would probably not want her calling me not only early, but not calling me at all. Alphonso picked up his cell phone in the living room.

"Hello, this is Alphonso."

"Hi, Alphonso this is Jason, I thought you might be up this morning because of your flight to Atlanta."

"I thought you had a wife and children, why are you up so early?"

"Yes, I do have a wife and children, so I go to bed early at night and get plenty of rest. Then, I am ready for the children when they wake up early. Your day is coming, when you will have small kids and a wife. You won't be single forever."

"I hope you are right because I'm ready for that special lady to wake up to in the morning and the children jumping on the bed in the morning wanting cereal."

"Sometimes they come running in when you don't want them to. Keep that in mind as well."

"Enough of family talk. I have the results from the autopsy for the current case you are working on."

"The exhumation occurred right away, once the Judge in Delta Junction signed the authorization, and the new evidence proved justifiable. I was surprised at how quickly they finished the autopsy," said Jason. "The results arrived via a courier service late yesterday afternoon. As I was glancing through the report, it appears to have the information you need for a breakthrough."

"The forensic pathologist who performed the autopsy noted the skeletal body structure was in reasonably good form. The teeth were still intact with a stain on them, and some rare decay that would not usually occur. This might indicate wine or some drink he had consumed before dying. It might also be some substance that would cause decaying on the teeth."

Alphonso replied, "that means he consumed some of the wine that was in the room by the nightstand."

"The report also states, that the positioning of the hole in the skull, indicates that this was not a suicide. The bullet position looked like someone turned around with their back facing the victim and fired one shot."

"The shooter whomever that was must have fired two shots because one bullet was in the wall beside the bed," noted Alphonso.

"Whoever did the shooting was an excellent marksman or someone with military or police type training. As a matter of fact, the pathologists said it looks like he had been killed twice, once with a gun and once with a liquid substance."

Alphonso said with a surprised look on his face, "that makes it a homicide. What type of gun was it based on?"

"The hole size in the skull and the type bullet indicates it was a Springfield XDs .45ACP. I have scanned in all the information and emailed it to you in case you need to print it before your flight this morning."

"Why don't you also send it to Jacoby in Atlanta, and they can have a copy for me when I arrive this afternoon?"

"While I have you on the phone, see if you or the police can get a last known or current address of Elliott and Madison. They are both in Alaska. If I am correct, Elliott lives in my condominium community in Fairbanks."

"That should be easy enough. I will speak with you later this evening. Goodbye and have a good flight."

"I will be back in Washington on Tuesday. Right now, I have four suspects."

I will log in to my email and download that autopsy report into a word document. Then I can review it while on the plane. I will need to check out of this hotel and check back in on Tuesday afternoon. Jennifer, the hotel manager, had arranged for me to check-in to the same room on my return, and store my second piece of luggage. The luggage will be placed back in my room when I return.

That was nice of her, and I will have to put an excellent rating for the DoubleTree on Yelp and Google. I am leaving my car here and using the hotel shuttle to the airport. They have a company car at the office in Atlanta, so I do not need to rent another one. Hotlanta here I come.

It is now Friday, and Elliott is sitting in the kitchen sipping a cup of coffee waiting for Cindy to come and beautify his Condo. I can't wait to see what she is going to do with the place. Decorating has never been my thing. As he was finishing his thoughts, the doorbell rang. That must be Cindy. First good sign, she is on time. It is ten a.m. straight up. He went to the door.

"Good morning Cindy I have been anxiously awaiting your arrival."

"Hello, Mr. Elliott I can tell by your enthusiasm and comment that you are excited about the rebirth of your condo?"

"Yes, I am excited Cindy."

WHO WOULD HAVE THOUGHT

"I believe that you are going to be pleasantly surprised and pleased. I have the truck outside and two guys to unload everything, and you do not have to lift a finger."

"That is ok by me."

"Let the fun began." The two men started unloading and placing furniture and hanging pictures on the wall per Cindy's instructions. They started with the living room. It was decorated with different shades of blue with silver accessories placed strategically throughout the room. The guest bathroom was renovated with varying shades of brown and beige with a touch of green.

The Master bedroom and bath were black and gold. The kitchen was decorated in gray and red. After a few hours everything was complete.

"Mr. Elliott it is time for you to assess and tell me how you like it?"

After Elliott looked at each room, he said, "I feel like I am living in a mansion on a retired police officer salary. Everything looks splendid and manly. I like how you infused the colors in each room. I only had one request for color, and that was the master bedroom, and it is incredible. My office that you decorated looks like an executive office in a fortune 500 company. That means I may have to do some work in there."

"I am happy that you like all the changes. If you are happy, then I am happy. You can make me happier by writing me a check," said Cindy.

Elliott laughed out loud. "I have your check right here, and what you and your men have done here is worth every penny, and some more."

"We are going to get out of here and let you enjoy your place and have a good weekend. Goodbye, Mr. Elliott,"

"Thank you and have a good weekend Cindy."

Elliott closed the front door and started thinking about how his wife would have loved what Cindy had done. If she were here, she would not have let me hire Cindy, she would have done the decorating herself. I really do miss her. She was the only thing I did right in my life. The time we had together was cut short too soon. May she rest in peace.

CHAPTER **18**

A BREAK THREW IN ATLANTA

ON this Friday morning I am on my favorite airline again, Delta. Alphonso is flying from Washington and will arrive at Hartsfield-Jackson Atlanta International Airport at eleven twenty-five a.m. A very smooth flight piloted by one of Delta great female Captains. Both my parents had taught all their children that women can do any job that a man can do, and sometimes even better. Today I say Amen to that.

Jacoby had arranged for me to be picked up at the airport. At twelve- fifteen I was walking out to passenger arrival pick up where Soco and Soco Attorney Karen was waiting. I like it everyone is on time today. She recognized me as soon as I walked out.

"Hello, Mr. Alphonso."

"Hello, you must be Attorney Karen? Thank you so much for picking me up and agreeing to be my chauffeur."

"No problem. It gets me out of the office for a while."

"We are going to the office where Jacoby has lunch waiting. Since you have a late check-in for your hotel, I will drop you off after your interview with AllTuck. It will only take about twenty minutes to the Soco office."

"Sounds like a plan," stated Alphonso. At twelve-forty we arrived at Soco & Soco. Karen parked the car in a covered parking garage. We took the elevator to the third floor and went straight to the conference room where Jacoby was waiting with food from Jason's Deli.

"Hey, Alphonso, you never age man. What is the secret?"

"As my grandmother use to say, you are a sight for sore eyes yourself, and the secret is living in a cold climate like Alaska."

"Are you telling me that I am going to look like an old man before I turn fifty if I don't move out of Atlanta?" They both laughed and embraced each other.

"Alphonso, I know you are on a tight schedule today, so we are going to have a sandwich, water, and chips. I hope this is okay with you? We can also discuss the autopsy and Atlanta police report while we are eating. Then you and Karen can be on your way."

"You have three choices of sandwiches, roast beef on rye, turkey on wheat and shaved ham on white."

"Turkey will be good for me."

Karen expressed, "I will have the roast beef."

"Only one choice left, that is the best, ham on white bread," Jacoby smiled. "The one thing about Jason's Deli, every sandwich is good."

"I have the autopsy report that Jason email over. I printed each of us a copy, so we can look through it quickly in case there is some reference you need for your interview today."

"When I talked to Jason earlier this morning, he stated that the handgun was a Springfield XD.45," Alphonso pointed out. "This is the same make and model that the son Landon and the father had."

Karen asked, "Is Landon a suspect and why?"

"I initially thought he was not until I interviewed him. He was unusually nervous as though there was something, he knew but was not telling me. He was angry, combative and could not answer some questions I thought he should have been able to answer. So, yes right now he is a suspect."

"Did you tell him that?" Jacoby asked.

"Not exactly, but in his outburst, he assumed he was."

Jacoby glanced at the autopsy report." It looks like this was not suicide on the part of the victim but quite the contrary. It looks like the deceased might have had a liquid substance in the wine that he drank that night. The substance either killed him or rendered him unconscious."

"The report further states that it appears that someone, not the victim was in the room with his back to the victim. Shot him over the head. In conclusion, the report states the victim was killed twice. To me, that means two people killed Daniels. It appears the first person killed with a substance in the wine. Another person assumed the victim was asleep and shot him in the forehead. We are looking for two murderers."

"Jacoby, how do you prosecute a crime such as this?"

"There is something called serial murder, but in this case, it is two people killing one person both premeditated. I will need to pull out a law book and do some research and get back to you on this."

"Of all the cases I have investigated, I have never run into something you call serial murder of one person. Let's go over the police report," said Alphonso.

"The police report states a Springfield XDs .45 ACP pistol was used in this incident. We now know this is a serial murder of one person. This gun might belong to the victim since it was not found on the scene. As I was questioning attorney Landon, he stated he has this same exact gun, but he did not remember if he had it in his car the night his father was found dead."

"At the time this incident occurred the police in Washington did not check Landon's hands for gunpowder residue, and it's a little too late for that now," noted Jacoby.

" The police report states a family had purchased a home from Madison two months ago and a contractor found a gun in the backyard while digging a hole for a pool. There is an ongoing investigation about the firearm, the family and the previous owner who was Madison. The family who purchased the home and the contractor have been cleared of any wrongdoing, but the report does not state that fact," mention Karen. Alphonso pointed out that, "the deceased was having an affair with Madison. That is a lot of information to process and digest in an hour." "I guess we need to start on our way to AllTuck for your interview, said Karen."

"I need to go to the bathroom first. Thank you both for lunch, transportation, and these reports."

"You both have made this trip less of a headache than I had anticipated."

"We aim to please," said Jacoby smiling. "I will be right back."

Once Alphonso returned from the bathroom, he and Karen left the office in the firm's car and arrived at AllTuck about two-ten p.m. We parked in the AllTuck parking lot and entered the building into the receptionist area and asked for Joseph, the Executive assistant.

Joseph was the point of contact for Matthew, the person I am interviewing today. Within ten minutes Joseph came to escort us to the office of Matthew.

"Hello, Mr. Alphonso."

"Good afternoon Joseph. This is Attorney Karen from Soco & Soco." "Nice to meet you, Attorney Karen. Mr. Matthew's was expecting only you Alphonso."

"I do work for Soco & Soco." Karen expressed with a little frustration. "I realize that, but let me just make Mr. Matthew aware that you will be escorted by an Attorney."

Joseph placed a call from his cell phone to Mr. Matthew.

"Mr. Matthew this is Joseph, just wanted to inform you that Mr. Alphonso has with him an attorney from Soco & Soco."

"That is okay Joseph, just put in a call to our lawyer that is onsite, to stand by in case I need his presence in the meeting."

Joseph returned to the receptionist area to escort investigator Alphonso and Attorney Karen to Mr. Matthew's office, where the door was already open.

"Hello, Mr. Alphonso and Attorney Karen. I am Matthew CEO of AllTuck."

"Hello," said Alphonso and Karen.

"Come in and have a seat at the conference table. Joseph, please close the door on your way out? Can I get either of you some water or a soda?"

"No, we are fine, we both had lunch before arrival here." "Where would you like to start?" Asked Matthew.

"First of all, thank you for taking time out of your busy schedule to meet with us. We will not hold you any longer than necessary. I will just reemphasize the reason for our visit. We are here today because the case of Mr. Daniel who died in Washington DC about three years ago has been reopened because of new evidence."

"I am familiar with the case."

"Did you know Daniels the deceased?" "I did know of him, but not personally."

"Did you know that he was an investigator and was investigating your company?"

"Yes, I did, but I don't know all the specifics of the investigation." "Can you tell me what you do know?"

"There was some false information on social media by some patrons of the military Exchange stores in several locations in Washington DC area."

"What exactly was being reported on the social media that was not true?"

"The comments stated that AllTuck software was being used to scan purchased items at checkout counters in exchange stores and were supposedly ringing up a greater price than the listed price on the shelf. It also stated we were stealing from the soldiers with these purchases." "Were the patrons correct in their assessment of the software or was this an intentional glitch?"

"We did find a glitch in the software and no, it was not intentional."

Matthew appears to be a little angry at this point of questioning.

"Mr. Matthew, you don't have to get upset. We are just trying to get to the bottom of this investigation. Once you realized there was a real glitch in the software, when did you report it to the exchange?" "It took a year to figure out what was going on. During that year, military customer was still getting charged too much for their purchases."

"Do you know Sergeant Major Rick was in charge of making sure operations at all exchange stores ran properly and a Sergeant Scott who was his assistant?"

"Yes, I knew of them both."

"Did you know that it was Sergeant Scott who discovered the problem with the software at the exchange stores?"

"No, I did not."

"Did you know shortly after Scott discovered this problem, he reported it to Sergeant Major Rick and shortly after, Scott was found dead in his apartment."

"The report stated it was an accidental shooting from his military- issued gun."

"Yes, I did hear that he shot himself."

"Do you think this was all coincidental that Scott finds this problem concerning AllTuck? Then is found dead by Major Rick."

"No, not really. You seem to be accusing me of this accident."
"No, I was not saying that. We don't have any jurisdiction to investigate military crimes or incidents. However, we do investigate civilian cases, and we do believe that Sergeant Scott and Mr. Daniel's deaths are tied into the millions your company would lose if you lost this contract."

"Did a Ms. Madison work for you during the time this software problem was found in the Washington area?"

"She may have, but we have thousands of employees you can't expect me to know all of them?"

"Well, you should know Madison because Sergeant Scott was her brother."

"I was not aware of that."

"Mr. Daniel submitted a final report to his company Q'UP concerning your company. In this report, he mentions Sergeant Scott discovery of the software problem. So, within days, Scott dies of the discovery of the software, and within a week of your company being reported to the Attorney General, Daniel dies."

"It looks like the only party that had something to lose were your company. My last question. Did your company have any involvement in the death of Mr. Daniel and Sergeant Scott?"

"AllTuck had no involvement in either one of these deaths to my knowledge."

"We have no further questions at this time."

"There may be questions asked later before this case is solved, but we do thank you again for your time and cooperation."

"I am glad I was able to assist you with this investigation. I will get Joseph to escort you out. You both have a nice day."

"You the same," as they walked out of Matthew's office, Joseph escorted them back to the receptionist area.

"Thank you, Joseph." "You are welcome."

Karen and Alphonso are back in the car and on their way to the hotel.

"Attorney Karen, I believe from that interview that Sergeant Major Rick was getting a financial kickback from AllTuck to look the other way. Sergeant Scott figured it all out and set up a meeting with Mr. Daniel."

"But someone whom I believe was a friend of Sergeant Scott sister killed her brother. Madison knew about the software as well and did not want to go to jail."

"She also found out about the communication between Daniel and her brother, whom she had not told him about. Even though she might have loved Daniel or maybe used him to get information for AllTuck, I believe she knows who killed Daniel, but I don't believe she committed the act herself," said Alphonso.

"I had some similar thoughts, but not all that you have just expressed. What is your next move?"

"I need to talk to Daniel's daughter Kathleen, and the Atlanta police department. I will get Jason to question Madison because she is in Alaska somewhere. He is checking with the police department in Fairbanks to see where she is living now."

"This is a complicated case. Looks like the Washington DC police department missed a lot of obvious clues," said Karen.

"You are absolutely right."

"Jacoby asked me to leave the car with you, and I am going to get Uber home. That way you can coordinate your own time to talk to other people you need to interview. It has been educational hanging out with you and seeing the investigative side of solving a case. Thank you for letting me tag along today."

"It was my pleasure, and we have arrived at your hotel."

"I am going to call Uber on my cell and be out of your hair." "I will wait with you to ensure you are safe. That's the least I can do."

"Thank you, Alphonso."

CHAPTER **19**

AN EVENING AT Le'DIPLOMATE

IT is finally Friday, and LANDON is in his room getting dressed for dinner at Le'Diplomate restaurant downtown. He, Connie and his mother Violet have a reservation for six p.m. They must pick Connie up at five to make their reservation on time. Landon was sitting at the foot of his bed thinking about the interview he had with Alphonso on yesterday. It appears Alphonso is trying to accuse me of my father's death and I don't know why?

I am glad my mother is flying out to Atlanta tomorrow to see my sister Kathleen. Maybe that will take her mind off this entire situation. Darnell has not even given me a call from Soco & Soco on any updates for the case. So, I am just in limbo right now, and I don't know how I will concentrate at dinner tonight or relax. But I must keep my composure for mother's benefit.

As he was finishing his thoughts, his mother called out. "Landon, I am ready if you are."

Landon walked out of his room and said, "yes mother I am ready. I will text Connie and let her know we are on our way. It is now

four-twenty, and it will take us about thirty minutes to get to her place."
"I am excited we are having dinner with Connie."

"Mother, can you hold that excitement, so we can get in the car and drive to Connie's place."

As they were pulling out of the garage, Violet was thinking about her visit with Connie yesterday. "Landon you did not discuss the meeting you had with Alphonso, and you have been unusually quiet since then. As a matter of fact, you seem somewhat worried. Is everything ok?"

"Yes, mother, everything is ok. I just don't want to talk about it right now."

"You can't keep it all bottled up inside like that son."

"Mother, I want you to enjoy dinner tonight. Let's talk about it later when we get back home."

"Okay, but Connie was worried about you as well. She told me how nervous your father made her feel the first time she met him. I told her that's how he treats everyone because he never turns off that work mind of his even when he is not at work. She also thought your father did not like her. I was surprised at some of the things she knew about him."

"And what might that be."

"She knew his favorite wine that he drank sometimes. Even though I knew he liked wine, I did not know that he had a favorite, called Pinot Noir. Did you know that?"

"Yes. Connie might have heard me mention that as well about dad." "She also seems to know your father loved me a lot, as a matter of fact, she seems to know a lot about your father. There was one thing that sort of concerned me about Connie on yesterday and that she was very nervous and broke out in a sweat at one time when she was talking about your father."

"Mother, I have no clue what Connie may know about my father except for what I have told her!"

"Son you don't have to get upset."

"Connie has only seen him a couple of times, and all those times she saw him, she was with me. Mother, I am not upset."

"Then why are you raising your voice at me."

"Mother, I am sorry, I just have a lot on my mind. We have arrived at Connie's place so let's act like we are excited to see her."

"She lives in a condominium, and these are really nice from what I see from the outside."

"They are just as nice on the inside."

"You have been to her place, sounds like more than once."
"Mother, we have been dating about three years. Of course, I have been
here on several occasions to visit."

Landon parks the car and opens the door for his mother. They
walk up to Connie's door, and Landon rings the doorbell. Connie
answers the door on the first ring.

"Hello, Landon and Ms. Violet, good to see you both." She
gives Landon a quick kiss on the lips.

"Hello Connie, so good to see you again." Violet gives Connie
a hug. "Connie are you ready to head out. I don't know what the traffic
will be like since we are getting out sort of late. At least we have a
reservation." "I am ready, come on in, just need to get my purse. Ms.
Violet do you need to use the restroom before we head out."

"No, I am good, but I am hungry."

"I better go just in case we get caught in some accident or
something, or whatever causes the traffic to be so bad all the time in
this city," said Landon.

"Ms. Violet come in and have a seat while we wait for Landon."
"Don't get too comfortable, I am only going to be a minute."

"I see you love flowers. You have the place decorated
beautifully." "With some advice from my mother, I do pretty good with
flowers."

"Because of the long hours at the hospital, I didn't have time to decorate. I paid for a decorating company to decorate for me. You just tell them what your ideas are and what colors you want, and they handle the rest."

"Well, you have great taste no matter who did the decorating." In comes Landon.

"Are you ladies ready." "Yes, we are ready."

"Let's get going." They walked to the door, with Landon going out first, then Violet, and Connie last.

"The alarm is set, and we are ready." Landon opens the car door for Connie and his mother.

"Connie you sit in the front. I don't mind sitting in the back."

As Landon pulled out of Connie's driveway and got onto the highway, no one spoke a word for ten minutes.

"Connie what is the name of this city you live in."

"It is called Falls Church, Virginia. It is supposed to take us thirty minutes to get from my Condo to the restaurant, but It is always traffic, so it might take forty-five minutes."

"That is what Landon said. Do you like this area?"

"Yes, I like it a lot but don't get to enjoy it that much, but when I do, I have a good time. I would recommend any newcomer to live here because It is a very culturally diverse city. It has lots of unique restaurants and shops located in each community."

"It is what they call live, work, and play type city that caters to every age group."

"It sounds like a place I might like to live in because I love unique restaurants and shops that you can safely walk to."

"Ms. Violet is that a hint you are thinking about moving to the area."

"I know Landon would love that very much and has said so to me on several occasions."

"Mother are you really thinking about moving."

"Hold on Landon, don't get too excited you might have an accident."

"No, I am not thinking about it, and I just said it would be nice."

"Okay, everyone, we have arrived at the restaurant, and I am going to valet park the car."

"It seems like we got here very quickly."

"No, actually it was fifty minutes exactly. I-66 was not as busy as I thought it would be."

The attendant came up to Landon to get his cell phone number and gave him a ticket to park his car. Landon must text his ticket number to the attendant when he is ready to leave. Landon gave him twenty dollars for the parking.

"Did you give the young man a tip Landon."

"No mother, I will give him a tip when he brings my car to me safely when we get ready to leave."

"Do you think for some reason he may not return it safely."

"No, that's just my assurance that he will return it." All three of them walked up to an open door from the host.

"Good evening everyone the host said. Do you have a reservation?" "Yes, we do for six p.m."

"We are glad you are dining with us this evening, just follow me, and we will get you seated." The host checked the reservation list for their table location.

"You have two choices this evening a booth by the window or a table across from a window."

"We will take the booth by the window."

191

"Follow me please." They followed the host where she seated them. "I hope this is to your satisfaction."

"Yes, this is great."

"Your waitress will be right over to take your order." "Thank you," said Landon.

"Landon this is a really fancy place you and Connie have brought me to."

"Wait before you thank us."

"We hope you will like the food as well," Connie said with a smile.

"If you two like it, I am sure I will like it as well. We don't have any French restaurants in Delta Junction, so this is a real treat for me."

"Good evening, everyone, my name is Amandine, and I will be your waitress for this evening. Is this your first-time dining with us?" Violet said so eagerly, "yes, it is my first time."

"We have been here several times. This is Violet, Landon's mother, visiting us from Alaska."

"I am so glad you have chosen to bring your mother to dine here with us, and Ms. Violet, I hope that you will enjoy all the food and the entire evening."

"Thank you," Violet said so graciously.

"Since this is your first time, what can I get for you to drink?" "I will have a glass of wine."

"Connie and Landon what can I get for you?"

"Amandine can we have a bottle of Sauvignon Blanc." Landon requested. "I would also like water."

"Why don't I bring water for everyone, and would anyone like an appetizer? Ms. Violet do you like seafood?"

"Yes, I do. Landon and I have had the petit plateau, and It is a beautiful presentation, and it would be enough for the three of us." Connie recommended.

"Sounds good to me," said Violet and Landon.

"We will have the petit plateau, and we will need a minute to look at the menu for our entrée."

"That is a great selection that will go great with your wine choice. I will be right back with wine and water," said Amandine.

"She is a really nice waitress, but I can't pronounce her name the way she says it."

"Don't worry mother, we can't pronounce it either."

Within five minutes the waitress brought the water and the wine.

Amandine poured wine into everyone's glass. "Enjoy, and I will check on your appetizer." "Mother, how is your wine?"

"It is good Landon. I would not have known what wine to order if I was not here with the two of you."

"Glad you like it."

"You would have figured it out, Ms. Violet."

The waitress is now back at their table with the appetizer with small plates for everyone. "Hope you enjoy."

"This is the most beautiful platter of seafood that I have ever seen. It has these large shrimps, oysters on the half shell, that I don't like, clams, crab, and lobster."

"Wait till you taste it, mother." They each filled their plates and dug in.

"The waitress was right, this is a perfect appetizer for the wine we ordered. This is some of the best seafood I have ever had. I may not have room for anything else."

"Mother, it is totally up to you if you don't want to order an entree." "Landon you have always been a big eater like your father."

"Ms. Violet, I did not know where he got that from, because he eats a lot when we go out."

"You better slow it down Landon, it will show up when you get older." "Mother you can stop telling jokes now. We need to finish looking at the menu if we are going to order anything else."

"I have already decided. While the two of you were discussing how much to eat or not to eat."

"I am going to have the Friday special bouillabaisse." "Connie, what is that?"

"It is a spicy seafood stew made with several different types of fish." "You are ordering more seafood. I guess you can say that, and it is tasty. I have had it before, and it is almost enough for two."

"Landon, I will have the short lamb loin."

"I guess I will have the half-roasted chicken. Mother everything here is in large portions so don't feel bad about not eating all your food." The waitress returns to the table. "I see you have almost finished with the appetizer, are you ready to order your entrée? Why don't we go to Ms. Violet first?"

"I will have the short lamb loin and the vegetables that come with it." Ms. Connie, what would you like?"

"I will have the Friday special bouillabaisse." "Excellent choice. And for the gentleman."

"I would like the half-roasted chicken with the vegetables that come with it."

"I take it the appetizer was good for everyone." Everyone repeated, "it was great."

"Amandine I could eat another one." Connie and Violet just laughed out loud.

"I will get your order. Why are you ladies laughing?" "We are laughing because Landon is a big eater."

"Landon, son, where is all that food going?"

"Mother it is going where it is supposed to go in my mouth and down to my stomach for processing." "You are funny," said Connie.

"I am having such a great time. Don't remember having this much fun in a long time." Violet expressed in gratitude.

"Mother, we could do this more often if you would move to the area." "Landon let's not get on that subject."

"Okay, Mother we will talk about your trip to see Kathleen tomorrow. Kathleen text me this morning and said that she will be so glad to see you."

"I will be happy to see her as well." While they were still talking the waitress brought their food.

"Lamb for Ms. Violet, spicy stew for Ms. Connie, and roasted chicken for Mr. Landon. Can I get you anything else? I will bring the dessert menu if you would like."

"With all this food Amandine we will not have room for the dessert." "Mother, speak for yourself."

"I will check back later to see how everyone is doing and see if anyone has room for dessert."

Everyone was just raving about how good their entrees were and savored every bite. There were no complaints except too much food. "Mother I thought you said it was too much food."

"It is too much food, but I did not want to leave any of it." "My bouillabaisse was wonderful as well."

" I don't have to tell you how great my chicken was because you don't see any of it left. I am thinking about that dessert, how about you ladies?" Connie and Violet said no at the same time.

"Well, I guess I will pass up dessert this time." "What about some coffee?"

"That would be excellent," said Violet. Amandine came over and noticed they all were finished.

"Can I get anyone dessert?"

"No, we are all going to have just some regular coffee and just bring the check when you bring the coffee."

"I am glad everyone enjoyed their meal. I will remove these dishes out of your way. Ms. Violet what did you think?"

"Amandine, I had a great time, and all the food was good. You were just an excellent waitress. I enjoyed being here with my son, and his friend Connie. It has been a perfect evening."

"You have made my night," stated Amandine. Your coffee and check are coming up. Within five minutes, Amandine returned with the coffee and check.

"It was my pleasure serving each of you this evening, and I hope to see each of you again. Mr. Landon, I will return with your receipt for the signature of your credit card."

"I will text the attendees so that when we walk outside our car will be waiting."

"Connie do you have to work tomorrow?"

"Yes, Ms. Violet, I have to go in for a couple of hours in the afternoon." "I hope you have a wonderful visit with your daughter. It was great having dinner with you, and I hope we can do this again soon."

"Me too, Connie and it is too bad you have to work on Saturday."

"It is part of the job. I work at least 2 weekends out of a month, but I do enjoy my work."

"Well, it was nice having dinner with you two ladies this evening, and we should do this again soon."

"Son, you have been quite the comedian this evening. I don't know how much more of that I can take." Violet laughed as she finished talking.

"Just think how much more money I could be making as a comedian." "Son you are not that good. Keep your day job."

They all were laughing when the waitress returned. "Thank you all again and have a safe trip home."

"You too," said Violet. They all walked toward the front entrance. "Ladies, since the bathrooms are in the front, I think I need to stop before getting on the highway. I advise you ladies to go as well."

"Son, we will meet you at the front door." They all used the bathroom and returned to the front entrance.

As they walked outside the car was waiting for them. Landon handed the driver a tip, and they all entered the car. "Everyone on board?" Asked Landon. "The next stop Falls Church, Va."

"Yes," said Connie.

After a few turns, Landon ended up on I-66. "We should be there in about thirty minutes."

Violet went right to sleep soon as she got in the car. "Landon, will you call or text when you and your mother get home. I really enjoyed tonight and hope we can do this again soon."

"I hope Mother will decide to move here. Maybe tonight caused her to think about it more," said Landon.

"Maybe she will have a change of heart once she gets to Atlanta. What time is her flight tomorrow?"

"She leaves at ten arriving in Atlanta at eleven-thirty." "How is she taking the reopening of your father's case?"

"I think she is handling it reasonably well, maybe better than me." "What do you mean?

"What happened in the interview with Alphonso?"

"He almost has accused me of killing my own father. I could not account for a thirty-minute window, in route to my father's hotel. I told Alphonso the same thing I told the police three years ago."

"Landon, I don't think they are trying to accuse you, they are just trying to get all their facts together and some that the police might have missed." "Things change, people forget, and evidence tools are better today versus three years ago."

"I guess you are right. Mother said you got upset when talking about my father. What was that all about."

"I am not sure what she meant I got upset. I did not want to upset her by bringing up your father. Maybe that is what she means."

"Maybe so. We are at the exit for your place."

As Landon pulled up to Connie's condo, he said "I had forgotten how beautiful this place is as mother stated. You picked a great location."

"I think so too. Maybe you will visit more often? You don't have to get out, get your mother home, she seems to be tired. Just wait until I get inside before you pull off."

Landon reached over and kissed her before she exited the car. "I love you, Landon. Good night."

"I will call when I arrive home. Good night Connie."

Once Connie was inside, he backed out of the driveway and headed for home, without bothering his mother. As he was driving, he thought to himself why Connie denies what my mother said, and I did not know she loved me. She is possessive of me, and I don't understand why. I really don't have time for a serious relationship.

Alphonso is trying to put a damper on my becoming a partner at Soco & Soco by making me a suspect in my father's death. I could lose my job, house, and everything if I am found guilty. I will have to wait for the results. Wow, we got home in twenty minutes.

Everyone must be out of town because there was hardly any traffic, and its only nine-fifteen on a Friday night. Landon pulled up in the garage. And let the garage door down.

"Mother, mother, wake up we are home." "Where is Connie?"

"We already dropped her off, and we did not want to wake you." "I wanted to say goodnight to her."

"You will see her again." "Okay, if you say so."

"Right now, we need to get you to bed so you can get some rest for your trip tomorrow."

Landon got out of the car and went around and open the door for Violet. "Landon I am going straight to bed without a shower tonight. I am more tired than I thought."

"I am going to call Connie and let her know we arrived home safely." "I will see you in the morning. Love you, Landon."

"Love you to mother. Goodnight."

After Landon reached his bedroom, he dialed Connie's number. "Hello, Connie we just made it in."

"I will call you tomorrow. Okay, talk to you later." Landon slipped into his pajamas and went to bed.

CHAPTER **20**

SURPRISE SURPRISE SURPRISE

THE doorbell was ringing while Madison was putting her mother Jamel back into bed per her request. She had given her a bath, put her clothes on and gave her breakfast. Who could be visiting at eight-thirty on a Friday morning? She looked out the window, and It was a police officer with another man at the front door. Could something have happened to my father, Violet or Elliott?

She opens the door. "How may I help you?" Madison said to the officer.

"My name is Detective Smith from the 15th precinct here in Delta Junction, and this is Attorney Jason from Soco & Soco law firm in Fairbanks." They both showed Madison their identification.

"Are you Ms. Madison."

"Yes, I am. Is there something wrong?"

"We are representing the brother of a man who died in Washington three years ago. The deceased name was Daniel. He was a resident of Delta Junction and worked in Washington for a company called Q'UP.

We understand that you knew him. This case has been reopened because of new evidence."

"What does his death have to do with me?"

"We would like to ask you a few questions about your relationship with the deceased," said Detective Smith. "Can we come in?"

"Yes, but we have to be a little quiet because my mother is sleeping and not feeling well."

"Would you prefer to come down to the police precinct to answer our questions?"

"No, here is okay because I do not have anyone to sit with my mother. She cannot be left alone." Madison led Detective Smith and Attorney Jason into the living room and asked them to have a seat on the sofa. Madison sat right across from them in her mother's favorite chair.

"We will begin if you are ready," said Detective Smith. "I am ready."

"We would like to get your consent to record our conversation?"

"Do I need my own counsel present before I start to answer any questions?"

"That is your right and privilege, Ms. Madison."

"Would you prefer we come back when your lawyer is present?" "No, I don't have anything to hide, and I will just see how this goes. If questions get to a point where I feel I need counsel. I will stop answering." "That's fair," noted Detective Smith. "We will proceed, and I will ask all the questions."

"Did you have a brother named Scott who was in the military?" "Yes, I did. You did not say we were going to talk about my brother." "We have to establish some of the relationships that Mr. Daniel might have had. What type of relationship did you have with your brother?"

"We were not very close, but he was my only brother."

"Did Scott know where and what company you were employed by?"

"I assumed he did because we talked about my job on several occasions." "Do you remember the last time you talked to him before his death?" "Yes, a couple of days before his death."

"Had he talked to you about a problem they were having with the barcoding software at the military exchange stores?"

"He mentioned it briefly, but did not give any details."

"Was he aware that AllTuck, the company you worked for, was the one who designed the software?"

"I assumed he did."

"It is hard for me to imagine your brother knew about the software problem and did not ask your assistance in helping to solve it."

"Maybe he did, and you are not relaying that info to us, and yet a few days after you talk to him, he was found dead. Do you know how he died?"

"I was told by military personnel that he had an accident while cleaning his army-issued firearm."

"Was there an autopsy performed after his death."

"No, because he requested that in the event of his death while serving in the military, he wanted to be cremated and no autopsy performed."

"We will never know what happened to your brother?" Said Jason.

Madison is now upset. "I just told you what I know, and I thought Detective Smith would be asking all the questions."

"Ms. Madison we are not trying to upset you, we are only trying to get to the truth about the death of Mr. Daniel. We need your cooperation as much as possible."

"Did you have a relationship with Mr. Daniel before his death? if yes, how long was that relationship going on?"

"Yes, I had a relationship with the deceased about two years." "Was Daniel wife and children aware of this relationship?"

"I don't think Daniel informed his wife or children."

"How did you feel about that and were the two of you in love?"

"We were in love, and we discussed that he would tell his family before he died."

"Did Daniel know your brother Scott?"

"I think so. I did mention I had a brother in the military."

"Do you know if Daniel had any communication with your brother?" "I am not sure, he did not mention it if he did."

"Were you aware Daniel's company had directed him to investigate your company concerning the barcoding software for the exchange stores?"

"Yes, I had some knowledge."

"Did Daniel discuss this case with you?" "No, he did not."

"How could that be?"

"You and he were having a relationship. He knew you worked for AllTuck. Your brother was working on the case from a military perspective, and the two of you never discussed it. I find that hard to believe Madison."

"Detective Smith, whether you believe it or not it is the truth."

"Did you know that Daniel had submitted a final report of his findings to his company on the eve of his death?"

"No, I was not aware of that."

"What could have happened to your company, if that report was submitted to the military exchange and to the Federal Contracting Procurement department for deception and fraud?"

"I'm not aware of any deception or fraud by AllTuck."

"I believe you do, and that is why Daniel and your brother are both dead today. The two of them were the key to that report Daniel had produced as proof of deception and fraud. What I don't know is what part or role did you play in these two deaths?"

"It is time for this questioning to stop, and I need to seek legal counsel. I am being accused of my brother and the man I loved death."

"Ms. Madison, you are right. At this point, you do need counsel present. We will stop the questioning. We expect you at the 39th precinct in Fairbanks on tomorrow morning with your lawyer, no later than ten a.m." Said Attorney Jason.

"Jason, no way can I get my lawyer that quick and get someone to sit with my mother by that time tomorrow."

"You either be there, or we will send a police escort," stated Detective Smith. "Okay, I will do my best. Will you see yourself out?"

"I hear my mother wakening up." Thank God she did not wake up while I was being interrogated.

Detective Smith and Attorney Jason left Madison home and return to their cars. "I think she is guilty of either participating or conspiring with someone in the deaths of Daniel and Scott," said Jason.

"I agree with you, but who would she have conspired with?" Stated Detective Smith.

"Alphonso asked me to question a guy name Elliott who is a retired police officer from the Washington office but was assigned to a particular detail in Atlanta. This Elliott supposedly lives in Alphonso condominium community. I think he is the connection we need with Madison. I meant to ask her if she knew Elliott. We will get a chance to ask her that question tomorrow."

It is now ten-thirty, do you think you could coordinate with Fairbanks police to talk to this guy Elliott this afternoon? I would like to speak with him before we finish our questioning with Madison tomorrow."

"Yes, I can coordinate that to happen this afternoon if they have an officer available," expressed Detective Smith. "I have already discussed the case with the Captain of Fairbanks police department. They are waiting for justification and motive."

"We now have a motive," Jason said and smiled.

Detective Smith agreed and said, "We need to take Elliott into the precinct for questioning not like we did Madison."

"We need to also coordinate with Detective Jones at the 39th precinct in Fairbanks to make preparation for Madison interview tomorrow. Will talk to you soon Jason. Have a safe trip back to Fairbanks.

Madison went into her mother's bedroom to see how she was feeling. She did not have time to think about the accusations that were just made against her. I will call Elliott because the detective and the lawyer possibly knew there is a connection between the two of them. She had to attend to her mother, call her lawyer and call her father to sit with her mother tomorrow.

"Madison, I thought I heard you talking to someone, and you seem to be upset?" Said Jamel.

"Mother, I was talking to someone, but everything is okay for right now. I must go out for a while tomorrow, and I don't know how long I will be. We discussed that daddy will come to sit with you, and you said it was okay. Well, I need him to sit with you tomorrow if that is okay?"

"Right now, I have no one else to sit with you. I would ask Violet, but she is out of the state visiting her children."

"Yes, it is okay Madison, and I hope Sam is not upset about the divorce and me getting married again."

"No mother he has gotten over that. I do believe he will be happy to see you. I am going to call him now."

"Are you feeling better after your nap?"

"I am much better since I laid down and rested. I am a little bit hungry since we ate breakfast sort of early this morning."

"I will fix us some lunch as soon as I speak with daddy about tomorrow." "Okay, Madison I can wait."

"Mother I left my phone in the living room. I am going to call daddy from there. I will be right back."

Madison walked into the living room, picked up her phone and dialed her father. Sam picked up on the first ring.

WHO WOULD HAVE THOUGHT

"Hello, Madison, how are things going with you and your mother?" "Hello, Daddy. Mother and I are doing great."

"Daddy, I have a last-minute request for you to sit with mother tomorrow. She said it would be okay with her. I have an appointment tomorrow that I don' know how long I will be. Can you come and sit with her? You will need to bring a change of clothes."

"Is everything okay with you Madison?"

"Yes, daddy everything is okay. I just had something come up at the last minute, and don't know how long it may take."

"Madison you know I would be more than happy to sit with your mother. Would you like for me to be there this evening?"

"Daddy that would be great because I have to get an early start in the morning."

"I will be there this evening about seven p.m. text me the address." "Okay, daddy I will fix us some dinner so don't eat before you get here." "Goodbye daddy, look forward to seeing you. Love you."

"Love you back honey."

One less worry out of the way. I will call my lawyer first and then Elliott. Madison dialed her lawyer.

"Hello, this is Attorney Michael's office." "This is Madison, is Michael in?"

"Yes, he is just coming in from an early court appearance."

"Hold on just a second. Attorney Michael, I have Madison on the line, she sounded sort of desperate."

"Let me get to my office and just transfer her to my office phone. Michael walks to his office and puts down his briefcase. Then sits at his desk and picks up the phone.

"Hello Madison, what can I do for you?"

"Michael I may be in trouble. I need you to accompany or meet me in Fairbanks at the 39th precinct tomorrow."

"For what Madison?"

"I was visited today to be precise at eight-thirty a.m. this morning by Delta junction finest police and a lawyer from the firm Soco & Soco in Fairbanks."

"And what prize did you win to get a visit from such distinguished visitors?"

"This is not a funny matter Michael."

"Madison, I know it. Did you already talk to them without my presence?" "Yes, I did."

WHO WOULD HAVE THOUGHT

"That was your first mistake."

"I know that now. Detective Smith and Attorney Jason are accusing me of Daniel and my brother Scott's death. I had nothing to do with either. I have to be in to talk with them at ten a.m. tomorrow, and I need you there to represent me."

"Okay, Madison. Who is Daniel?"

"Daniel is the man I was dating. He was found dead in his hotel room three years ago. My brother was accidentally killed with his army-issued gun."

"Are you innocent?" "Yes, I am innocent."

"Will see you in the morning." "Thank you, Michael."

"That's why you pay me to represent you." "Goodbye, Michael."

Last call to Elliott before I prepare lunch for mother. Madison dials Elliott's number.

At the same time, Elliott phone is ringing, his doorbell is ringing also.

He knows it is Madison. "Hello, Madison will call right back, someone is at my door."

Elliott opens the door without looking through the peephole, and two police officers are there. "Hello officers, how can I help you?"

"We are Detectives Smith and Jones, from precincts 15th in Delta Junction and 39th precinct in Fairbanks." They both displayed their identification to Elliott. "We are here to take you to precinct 39th for questioning. A resident of Delta Junction by the name of Daniel died three years ago in Washington DC. You are a person of interest in this case. We need you to come down for questioning."

"I would like to call my lawyer first. You can do that from the precinct, we will not question you until your counsel is present," said officer Jones. "I need to get my keys to lock the door."

"We know that you are a retired police officer and you know the procedure for taking a person of interest in for custody."

"Yes, I do know the procedure and so for you guys have done everything right."

"Are you ready sir?"

"Yes, I am." Detective Jones placed Elliott in the backseat of the squad car, and they both got in the front seat. Elliott was thinking to himself, was Madison calling to warn me about the police? Once reaching the precinct, Elliott was escorted to an interrogation room. He was allowed to call his lawyer, and then his phone was removed from his possession.

I forgot to put a password on my phone. The detectives will be able to see who I have called, text, and emailed in the last few days and weeks. That was careless on my part. Detective Jones came back to the room. "Would you like some water, or do you need to go to the restroom?"

"Some water would be great."

Detective Jones returned with a bottle of water. "Thank you, detective."

"You are welcome. Your lawyer is in the building and is being briefed by the Captain. In a few minutes, we will start questioning you."

As soon as they finished talking, Elliott's lawyer Steven, Attorney Jason and Detective Jones reentered the room.

"We are here today because the relative of a deceased resident from Delta Junction requested the reopening of this case. Steven, we believe your client Mr. Elliott may have had some involvement in this case, that is why he is here. He did request counsel be present, so we have not asked any questions in your absence. We are also aware that your client is a retired police officer from Washington and now living in the state of Alaska. He is aware and understands due process, and interrogation practices.

"Currently, he is not being charged for any crime." "Do you have any questions, Attorney Steven?"

"I would like a few minutes alone with my client since this has all happened so quickly in a videoed non-screened room."

"You can do that in this room without leaving. All recording devices will be turned off, so you can have privacy."

"Thank you," said Steven.

Everyone left the room except Steven and Elliott.

"Elliott tell me what the hell is going on? It appears that in our phone conversation you left out a few significant details. Tell me what you do know and why would you be a suspect."

"I worked on this case for a month three years ago, and I was aware of its reopening. They think I am a suspect because I know the woman who was having an affair with the deceased."

"What is her name?" "Her name is Madison." "How did you meet her?"

"She and I met at a restaurant in Atlanta during the time I lost my wife.

She and I have been friends for a couple of years."

"Did you handle some type of police work for her while you were on the force?"

"No, I did not. I did start to like Madison, but this Daniel guy got to her heart before me."

"Is that the extent of your relationship with Madison."

"Did you know this Daniel guy or arrest him at any time?" "No, I did not."

"Elliott, I don't want any surprises with this interrogation."

"There won't be any." Steven stepped out of the room and returned with Detective Jones and Attorney Jason.

"Mr. Elliott we only have a few questions to ask you. We have already explained to you and your lawyer why you are here. Where is your official residence, and can you state it for the record?"

"My current address is 206 Only Dr. Fairbanks." "How long have you lived at this address?"

"I have lived at this address for one week." "What is your previous address?"

"It is 922 Misty Trail Washington, DC."

"How long were you there?"

"I lived their twenty-five years." "What is your current occupation?"

"I am retired from Washington DC Police Department."

"I was a police officer in Washington DC for twenty-five years."

"Were you employed at any other department before DC or while in DC?" "Yes, I worked a special assignment in Atlanta Georgia for two years before retirement."

"Were you forced to retire?"

"No, I was not. I had the time and the age."

"Did you have a good repour with your fellow officers?" "Yes, I think so."

"Did you develop any close relationships while you were in Georgia?" "I did find a good friend right after I lost my wife."

"Who might that be?"

"A lady by the name of Madison."

"Did you just have a friend relationship or a romantic one?" "It was just a friendly relationship."

"Was Madison employed at the time you met her and if so with whom?" "Yes, I believed she worked for a company named AllTuck."

"What type of company is AllTuck?"

"I think they are a technology firm that specializes in software and hardware design and implementation."

"Were you aware of a contract that AllTuck had with the military exchange stores?"

"Yes, I read about it in the paper."

"What project were you assigned to at the precinct in Atlanta?"

"There was a drug ring task force or special services department developed in Washington. The drug ring had spread or migrated into Atlanta. To stop this ring from migrating to other states, I was assigned as the DC. point of contact to work with Atlanta drug task force."

"When did this task force end for you?" "It ended two months before I retired."

"Did you ever discuss with Madison this special task force you were working on?"

"No, I did not."

"Did this task force cause you to get involved with any military personnel?"

"Yes, it did. "

"Was that military contact name Sergeant Major Rick?" "Yes, it was."

"Was Sergeant Major Rick also responsible for ensuring the military exchange stores operate successfully?"

"I do not know."

"Did you know that Madison had a brother named Scott?" "Yes, I did."

"Did you ever arrest Scott while in your position in Washington?" "Yes, I did."

"What was the nature of the arrest?"

"He had too much to drink one night at a club and decided to drive back to the base. He was driving, across the highway. After a breathalyzer test, I knew his mental and motor skills were impaired, so I arrested him."

"Did you know Madison before you arrested her brother?" "No, I did not."

"When you learned that Scott was her brother, did you tell Madison you had arrested him?"

"No, I did not."

"Did you know Daniel the victim's case we are investigating?"

"I did not know him personally, but I knew of him through Madison because she was dating him."

"Were you aware that he was married?" "Yes, I was."

"Did you try to talk Madison out of having an affair with Daniel?" "No, I did not try to talk her out of it, but I did tell her it was wrong." "It appears that you and Madison are more than just friends."

"Why did you move to Alaska?"

"It was a recommendation from Madison."

"Were you following her and hoping you and she could have a closer relationship now that Daniel is out of the picture?"

"No, you have it all wrong. Madison knew I was retiring and did not want to move back to Washington. So, she suggested that I check out moving to Alaska to live when I retire."

"Detective Jones if you are not charging my client with anything, then we are getting out of here."

"You have held us here long enough. It appears you are just badgering, and we are not going to stand for anymore," said Attorney Steven. "No, we are not pressing charges at the moment, but we don't want your client leaving town, because we may have more questions."

"Come on Elliott let's get out of this place."

Detective Jones said, "Thank you for your cooperation, and you both have a nice day."

Elliott and Steven walked out of the interrogation room, exited the building and headed for their cars. "Elliott you do not need to contact whoever this Madison is. If they are talking to you, you better believe they are talking to her as well. Is there something you are not telling me?" "I have told you everything. You were in that room while I was being questioned."

"Yes, I was in there, and they were asking some pretty incriminating questions. Now is the time, if you need to tell me something?"

"I don't have anything to tell you."

"Okay, I am going home to have dinner with my wife."

"I am going home as well, thank you for everything," said Elliott.

CHAPTER 21

EVIDENCE SPEAKS FOR ITSELF

AFTER Alphonso phone call with Kenneth to confirm their appointment on Saturday morning, he had an early dinner and went to bed around nine p.m. Kenneth works for the Atlanta police department and is a forensic fingerprint analyst.

Alphonso arose early on Saturday morning, took a showered and had breakfast in the hotel. At eight-thirty, he was getting in the car provided by Soco & Soco and drove to his appointment at nine at the 100th precinct in Atlanta with Kenneth.

Everyone calls this city Hotlanta, I call it hot traffic. Everything you want and need you can find in the heart of the city. I could probably get used to living here, especially if I could find that special lady. Alphonso arrived at 100th precinct in twenty minutes. This is a upscale police precinct, you won't see this in Alaska.

Alphonso was stunned when he walked in the front door of the precinct at the reception area. It looks like a small futuristic city with flat screens on every wall and ergonomic sit-stand desk.

Alphonso let the officer on duty know he was there to see Kenneth. Kenneth came right away to escort him to his office. "Hello, Alphonso." "Hello, Kenneth and thank you again for seeing me today."

"No problem. It is a normal day for me. My wife and children are away for the weekend visiting her mother in Tennessee, so I am on my own this weekend."

"I like how modern this precinct is."

"Our Mayor spares no expense when it comes to the police department. Why don't you have a seat?"

"The gun report is here for us to review and I printed an extra copy for you. Let's go over it and see what you think."

"I glanced at the report earlier today at the Soco office, so I have an idea of what's in it."

"Excellent. The gun that's in our custody we are positive it was used in the death of Daniel. It was dusted for fingerprints, and to our surprise, we found prints of a former police officer by the name of Elliott."

"He was on a special assignment here in Atlanta from Washington. For a couple of years, he worked with our drug task force unit. There was talk he was a dirty cop. The Captain, an outstanding officer, runs a very ethnical precinct. There was whisper around the office that the captain was glad when Elliott retired."

"What kind of things had Elliott been known to do while working here?"

"He was known to rough up victims when arresting them unnecessarily, placing false evidence on them like drugs, just to name a few."

"What about murder?"

"Until we found his prints on this gun, we did not think he would go that far. This gun was a Springfield XD .45 ACP, and not registered to Elliott, as a matter of fact, no registration or serial number was found."

"Prints found on this gun were not like normal prints would be placed."

"The person who shot this gun was not facing the victim but was turned away from the victim and then fired the gun. This would make the incident look like the victim committed suicide," said Kenneth. "Kenneth, that's interesting you say that. The victim's skeletal body was exhumed a few days ago for an autopsy. This autopsy report confirms that the gunshot wound position to the head of Daniel proves he did not commit suicide."

"Were their other prints on the gun?"

"There was a small smear on the gun, that we have not been able to identify." The Leeson's family lives in this house where the contractors found the gun in the backyard. They are having a pool put in, and the contractor they hired found the gun while digging the hole for the pool."

"We set up a crime scene and searched the backyard, to see if there was other evidence, but there was none. Before clearing both contractors and the Leeson's, we were able to get an affidavit from everyone. Would you like to view it?"

"Yes, I would like to see it. I have an appointment with the Leeson's this afternoon, but this report may save me from having to talk with them."

"If I have to go visit the Leeson's after reading the report, do you think it possible for an officer to escort me?"

"Yes, as a matter of fact, Captain Ray thought you might want to talk to them. He has assigned detective Shelia to accompany you, and he would have been here today, but he was called in for a family emergency last night."

"Your Captain has thought of everything."

"He is the best I have ever worked for."

"I have two more requests. Can you find out if the deceased son is registered for a gun and I would like to see the gun that you guys found?" "I have other cases to work today, so detective Shelia will be able to help you with those requests. She was waiting for me to finish giving you my report before she introduced herself. If you don't have any more questions for me, I can take you to her office."

"No, I don't. Thank you, Kenneth, for being so thorough and providing all this information. You have almost solved this case for me. I want to make one phone call."

"You can use my desk, and I will go get Detective Shelia." Alphonso dialed Jason's number in Alaska. "Hello, Jason." "Hello, Alphonso. How are things going?"

"Believe it or not, I was getting ready to dial your number, and here you are calling me, great timing."

"I am at the Atlanta police department, and they have found the gun that was possibly involved in the death of Daniel. Elliott's fingerprints are on the gun. They have concluded the same thing as the autopsy report. The gunshot to Daniels' head proves it was not a suicide."

"We talk to Madison yesterday morning at her mother's home in Delta Junction and Elliott and his lawyer at the precinct in Fairbanks on yesterday afternoon. Madison will be at the precinct this morning with her lawyer. There were some questions we asked her that she felt she needed to have a lawyer present," said Jason.

"Jason, we have enough evidence on Elliott that you can arrest him officially as a suspect in the murder of Daniel."

229

"Man, you guys are on it in Alaska, and I believe we will have this case solved in a few days. Therefore, I will have more time to look for that special lady."

"I'm pulling for you, but I don't know what woman would want you?" "She is out there, I just got to find her. If you don't find her on this trip, I will introduce you to some ladies when you get back."

"Now you tell me." "You never asked."

"I thought since you been married for a while you did not know any single women."

"That's what you get for thinking." "Jason, let's get back to the case."

"The gun the police found in the backyard of a home previously owned by Madison is the type Landon owns, and the same type used to shoot Daniel. I have an appointment with the Leeson's today at eleven a.m. It is just a formality."

"Alphonso, the only other question I have is who put a substance in Daniel wine or soda he was drinking that night?"

"Jason, I don't believe Joshua had anything to do with it because he had no motive. Daniel was dead when he brought room service. However, we know Landon his son visited him at the DoubleTree the same night. He had a motive because he tried to get him to end the affair. Daniels' daughter Kathleen was at her dental office at the time of the incident. She and her brother are close, she could be hiding something. I have an appointment with her on Sunday."

"If all goes well here, I will be back in Washington on Tuesday, maybe Monday. Jason, I will give you a buzz later this evening for an update." "Okay, talk to you then."

As he was finishing his phone call, detective Shelia and Kenneth returned to his desk. "Hello, I am Detective Shelia, and you must be investigator Alphonso?"

"Yes, I am, but please call me Alphonso."

"Only if you call me Shelia. It is a pleasure to meet you. Kenneth tells me he has provided everything you needed from him. We will go to my office and complete the other request. Kenneth, I forgot the Captain called and will not be in the office until Monday. We will see you later."

Shelia and Alphonso walked to her office next to the Captain's.

"This is the most innovative precinct I have ever seen, and I have been in quite a few."

"We have an excellent Mayor and Council that wants us to do our best for the city. They make sure we have tools we need to do our job, but also a work environment that helps us do our best."

"That is great. I am impressed."

"Come on in and have a seat. I understand you want to see the gun we found at the Leeson's and to see if Landon's gun is registered in our database."

"We do have access to a national database we can search. We will do that first. It will take a few minutes because of the size."

"Shelia, this department has already provided me with more information than I had expected."

"Landon is registered in DC for two Springfield XD .45 ACP guns. He purchased both at the same location."

"The first one he reported stolen but never recovered. It appears in the community and in the surrounding area where he lives, there has been more than a normal number of break-ins. It does not say here if he had a break-in at his residence."

"When I interviewed Landon, he failed to tell me one of his guns was stolen."

"I can look for stolen or lost guns in this database."

"Landon did have a gun stolen while in one of the parks in Washington. It states here he accidentally left his car unlocked. The gun was taken from his glove compartment, about three years ago. This database also indicates the last three years, this handgun has been the number one purchased throughout the country. That is interesting. I will print you a copy of the report."

"Will, you also look to see if his sister owns a gun, her name is Kathleen?"

"No records were found."

"I did not think you would find anything. Kathleen does not appear to be the type to own a gun. I have not met her. Not sure how I came up with that conclusion," said Alphonso.

"You know that is just investigative instinct. Most law enforcement officers solve cases from instinct all the time," stated Shelia.

"If you will walk me down to the evidence room, we can look at that gun. "This is a huge precinct."

"Wait till you see the evidence room."

As they approached the administrator desk for the evidence room, Shelia gave the officer the information she needed to find the gun. He put the data into the computer and then asked us to follow him. I could not believe the size, and how organized this evidence room was.

The officer led us directly to the gun, and we were able to sit in a small office and examine it.

"We have pictures of the gun for courtroom appearances, and you can take a copy of it."

"We have a request to transfer the gun to the precinct in Washington."

"Can you hold up on that request until Thursday next week? I may have solved this case, but I need to talk to two more people. One here in Atlanta and one in Washington."

"Yes, we can do that. Captain Ray said we might not have to send the gun anywhere unless there is going to be a trial. We will wait for directions from you and your law firm."

"I do appreciate all that you and Kenneth have done for me today and what this entire precinct has done. Can we now go to the Leeson's, they are expecting me at eleven a.m.?"

"Let's take an official car," suggested Shelia.

Shelia and Alphonso walked out to the parking lot and got in one of the precinct detective cars. "It will take us about fifteen minutes. The traffic is great for a Saturday."

They arrived at the Leeson's home at precisely eleven. Shelia parked the car, and they walked up to the door. Alphonso rang the doorbell. Mr. Leeson answered. "I am detective Shelia, and this is investigator Alphonso from Soco & Soco law firm." Both Shelia and Alphonso presented their identifications.

"I am Mr. Leeson. Please come in; my wife is waiting for us in the living room."

"The children are at our neighbor's home for a birthday party today." They walked in the living room and joined Mrs. Leeson.

"Honey this is detective Shelia and investigator Alphonso whom we talk to on the phone."

"Good to meet you both," said Mrs. Leeson.

"Nice to meet you as well," said Shelia and Alphonso in unison. "Have a seat on the sofa."

"Mr. and Mrs. Leeson's as I stated on the phone, I am investigating a case of death that happened in Washington three years ago. It was a cold case and now reopened because of new evidence? One of the people of interest is Madison, whom I believe sold you this home. We are aware your backyard was being prepared to put in a pool when the contractor found a gun. Is that true?"

"Yes, that is true."

"Did the contractor come in right away and tell you about the gun or did they call the police first?"

"They called the police first and then notified us. We agreed with the way they handled it."

"What happened after police were called?"

"The police came out the same day, bagged the gun, put yellow tape around the area and declared it a possible crime scene."

"How did that make you feel?"

"It made us wonder if we had made a mistake purchasing this house. We were able to purchase from Madison at an unbelievable low price in comparison to other homes in this area. The owner was anxious and wanted the loan to close sooner than we planned, but it all worked out," said Mr. Leeson.

"When the police came and questioned us about the gun, we thought someone had died or was killed here and buried the gun in our backyard." "The police found that no crime had been committed here it put us at ease."

"Have you been in contact with Madison since you closed on the house?" "She called once and wanted to know if we had gotten settled in and how was everything going. We have not heard from her since."

"Has anyone else come to this home looking for her?" "No one has come by while we were home."

"Have you noticed any strange cars watching the house?"

"No, we have not. We did get a strange phone call last week. Someone called about six p.m. and asked to speak to Carol."

"I answered the phone. said Mrs. Leeson. I told them Carol did not live here. But they kept insisting that our number was Carol's number and sounded like they were upset because they did not reach her."

"Was it a male or female?"

"It was a male I believe from the tone of his voice."

"Is our family in danger by living in this house?" Asked Mr. Leeson. "Mr. and Mrs. Leeson, I am from the local police. I assure you that you are not in any danger, and this home you purchased is not part of any crime so feel free to continue to enjoy living here."

"Mr. and Mrs. Leeson's, we have no more questions."

"Thank you for all your help and honesty surrounding the case. I hope that we have not inconvenienced you too long?" Said Alphonso. "Thank you both for clarification and honesty about this entire situation," said Mr. Leeson. We will walk you out. You both have a nice rest of the day."

"You too," said Alphonso.

"Detective Shelia and Alphonso walked back to the car and got in. They were in complete silence in the car for about five minutes driving back to the precinct. "Do you think you got all your questions answered?" Asked Shelia.

"Absolutely. The main thing I wanted to know was the process and how quickly Madison wanted the home to sell."

"Do you think it was Elliott, calling asking for Carol to see what kind of information he could find out about the people living in the house?"

"Shelia, yes, I do believe he called, and I think he planted the gun in the backyard. I'm wondering if Madison knew about the gun?" It was obvious the Leeson's were not involved in this case."

"Thank you again for your help and assistance today."

"Glad I could help, and Alphonso I try to always learn something from other people such as yourself."

"I have one more interview tomorrow with Kathleen at one p.m. I don't suspect she was involved in her father's death. She might have some information about her brother that could be helpful."

"It looks like I will be flying out of Atlanta on Monday instead of Tuesday. This trip to Atlanta has put a lot of pieces together. Some of the evidence I have found, makes me think the Washington police did not try very hard to solve this case. I don't normally have doubts about the police department, but this time I do."

"The Alaska police department has questioned Elliott and Madison. According to the detectives that question them, they both appear to be hiding something. With the information this precinct has

WHO WOULD HAVE THOUGHT

uncovered concerning the gun, we can now arrest both. Hopefully, that arrest will cause one or both to confess."

"I'm going back to my hotel room and read these reports I have received from your department, the report from Q'UP, and the autopsy report from the coroner in Alaska. Hopefully, I can figure out what else happened in Mr. Daniel's room. I need to figure out what substance was in his system."

"The autopsy report states he was killed twice, how can that be?" Said Shelia.

"Jacoby told me it was a serial murder of one person."

"Do you mind if I get a copy of the autopsy report and let us help you do some research on this second death? I believe Kenneth can find it for you. We will get back to you."

"If you guys find anything, no matter what time of day or night give me a call."

"We will do just that."

Shelia and Alphonso arrived back at the precinct within fifteen minutes. "If you hand me the autopsy report, I will make a copy of it, and then you can be on your way."

"Do you have any recommendations for lunch? I want to eat before driving to the hotel."

"If you like Chinese food, there is one that is two blocks from the precinct called HSU's."

"That would be great."

"The precinct personnel to include myself eat there at least once a week sometimes twice."

"I will check it out and thanks again."

CHAPTER **22**

TRUTH AND CONSEQUENCES

THE flight to Atlanta for Violet is scheduled to leave at ten a.m. from Ronald Reagan National and arrive at Atlanta Hartsfield-Jackson at eleven. Kathleen will be waiting to pick her up.

"Landon I'm going to be so excited to see your sister. It has been a longer timeframe since I saw her versus how long I had seen you."

"Mother you have to realize she is a dentist and her patients dictate her schedules."

"I know she would visit more often if she could."

"Another reason for you to move to this area so we can take care of you." "Landon, I really feel good that you and your sister want to take care of me now that your father is gone. However, I can take care of myself. I am in good physical and mental health as you said. If I get to the point, I can't take care of myself, I will move here."

"That's just it mother, we want to spend time with you now while we are all in good physical and mental health. It is time for you to board. You and Kathleen are going to have a great time together. I look forward to seeing you and her on Thursday."

"You did not tell me she was coming back with me. That is our surprise for you. The three of us are going to spend time together until you go back on Monday."

"That is the best surprise a mother could have, to spend time with her children. Your father would be happy to know we are spending time together."

"I guess so."

"What do you mean Landon, you guess so? Did something happen between you and your father? You have been acting a little out of character since you had that interview with Alphonso."

"No mother there is nothing wrong or anything I need to tell you. I am just excited about you being here."

"You could do a little better in show and the tell department of how happy you are to see me. It is nine-twenty, time for me to head to security and get to my gate. Give me a hug."

Landon walked closer to give his mother a hug. "You know when you were a little boy, I did not have to ask you for a hug, you would just always give it to me."

"I remember mother."

"I hope you are more compassionate with Connie."

"Mother go to your gate and give Kathleen my love when you get there." "Love you Landon and goodbye."

"Goodbye, mother."

Violet was able to get through security quickly and to her gate just in time to hear the attendant calling for first class passengers.

I am so glad my children purchased first class seating. I can get on the plane first and get off first. They have spoiled me, I will not want to travel any other way after this.

After all passengers boarding was complete, the flight attendant did the safety drill and announced we would be taking off in four minutes. Being distracted by my son's attitude, getting through security and boarding the plane I did not realize my seat assignment was the same coming from Alaska to Washington sitting next to Alphonso.

I am going to have to do more vacationing and enjoying my life as my children have been trying to get me to do. After about an hour we were landing in Atlanta. While exiting the plane, I remembered that Kathleen said the Atlanta airport can be confusing, so pay close attention to the direction signs. I did everything she told me to do. Therefore, I arrived safely at baggage claim where she was waiting for me.

"Hi, mother," said Kathleen.

"Hello, Kathleen. They both hugged each other, and Violet did not want to let her go.

"Mother that's how you use to hug me when I was a little girl." "You are still my little girl just taller, and you look just like me."

"I wonder how that happened?" Kathleen and Violet both laughed out loud.

"You look like me, but you were a daddy's baby." "I miss daddy so much, mother."

"I miss him too Kathleen."

"Let's get your luggage, get to the car, then we will stop and have lunch on the way to my place. When we get home, we can just sit, relax and catch up."

"Sounds like you have it all planned Kathleen. You are still that very organized person you were when growing up at home with me, and your father."

"Some things don't change mother." Once in the car, they exited the airport.

"Where are we having lunch?" Violet inquired.

"You were at an Asian restaurant the last time we talked, so I decided we would go to a Chinese restaurant called HSUs. I think you will like it."

"If you have been there and liked it, I am sure I will like it?"

"I have been on several occasions and have not been disappointed." Within fifteen minutes they were at the restaurant.

"We are here, mother." "That was quick Kathleen."

"The traffic is not bad today as it normally is on a Saturday. We will park the car, and we have a short walk to the restaurant."

They exited the car and reached the restaurant in five minutes. The hostess said it would be a ten-minute wait.

"Kathleen, let's go to the bathroom while we are waiting. This is a beautiful restaurant. I like the decor."

"Mother glad you like it. They are busy most of the time, just glad they not busy today."

As they were returning from the restroom, the hostess approaches to seat them and asked if they preferred a booth or table. They both said table. Once seated the waiter brought their menus and asked what they wanted to drink. They both ordered sweet tea and water.

"Kathleen, what are you going to eat?"

"I am going to have the vegetable egg rolls as an appetizer and hot and sour soup. For an entree, I will have lemon chicken. Their egg rolls are the best in Atlanta. Have you decided mother?"

"Yes, I am going to try the egg rolls as well since you say they are the best, soup choice will be wonton and my entree basil chicken." "Great choices mother, everything I have had here is good."

Once they finished talking, the waiter came for their orders. The restaurant was a little dark, so they were adjusting their eyes to the lighting Violet looked around the restaurant and sitting at a booth behind her daughter was Alphonso. He looked up from eating as she looked straight at him, and they both looked surprised. Alphonso immediately got up from his booth and came over to their table.

"Hello, Ms. Violet, it is good to see you again." "Hello, Alphonso, surprised to see you here."

"This is my daughter Kathleen. Kathleen this is Mr. Alphonso."

"I am pleased to meet you. As a matter of fact, we have an appointment tomorrow," said Kathleen.

"I am open for date and time change if you are." "Let me think about that.

"My schedule is completely free for this afternoon," said Alphonso. "If you change your mind let me know."

The food here is excellent. It was recommended to me by a local resident."

"My daughter has been here several times, and she says the food is excellent as well."

"I won't keep you any longer. I need to finish up my lunch, and you can get started on yours. It is good to see you again, and good to meet your daughter."

"Mother how do you know this guy, you have only been in Atlanta for several hours."

"I met him on the plane from Alaska to Washington. Then I met him again at a dinner party with your brother's law firm. He works for the same law firm as Landon, but as an investigator."

"It seems like you know a lot about this man."

"I don't know any more than you do about this guy. Why didn't you tell me he is interviewing you?"

"It has to do with daddy's death, I don't know exactly how I can help him?"

"Well, you know that he has interviewed your brother and he has not been the same since that interview."

"What do you mean?"

"Landon has been nervous, on edge, not focused and just seem downright worried about something."

"Mother, I just think Landon does not want us to have to go through this investigation all over again, especially you. If he is rattled, that is the reason."

"Well, I hope you are right."

The waiter brought their soup and egg rolls because they ask for them to be brought out together.

"These egg rolls are good just as you said, Kathleen. Glad I ordered my own."

As soon as they finished their appetizer, the waiter brought their entrees. "It looks and smells good. I hope you like it, mother."

"Wow it is good," said Violet.

"So is mine," stated Kathleen.

"Kathleen why don't you go ahead and talk to Alphonso this afternoon. You will be done with it and won't have to anticipate what he wants to ask you tomorrow. That way I believe we will have a better time these few days we have to spend together."

"Are you sure mother?" "Yes, I am sure."

"If he is willing to follow us home, I will get this over with." Violet and Kathleen had finished eating their food, and while they were waiting for the check, Kathleen walked over to the booth where Alphonso was sitting. He was enjoying a dessert.

"Mr. Alphonso, I was wondering if you would like to question me this afternoon at my home?"

"Yes, I would be happy to."

"We are waiting for our check, and you seem to be finishing up. Are you parked in the parking lot?"

"Yes, I am on the first level."

"As soon as we get our checks, we can walk out to the garage, and you can follow me home from here."

"I really appreciate you consenting to talk to me today especially since your mother is visiting."

"It was actually her idea."

"You can thank her for me," said Alphonso. When they got to the parking garage, Alphonso was parked right next to them. "How convenient," said Kathleen. "Kathleen, remember we parked after him."

"Yes, mother you are right."

"You are already upset, and you have not been asked one question by Alphonso."

"Mother, I am not upset."

"I know I have not seen you in a while, but I have known you all your life, so I do know when you are upset."

"If you put it like that, I guess I am a little irritated. It will only take us about fifteen minutes to reach my place. The quicker we get there, the quicker this will be over."

About twenty minutes they reached Kathleen's condo. "Kathleen this is a beautiful place."

She pulled her car in the garage and signaled for Alphonso to come to the front door. She retrieved her mother bag from the trunk, and they went inside.

"Mother your room is the one to the right. I will get you settled soon as I let Alphonso in."

Kathleen opens the front door for Alphonso.

"I am going to take you to my office, and we can talk there in private. I need to get my mother settled in."

"She just got off the plane from Washington. I am sure she is tired." "Do what you have to do, I am in no hurry."

Kathleen picked up her mother's bag and carried it to her room. "Mother are you okay?

"Yes, I am doing fine. This is a beautiful master suite with a bathroom."

"My room is the same. You might want to unpack your things, take a shower and get comfortable while I am talking to Alphonso. Hopefully, this won't take long. We will talk in the office that way you won't be disturbed."

"Go ahead I will be fine, and we will talk later." Kathleen walked back to her office.

"I am ready," said Kathleen.

"I will show my identification to you first. I am an investigator for Soco & Soco law firm from Alaska. We have offices in Atlanta and Washington DC."

"The reason I am here is about your father's death."

"Your uncle Johnny came to our firm and requested we reopen his case. Your mother had to agree to have his body exhumed, and an autopsy performed as a condition to open the case. We have done all that, and we are now questioning people that knew your father, and some that did not know him. That brings me to our interview."

"Where were you on the day your father was found dead?"

"I was in my dental office with a patient. I have evening hours at my office on Wednesdays, to accommodate parents who work and want to bring their children to the dentist."

"How can you be sure?"

"I am sure because my patient was a little boy who had come to the dentist for his first visit, and he was terrified."

"Is that his picture on your wall?"

"You are very observant, and I keep it there as a reminder, that not only are children afraid of going to the dentist, but adults are as well."

"Did you know what type of work your father did for a living?"

"I thought I did until he was found dead. Social media and the company Q'UP let me and Landon know he was an investigator."

"We were told that his job put him in danger sometimes. He did everything he could to protect us."

"What kind of relationship do you have with your brother?"

"We have a close relationship since we were kids. Our parents always told us that we needed to stay close because when they were gone, we would only have each other."

"At the time they told us that, I did not understand what they meant until my father died."

"What was your mother and father relationship like?"

"They loved each other very much. My dad was away on his job for long periods, but my mother understood."

"Was your father in a relationship with another woman besides your mother?"

"Yes, he was?"

"How did you know, and did you know whom this person was?" "My brother told me that he was involved with a woman name Madison." "How did that make you feel?"

"It made me angry. I could not believe my dad loved my mother and had an affair with another woman."

"Are you still angry today?"

"No, I am not angry, I am just glad my mother did not see him with this woman."

"Did you know that Madison lived in Atlanta for a short period?" "No, I was not aware."

"Are you sure your mother was not aware of the affair?"

"No, I am not. I assumed mother had no knowledge since she did not mention it."

"How did your brother feel about your father having an affair?" "He was very angry with him because mother loved our father. He knew this would break her heart."

"Do you think your brother was involved in your father's death?" "Absolutely not. Landon and my father had such a close relationship, and Landon loved him very much."

"Who notified you that your father was dead and how he died?" "Landon notified me the same day that dad had supposedly committed suicide. Dad was careful to keep guns out of our home while growing up. I do believe someone got this wrong, during the first investigation." "Did you know that your brother Landon visited your father the same day he was found dead?"

"No, I did not?"

"How close are your brother and his girlfriend Connie?"

"I think she is overbearing and is more in love than my brother." How do you know that?"

"Landon has told me that on several occasions." "Kathleen, that is all the questions I have."

"I am sorry that I interfered with you spending time with your mother. Thank you again for consenting to speak with me. Would like to leave my card with you in case you have any questions or think of something that will help the case."

"Will you let me, and my brother be the first to know when you find out what really happened to our father before it gets in the news."

"I will do my best to make sure that happens. You know social media gets information quickly these days," emphasized Alphonso.

"I understand, and I will walk you to the door."

Kathleen went to her mother's room to see how she was doing. "Mother, we are finished."

"Kathleen as you can see, I have my comfortable pajamas on. I am ready to sit and have a talk with you."

"Why don't you come to the kitchen and let's just have a cup of tea," said Kathleen. "You used to say that a cup of tea is good for relaxing the mind and soul. I didn't know what you meant, by that when we were young. I have a clear picture of what it means now. When I come home from work in the evenings, I have a cup of tea to relax my mind from all that I have experienced during the day."

"Kathleen, why do you need to relax today?"

"Mother let me put the water on before we start a conversation."

"Did your father get a chance to visit you here in Atlanta before he passed?"

"No mother he did not. His job kept him busy when he was in DC. When he was not working, he was in Alaska with you."

"Is there something you need to tell me about your father? I asked your brother this same question. The two of you seem to be hiding something from me."

"I need to tell you this now because I believe it will come out in the press since my father's case has been reopened. Let's make our tea first. Mother, I love this lemon and ginger tea, is that okay for you?"

"I can't believe that's the same tea I drink at home."

"What does that mean, that I not only look like you, but I love the same tea you like?"

They both had a good laugh. "Here is your cup and I will set mine down and bring the water over to where we are sitting."

"This tea is good, as a matter of fact, I believe it tastes better than the brand I use at home. You will have to take me to get some of this to take back with me when I go home on Monday."

"Mother before dad died, he was having an affair with a woman named Madison. According to Landon, this had been going on for at least a year. Landon saw them together on several occasions, so he approached dad about it. Dad had planned to get a divorce from you, but we don't know when he was planning on telling you. That is one of the reasons why he was not coming home to you as often as he had been in the past." "Why did you and your brother not inform me. Is this why the investigator has been talking to you, and your brother?"

"Yes, mother. We did not want you to be hurt. The investigator Alphonso thinks that Landon had something to do with dad's death because he knew about the affair."

"Do you really think your brother had something to do with his death?" "No, mother Landon would not harm daddy, because he loved him so much."

"Now I understand why your brother was acting worried after he was interviewed by Alphonso. I have lost your father, and now I may possibly lose your brother to prison. What are we going to do?"

"Mother there is nothing we can do except wait until the truth comes out.

In the meantime, we will have to hope and pray that Landon is not involved. After being interviewed by Alphonso, I believe he will find the truth and Landon will be okay. We are going sightseeing as we planned tomorrow to The World of Coca-Cola museum, Georgia Aquarium, and the CNN Center."

"That sounds like a full day for us. Maybe it will keep our minds off things. Let's find a good movie to watch on TV. By the time we finish watching a movie, we will probably be hungry for dinner. I will fix us a salad, but first I am going to take a shower and get in my PJs like you."

"I am going to make another cup of tea while you are in the shower." While sipping her tea, Violet was thinking to herself.

Did I hear Kathleen say Daniel was having an affair with a woman named Madison? Is it a coincidence that my best friend Madison lives in Delta Junction had a relationship with my husband? If it is the same person how could she do that to me? Maybe this why she never talks about her past. I should call and confront her."

"She is the only friend I have. It could be another Madison, at least I hope it is."

Madison arose early Saturday morning to help her father with her mother. I was so glad that he still cares for her. In her own way, she still cares for him. The reunion we had over dinner last night, brought back memories of how things used to be when we were a family. Maybe this is the way things were meant to be.

"Mom if you and daddy are okay, I am going to leave for my appointment. It should not take any more than four hours. Mother, you be good, until I get back, and do whatever daddy tells you."

"That will be a miracle," said Sam.

"Yes, daddy, you are probably right. My appointment is at ten so I will see you both later."

Madison got in her car and headed for the 39th precinct. It would take her about two hours to get there. While driving, her cell phone rang. "Hello, this is Madison."

"Hello, Elliott. Why are you calling me so early in the morning, and I told you don't call me unless it is an emergency."

"Do I not get a how are you doing Elliott. I am doing fine, hope you are doing the same?"

"I am sorry Elliot, but I have a lot on my mind right now."

"After you hear what I have to say you may have more on your mind. I had a visit from the police yesterday, and I had to go downtown for questioning with my lawyer."

"They said I was a suspect in the death of Daniel, but they did not have any evidence to prove their case, so they let me go."

"They did ask me about you, and I had to tell them I knew you." "Well, I had a visit yesterday as well, but I stopped them in the middle of their questioning and told them, I needed my lawyer present. I am headed to precinct 39th now. My lawyer is going to meet me there."

"Be careful what you say. The police have evidence, and I am not sure what it is. Just make sure you tell the truth, no matter what."

"Who is sitting with your mother?" "My daddy is with her."

"I did not know you were talking to your father."

"I have not for a long time, but I did not have anyone else. And I feel good knowing mother is with someone that cares about her."

"It was good talking to you, let me know how your interview goes." "I will do that. Talk to you later."

I got about forty-five minutes to go, and I will be at the precinct. Detective Jones was sitting in his office at the precinct waiting for Madison to show up, and his cell phone rang.

"Detective Jones, this is Attorney Jason. How are things going?" "Hello, Jason, what can I do for you this morning?"

"I thought lawyers only showed up in the office after twelve p.m." "That's not true of all lawyers, some of us come to work at seven a.m. as I do daily."

"Well you are the exception, and it is a Saturday morning, you are indeed exceptional."

"I talk to our investigator Alphonso who is working this case, and he found some information that will be helpful when you interview Madison this morning. He was at the Atlanta police department yesterday."

"They have a gun that was found in the backyard of the home Madison lived in before she sold it, to the current owners the Leeson's. The weapon has Elliott's fingerprints on it. I don't know if Madison was aware that the gun was there or not."

"We actually have enough evidence to arrest Elliott for murder, but Alphonso thinks there are two murderers. He wants us to hold off arresting him."

"Elliott could possibly be tied to Madison brother death whose name is Scott as well. We were not investigating that case."

"If we find evidence, we will pass it on to the district attorney in DC. I believe Elliott wanted a relationship with Madison. Therefore, he would do anything for her. He thinks because he was a cop, he covered his tracks."

"Jason that is some real hard evidence that makes it easy for us to arrest him. Just give me a call when we need to move forward. In the meantime, I will put together an arrest warrant and have it ready for the judge. Talk to you later Jason."

Jones went in to brief his Captain on the breaking news he had received from Jason about the case. We need to submit an affidavit to the judge for his signature to arrest Elliott after they receive that official evidence from Soco & Soco.

Madison arrived at the 39th precinct and parked her car in one of the visitor spaces. She mumbled to herself, I hope my lawyer Michael is already here. I don't know what questions the detectives will be asking. Based on the information I got from Elliott, I must put my honest, innocent, confident attitude hat on. As Madison walked into the precinct, her lawyer was waiting for her in the reception area.

"Hello, Michael, how are you doing?" "I am okay. How are you Madison?"

"I am doing okay and thank you for coming on a Saturday morning."

"I go where and when the client needs me. Detective Jones is waiting for us."

They walked to the detective office, and he directed them to the interrogation room.

"Ms. Madison thank you and your lawyer Michael for coming in this morning. We only have a few questions that we would like to continue with from the interview yesterday."

"We have already briefed your attorney on the case and why we want to interview you. Can you state your current address for the record?"

"My current address is 798 Just Circle Delta Junction, Alaska." "Did you have any knowledge concerning the death of Daniel?" "No, I did not."

"Did you have any knowledge of the death of your brother Scott?" "No, I did not."

"Did you sell a residence in Atlanta and if so, what is the address?" "Yes, I did. The address is 2090 Love Terrace Atlanta Georgia." "Who are the current owners of that residence in Atlanta?"

"The Leeson's are their last name. I don't recall their first names." "Have you ever owned a gun or shot one?"

"No, I have never owned or shot a gun."

"Have you spent any time at the DoubleTree in Washington DC?"

"Yes, I stayed overnight their several times with Daniel when he was living, but don't recall the exact dates."

"Do you know if they had security cameras there the times you visited?" "No, but I know most hotels have them."

"The times you went there you were not concerned about someone seeing you there with Daniel?"

"No, I was in love with him, and I wanted everyone to know it." "Did you and Daniel have plans before he was found dead?"

"Yes, we had talked about getting married, but we knew he had to get a divorce first. I am aware that sometimes relationships with married men don't work out."

"Did you have a romantic relationship with a man by the name of Elliott?" "No, I did not. We are just friends."

"Madison, I think we can wrap up our questions. I want to thank you and your lawyer again, for coming in and answering our questions. I would like to reserve the right for you and your lawyer to come in together if we have further questions," asked Jones.

"You will have our full cooperation detective," stated Michael. "Detective, you have a nice day, and we are going to try to enjoy some of the rest of this beautiful Saturday afternoon." Madison and Michael exited the building.

"Madison, I asked you this before. Is there something you are not telling me?"

"You were in that room with me. I answered all the questions they asked." "They seem to think or have some evidence that makes you a suspect. Do you have some knowledge about Daniel or Scott's death that you could share with the police? If you do and you are not telling the truth, they will find it out."

"Now is the best time, to tell the truth." "I have been telling the truth all along."

"Okay, Madison, I am going home and spend some time with my family. You do the same, and I will send you my invoice for today."

CHAPTER **23**

WHERE DO I GO FROM HERE

IT was only five p.m. on Saturday, and Alphonso was happy about all that had been accomplished in Atlanta. Taking a break in the hotel and thinking about all the evidence that has been gathered and analyzed, we are still puzzled by why Daniel was in a coma-like state. I believe Kenneth the forensic guy will find something in the autopsy report that will be critical to this case that everyone else had overlooked. I wonder if he had any health problems. The Washington DC police department transcripts do not mention any.

I am going to give his boss at Q'UP a call maybe he knows something. Alphonso searched his contacts in his cell phone until he found the number.

Peter was home watching his favorite TV channel that had westerns on all day, and his phone rang.

"Hello, this is Peter."

"Hi, Peter, this is Alphonso, hope I'm not interrupting your afternoon, but I have another question concerning Daniel.

"How can I help Alphonso?"

"You and Daniel had a close relationship. Did he ever mention to you about any health issues?"

"Well, I do recall that he said when he completed his last physical, his doctor said he was type 1 diabetic."

"Did he also mention any fainting episodes because of the diabetics?" "As a matter of fact, I had encouraged him to go to the doctor because while on assignment in Florida he did have an episode of fainting."

"Was he on any diabetic medication."

"I don't know because he was somewhat of a private person."

"You have really been helpful. Sorry to have bothered you on a Saturday." "No problem, anything I can do to help you find out what really happened to Daniel. He was one of the best employees we had. I really do miss him, as I am sure his family does as well."

Alphonso had an incoming call from Kenneth according to his caller ID. "Hey, Kenneth you must have known I was hoping you would call me. What is going on?"

"Hello, Alphonso this is Kenneth and Shelia we have you on speaker phone."

"Hello, Kenneth and Shelia."

"I know you were trying to determine how Daniel could have been killed twice. I think I may have a clue from looking at the autopsy report.

"What did you find Kenneth?"

"It looks like there may have been a large amount of insulin in Daniel's body. This is based on the stains on his bones, and the deterioration of his teeth. If you did not look really close at the report, you could have easily missed this. The forensic scientist that performed the autopsy put some words in the report that only another forensic scientist would recognize."

"Kenneth you and detective Shelia have made my day and have found the missing evidence that will help solve this case."

"I am glad we were able to help."

"Alphonso, I give all the credit to Kenneth. As soon as I gave him the autopsy report, he dug right into it. We were going to wait until tomorrow to give you this news, then Kenneth and I discussed it and said this is too important to wait."

"I am happy you did not wait. I would like to let your Captain know what great and efficient team of people he has working for him. I am sure he already knows."

"We will pass on your comments."

"Shelia, thank you for the recommendation on the restaurant, I stopped there on my way to the hotel, and the food was outstanding. Coincidently, Landon sister Kathleen and his mother were there."

"She agreed to my interview with her after we all left the restaurant, instead of waiting for tomorrow."

"It looks like I will be flying back to Washington tomorrow instead of waiting until Monday. I am so glad I had an open ticket for travel." "Thanks, both of you again, for all you have done and contributed to solving this case."

"We are out here, have a good trip back to Atlanta. Keep in touch," said Shelia.

I will make a quick call to Jason in Alaska and make him aware of the new evidence. Jason was sitting in his office at home, looking over some paperwork from another case and heard his cell phone ringing. "Hey, brother Alphonso."

"Hi, Jason. Did I catch you in the middle of something?"

"No this is actually a good time. My wife and kids went to a movie, and I was sitting in the office going over some paperwork from another case. What can I do for you?"

"It's not what you can do for me, but what I have to tell. I talk to Kathleen today and have eliminated her as a suspect, but not her brother. Kenneth and Shelia from the Atlanta police reviewed the autopsy report and found that a large dosage of insulin was in Daniels' body." "Alphonso, how did we miss that?"

"I said the same thing. Turns out there was forensic lingo that neither one of us would have understood in the report."

"Alphonso, that could mean he was a diabetic."

"According to Peter, he had been diagnosed as type 1, but I was not aware if he was on insulin."

"Jason, I thought you could talk to Daniels' brother Johnny and see if he knew anything about his health and who was his doctor."

"Getting that information from him and Daniel's doctor may be complicated."

"What do you mean Jason?"

"There are Health Insurance Portability and Accountability (HIPAA) laws we have to consider. HIPAA is still in effect even after a person dies. But they now have something called HITECH-HIPAA Privacy law that can protect a person's health records for fifty years after death."

"If the deceased authorized the executor or executrix to access their health records, you could get it. In Daniels absence that would be either his wife, children or brother."

"Jason, let's start with his brother, and if we have no luck there, then we would have to make a legal HIPAA request from a judge. This could force Violet to release his records, or she may volunteer to give us that information."

"Alphonso, she did authorize his exhumation. I believe if asked she will release the health records."

"Since it is still early here in Alaska, I will give Johnny a call about this matter."

"Jason it would be good to know if Jacoby needs to make a request from Violet while I am here in Atlanta."

"I will keep that in mind."

"One more thing from the Atlanta police. The gun they found with Elliott's prints on it belongs to Daniel. They used a beta test software to find the serial number. I will let you get back to your other case."

Jason immediately dialed Johnny's number.

"Hello, Johnny this is Attorney Jason, how are you doing?"

"I am doing okay. Did not expect to hear from you this soon. How is the case coming along?"

"We think we have evidence to prove your brother did not commit suicide, but we have to validate, and we have positive

270

identification of one person involved in his death. I can't reveal that today. Our plans are, to make arrest next week. I need to know if Daniel was a diabetic and was, he on insulin?"

"Yes, he was a diabetic and was giving himself insulin shots every day. He made me promise not to tell his wife and children. He did not want them to worry."

"How long had he been on the insulin and what was his unit of dosage?" "He had been on insulin about six months before his death, but I don't know what unit of dosage he gave himself. He hated the shots more than anything."

"Johnny, you have been very helpful, and as I said we are expected to make arrest next week. Thank you for the information, and I am sorry to have bothered you on a Saturday."

"Feel free to call anytime. Goodbye Jason, look forward to hearing from you soon." Johnny ended the call and said to himself. Our mother and father taught us to face up to battles in our lives and not find an easy escape from them. I really do miss my brother.

Alphonso has an incoming call on his cell as he is getting out of the shower. He grabbed a towel from the rack in the bathroom and ran to get his phone on the bed.

"Hello, Alphonso, you were right, I had a conversation with Johnny, and he confirmed your suspicions. Daniel was a diabetic, and he was on insulin the last six months before his death. According to

Johnny, Daniel did not want his wife and children to know. He has kept that promise all these years."

"Jason, that is great news, and you know what this means?"

"We can arrest Elliott for one, maybe both of the murders because this is no longer a suicide."

"You are absolutely right Alphonso but, one thing I have not figured out and that is how do we tie Madison in with Elliott and the death of Daniel." "Jason, the only thing we can hope for is Elliott confesses."

"I am going to cut this phone call short. I need to call the airport for the first flight out of Atlanta back to Washington in the morning."

"Jason see if you can get the police to arrest Elliott on Monday." Alphonso was able to secure a seat on Delta Airlines for nine Sunday morning. He coordinated with Karen from Soco & Soco to pick him up at his hotel and drive him to the airport.

Kathleen was awakened by the ringing of her cell phone. Who could be calling me at eleven-thirty at night? Mother and I just went to bed at ten- thirty.

"Hello, who is speaking?"

"Hello, Kathleen, wake up sleepy head you don't want to talk to your one and only brother?"

"Why is it my one and only brother is calling me this late at night?" "Well, I figured mother might be asleep, and we could have a few minutes to talk."

"She is asleep, and I hope my ringing phone has not awakened her." "How are you doing sis?"

" I was doing fine until you woke me up."

"I called to see how you are feeling about the interview tomorrow with Alphonso?"

"Surprise, surprise, I had my interview today." "Why did you have an interview today?"

"Mother and I stopped for lunch at a favorite Chinese restaurant after I picked her up from the airport. While we were there, Alphonso was there as well. He recognized mother and came over to speak. And after some conversation, we decided to do the interview today."

"After two hours of questions, we were done. He asked a lot of questions about you, it made me think he was trying to accuse you of father's death."

"Kathleen you know I would not hurt dad."

"Landon, I know that. Alphonso thought since you knew about dad's affair you might have done something. For your information, I told mother about dad's relationship with Madison."

"How did she take it?"

"She was in total shock and had no clue. I felt like we have kept this secret from her long enough."

"She is worried you might go to prison and so am I. Have you told me everything? You have not been lying to me as dad did to mother."

"No, I have not been lying. I can't believe my one, the only sister does not believe me."

"What do you and mother have planned for tomorrow?"

"We have a full day of things. We are going to The Coca-Cola museum, Georgia Aquarium, and CNN Center if she is up to it."

"That sounds like a lot of fun. Take lots of pictures. You and mother are still planning on coming to Washington DC on Thursday?"

"Yes, we will be there at one p.m. I can't wait till the three of us can spend time together. I guess I've kept you up late enough Kathleen. Give mother my love, and I will talk to the two of you tomorrow."

"Goodnight, Landon." "Goodnight, Sis."

CHAPTER **24**

THE FACTS ARE IN

AT seven a.m. Violet had awakened, taken a shower and dressed. She was now in the kitchen making coffee and excited about spending the day with her daughter at tourist places she had requested. About seven-thirty Kathleen comes into the kitchen.

"Good morning mother, how are you?"

"I am doing great. I smelled the coffee from my bedroom." "I did not want to wake you."

"That would have been okay, mother. Landon called me after we went to bed last night, and we talked a long time."

"What is he up to?"

"He is looking forward to the three of us spending time together on Thursday."

"I have started breakfast if you are hungry."

"Mother, I am always hungry if I can eat a meal you have cooked."

"This reminds me of how it was when dad was living, and we were all at home. We would get up early and go on our weekend trips to Fairbanks. Those were some of the best days of my life. You and dad gave us unconditional love."

"You are going to make me cry and mess up my makeup. One day you and your brother will make me a grandmother, and you will find there is no handbook to raising children. You just do your best and hope your children turn out okay."

"I thank God each and every day with how you and Landon have been so successful."

"I am concerned about Landon but, I don't believe he would hurt his father. But he also has a good relationship with me. To find out his father was having an affair with another woman, I can only imagine how he felt."

"Mother, Landon did not do anything."

"How do you know? Were you with him the day his father was found dead?"

"No, I was not. Mother I don't want to upset you."

"I have been upset ever since that investigator rattled my son, and you told me about the affair. While we are on the affair."

"Did you say that the woman my husband was having an affair with was named Madison?"

"Yes, I did mother, why do you ask?"

"I don't know if this is a coincidence or not. Do you remember when I told you this woman had moved to Delta Junction to take care of her mother and we had become friends?"

"Her name is Madison."

"Mother, do you think this is the same person?"

"I really don't know, but will find out when I get back home."

"Mother, about going back home, Landon and I would like for you to either move to Washington or to Atlanta. You don't have to live with either of us, we can help you find your own place. Dad would not want you to live alone in Alaska."

"You are probably right. Your brother and I have already had this conversation. I guess it is something I need to do some serious thinking about. I am not getting any younger. Being near the two of you would really be great."

"Do I hear you correctly, that you are going to reconsider the move?" "Yes, Kathleen."

"Hold that thought I need to get showered and clothes on, so we can start our sightseeing. Otherwise, we will be here talking all day."

"Okay, I will clean up the kitchen while you are getting ready."

Alphonso arose at six a.m. and took a shower. Karen was going to be at the hotel at seven a.m. I will grab some breakfast at the airport. The first thing I need to do when I get back to Washington is meet Darnell at Soco & Soco to discuss our next steps in this case.

Alphonso headed for the lobby, and when he got off the elevator, Karen was at the front desk waiting.

"Good morning Karen, you are early."

"Yes, I am an early riser. It is more habit than anything else."

"Thank you so much for being here this morning. I can't thank you and Jacoby enough. I am sorry we did not get a chance to have dinner, but I have been working non-stop since I arrived here in Atlanta on Friday."

"I have all my things, so we can head to the car. Why don't you just drive us to the airport, and when we get there you can just drop me off, and you can be on your way?"

"Did you already have breakfast?"

"No, I thought once I got checked in at the airport, I would grab something light."

"It is so early in the morning, it may not be as crowded as it would normally be on a weekday."

"You will have enough time to relax and have some breakfast." "When I talked to Jacoby last night, I gave him an update on the case."

"Alphonso, he called me last night when he finished talking to you. Sounds like you have almost concluded this case."

"I need to talk to Daniel's son Landon again, and possibly one other person. We have established from the autopsy report and the gun that was found, that there were two people involved in Daniels's death."

"Jason is coordinating Elliott's arrest for tomorrow. I need Darnell to handle his extradition to Washington. I thought we would be able to arrest Madison, but I have not proved her connection yet."

"I believe she had something to do with her brother's death to save her company from the potential loss of a contract."

"Do you think it is possible that Elliott might have killed her brother and Daniel?"

"I don't know unless she and Elliott had a romantic relationship that we don't know about."

"I thought you said she was having an affair with Daniel. She was, but she could have been using Elliott. The two of them were living in Atlanta at the same time for at least two years. There is something I am missing about those two."

"I know you will figure it out."

"I surely do hope so. We arrived at the airport in record time. Hopefully, check-in will be the same."

"So here we are at the Delta departure area. Thank you again, Karen." "You are welcome, have a good trip and keep in contact."

Alphonso got through security within five minutes, must be some record. I love this airport. It has an art theme for every concourse that makes you feel like you are walking through a museum. My final stop is concourse B for boarding where they have several choices for breakfast. I think I will try Freshens.

They have breakfast crepes, something you don't see in restaurants in Alaska. I'm going to pick up a Denver crepe and coffee. I will find a seat at my gate and enjoy my crepe. As he was about to sit down and relax his cell phone rang.

"Hello, Shelia."

"Good morning, Alphonso, we have some more good news for you. I am going to put you on the speaker phone and let Kenneth talk."

"Kenneth what can I do to get you, your family and Shelia to move to Alaska. I love working with the two of you?"

"Alphonso, I believe we both are happy working in Atlanta, besides it is too cold there. Enough of moving talk."

"I relooked the gun report and used a beta test on the gun that is available only to our police department. We were one of the first precincts that were selected to do the testing. What I found was an embedded serial number which had been erased inside the gun, and this test can reconstruct that serial number. When I did this test, I found that this gun definitely belonged to Daniel."

"This is the additional evidence I needed, and Atlanta police department has come through again."

"Shelia, Kenneth, you guys don't know how grateful I am at the hard work you have put into helping to solve this case. I will be forever grateful."

"You are welcome. Come back and visit us sometime. The Captain does give us time off for good behavior," said Shelia.

"I will keep that in mind."

"Alphonso, we will talk to you later. Have a good flight."

While finishing up his breakfast at gate B7, Alphonso was thinking, I have been in contact with four single beautiful women on this trip. I have not had a chance to reach out to any of them for a date or a phone call, not even a text message.

First, it was Jocelyn the airline ticket agent at Alaska airport that I see each time I'm flying out of Alaska. She is always throwing me hints. Second, it was Violet on the airplane that I met for the first time flying from Alaska to Washington, and I did get her phone number. This could be a conflict while I am working on this case. Third, in Atlanta Karen a lovely and intelligent lawyer at Soco & Soco, and Fourth, there was Detective Shelia in Atlanta. A very aggressive, smart, and respectful lady.

I have seen all four of these women, and all I can do is work on this case, that is sad. I have got to do some me time when I get off this case. I am missing out on my future wife and children. Alphonso thoughts were interrupted by the call for first class passengers to board. I thank Soco & Soco, for sparing no expense for me on this trip, especially the first-class airplane seating, and the hotels they have put me in have been nice as well. There is nothing I would change about the owners. I do think the way they treat their employees and people in general stem from how their parents raise them to be loving and kind.

My first-class seat was the same seating I had when I met Violet. Through all this investigating and interviewing her son and daughter, she probably does not have a reasonable criticism of me.

I am just going to take a nap to distress on this flight to Washington. By the time we land, I will be ready to hit the ground running. Alphonso was awakened from his sleep by the stewardess saying everyone needed to prepare for landing.

I just went to sleep; how could we have flown that quick from Atlanta. Deplaning of the passengers happen quickly. It appears that everything is in some sort of fast motion for me today. I like it that the pilots come out of the cockpit and greet everyone because we put a lot of trust in them to get us safely to our final destinations.

The DoubleTree van transports to and from the airport, so I don't have to think about how to get there.

I talk to Jennifer the hotel manager earlier, and she said my same room is ready. Darnell, text me while I was asleep on the plane. He wants to have lunch today at his home to discuss the case, and I must get there on my own.

By the time I get my luggage in the baggage claim area, catch the shuttle, and get checked into the hotel, it will be time to join Darnell.

When I reached my room, there was a welcome package on the bed.

My luggage was also sitting by the bed. This is excellent customer service. I wonder if they do this to all their guests.

Alphonso unpacked his luggage because he did not know how many more days, he would be in the Washington DC area. It was now twelve-thirty p.m., and this luncheon with Darnell was at one-thirty.

He quickly went to the bathroom to brush his teeth and freshen up. The hotel had left a robe for him, in addition to the welcome package. As he was leaving the bathroom, he said wow! I must be a distinguished guest. He picked up his laptop and car keys then headed for the elevator to the first floor. Once on the first floor, he picked up a cup where they had infusion water and filled it up. I am going to have to learn how to make this.

I don't like just plain water, and I would drink more if it were like this. Alphonso was now in the rental car and headed to Darnell's. In about fifteen minutes into his trip, Darnell called.

"Hello, Darnell."

"Alphonso. Are you already on your way?" "Yes, I am about fifteen minutes away."

"Just calling to let you know lunch is going to be a little late. Since you are already on your way, it will give us a little time to talk about the case. See you when you get here."

Darnell must have heard the car pull up. He was standing with the door open when I pulled into the winding driveway. As soon as I exit the vehicle. Darnell called out, "Come on in, good to see you again."

284

"You know my wife must have everything perfect, so that is why our lunch is late. Shanta, our daughter, is helping her. I told her we do not have guest today, it is just family, because you are like one of the family members."

"I told her we could have hotdogs and you would be satisfied."

"The hotdogs would be okay, but you know everyone to include me and you love her cooking."

"You are right about that she is a great cook."

"I would like to greet her and Shanta before we get started. It has been a minute since I saw your daughter."

"Let's just walk to the kitchen where they are." Darnell and his wife have this huge house, so the kitchen is on the opposite side of the house from Darnell's office. As they entered the kitchen, "do you ladies know this old guy?"

Shanta ran to hug Alphonso.

"Hello uncle Alphonso, you are getting old, but I am happy to see you. Did you bring me anything from Alaska?" Asked Shanta.

"No, I am afraid I only brought me this time. Your dad and his brothers have me working so hard, I forgot to bring my favorite niece a gift, I won't forget the next time."

"You better not."

Juanita, Darnell's wife, walked over and hugged Alphonso.

"Hello Alphonso, it is good to see you again, and don't pay any attention to our daughter. She thinks that everyone that comes to this house must bring her a gift."

"Juanita it is good to see you also. You and Darnell did well. You have a beautiful daughter."

"I am smart too," shouted Shanta.

"I bet you are." Alphonso complemented Shanta.

"Honey, how much longer before lunch will be ready?" "About forty minutes maybe longer."

"Well take your time, Alphonso and I are going to go to my office and talk some legal stuff."

"Shanta and I will get it ready as quickly as possible." Darnell and Alphonso walked to his office.

"Alphonso have a seat. I know you have a lot of information because you have been keeping all my brothers up to date to include me about this case. What is your next step?"

"We know that Elliott is guilty of shooting Daniel, and he intended to kill him. He might have been dead when Elliott shot him, so I don't think we will have a legal battle with him."

"The Atlanta police have the gun that was used in the shooting with Elliott fingerprints on it."

You are absolutely right. There is a legal term called "implied by one's action," which is the same as intent. In this case, Elliott not only had intent, but he carried it out. This is first-degree murder which carries a death penalty," explained Darnell.

"Detective Shelia from Atlanta called me just as I was about to head for the airport. Their forensics guy Kenneth found that the gun did belong to Daniel. The second part of this murder is that Daniel was dead before the shooting or he was in a diabetic coma."

"Daniel was a diabetic, taking insulin according to his brother Johnny." "Alphonso, how would Elliott have known that Daniel was a diabetic?"

"I don't think he did, but I believe that Madison knew. Daniel had an overdose of insulin in his system. It was administered either by Madison, Elliott, or his son."

"Why would you think Landon had something to do with his death?"

"Landon knew about the affair with Madison. He confronted his dad on several occasions and did not want his mother to be hurt."

"Daniel's brother Johnny stated to Jason that Landon nor his sister Kathleen or wife knew about his diabetes."

"Alphonso, suppose that Landon did know. Where would he have gotten the insulin from?"

"I don't know. Landon sister maybe, she is a dentist so she would not have had insulin in her office except maybe in an emergency for one of her patients."

"Darnell, Landon did visit his father on the day of his death. There were thirty minutes he could not account for. I want to question Landon again sooner than later."

"Can you arrange for me to question him again tomorrow morning around ten at the office?"

"Tomorrow is his normal day at the office."

"I just don't believe Landon had anything to do with his father's death. They had such a close relationship. Landon would not do anything that will cause him to lose his law license. He truly loves being a lawyer and is one of the best we have in the firm in this area. We were planning on making him a partner sometime the end of this year. Landon has not been told yet so come up with another theory."

"If Landon is guilty, I will be the first to support you. What else do we know about this case?"

"Elliott planted the gun in the backyard of a house Madison sold to the current owners the Leeson's. My question is why Elliott planted the gun in her backyard unless he and Madison were having a relationship?" Or she may not have known about the gun."

"That's the same conclusion that Karen came to except Madison was having an affair with Daniel. Elliott could have thought if Daniel were out of the picture, he would have Madison to himself."

"Darnell that still does not explain the insulin."

"Maybe Landon will reveal something in our interview tomorrow." "Did you question Daniels' wife."

"No, if I were going to interview anyone else it would be her. She was in Alaska at the time of his death, as a matter of fact in earlier testimony she had not been out of the state in over a year. We can exclude interviewing her."

"Are we sure she was not aware of the affair?"

"I am confident she had no knowledge."

"I did find out that Madison and Violet have been friends since she moved to Delta Junction."

"What about the death of Madison brother?"

"I believe that Elliott was involved in that as well. I did find out that Elliott arrested Scott for DUI in Washington DC before he met Madison."

"Could Elliott have been holding that DUI conviction over Scott because he revealed the information about Madison company AllTuck?"

"The Atlanta police told me that Elliott was a dirty cop, and their Captain Ray could not wait until he retired. Elliott also knew Sergeant Major Rick who was Scott's boss."

"Alphonso, it looks like Elliott had a relationship with all the players, Madison, Scott, Daniel, and Sergeant Major Rick."

"When he is arrested on Monday, all this will have to be brought up in the interrogation."

"If we find evidence of Scott's death from Elliott, Soco & Soco, will have to put together a report and submit it to the military commander here in Washington DC."

"I will start to work on that today."

"Alphonso, man you have uncovered a lot of evidence in a short period. The good thing is that this case was reopened in Alaska, so Elliott will not have to be extradited to Washington DC."

"If he confesses, there won't be a trial. Daniel was well liked by a lot of people in this area and in his hometown Delta Junction. Have you ever thought about moving to Washington?"

"No, but I would if I found that special lady here."

"You would have to stay here longer than a week to find her. I could help you out."

"That's what all you Soco brothers say, but no one has come through yet." "Well, all of us have wives."

"You have a point there." They both laughed out loud. The door to the office open. "What's so funny?" Asked Juanita.

"I am trying to get our brother by another mother married."

"He is listening to the wrong one. Alphonso needs to hang out with me for a few months, and he would be married in no time. Okay, guys time out for business. I hope the both of you are hungry. Lunch is ready. Wash up and come into the kitchen we are going to eat there."

"Okay honey, we will be there in a minute, you made us wait long enough."

After Darnell and Alphonso wash their hands, they walked to the kitchen.

"What have you fixed for Alphonso. You never fix fancy food for me. The only time I get anything besides a bologna sandwich is when I invite guest over."

"Darnell you need to stop it," said Juanita. Everyone was just laughing out loud at Darnell.

"We are having baked sea bass, grilled asparagus, new potatoes, homemade rolls from the deli, spinach salad, beverage of your choice and pound cake. How does that sound?"

"Sounds good to me," stated Alphonso. "Sounds pretty good to me to," said Shanta.

Everyone laughed. "Mom I am starving. We ate breakfast to early." "Did you not get a snack in between?"

"Yes, I did. You forget I am a growing girl, so I need a lot more."

Juanita table setting was just like eating in a fancy restaurant. "As soon as everyone sits down at the table we can eat. Alphonso, have you been able to do any sightseeing while here in DC or while you were in Atlanta?" Juanita inquired.

"Does that involve fun. No, I have not. Your husband and his brothers have had me working twenty-four seven since I left Alaska."

"When you are the best, you want the best working on your cases. You are Soco's best investigator. I wish we could clone you at each of our branches," said Darnell.

"You guys treat me like family, so you want to do your best for your family. That's how I feel about Soco & Soco. I have been with the firm for a long time, and I hope to retire with the firm as well."

"We hope to have you around for a long time." "Me too," said Shanta.

"Thank you, guys, and especially my favorite niece, Shanta. It is always a pleasure to be in the company of your family. You always make me feel like I am one of you. Hopefully one of these days I will have my own family and invite you guys to dinner."

"Alphonso is there something you have not told us that we need to know?" Said Juanita.

"Not yet, but when it does happen, you will know."

They finished their meal, had dessert, some more conversation and then Alphonso drove back to the hotel for a little relaxation.

CHAPTER 25

PREPARING FOR THE WORST

MADISON was sitting talking to her mother and father when her cell phone rang. She realized the number was Elliott. Mom and dad, can you excuse me I need to take this call. She walked out of the living room and walked outside.

"Hello, Elliott, how are you doing?"

"Not doing too well. I think I am in trouble. Why do you think that?" "When I went in for my interview on Friday at the police station in Fairbanks, they asked me questions that I thought only you and I would know. I could not lie. All the questions they asked were straightforward. They might have others later."

"Did you try to make contact with the police in Atlanta?"

"No, I did not, because that would make me look even more guilty calling to inquire about this case."

"Do you think this Alphonso investigator knows what we did?" Asked Madison.

"You mean what I did?"

"If they know your involvement, then they know how I was involved as well."

"They did not indicate that in the interview. My lawyer was present," said Elliott.

"I have no contacts anymore, so there is no one I can call to find the latest in this case. We must wait and see. In the meantime, I suggest you make plans for the worst," said Elliott.

"What kind of arrangements do you think I need to make?" "Look at your finance, care for your mother."

" My father is the only one who could care for my mother. They only have me."

"At this point, I am glad that it is just me and that no one will have to worry about what will happen to me," said Elliott.

"Madison there is something I have wanted to tell you for a very long time and I think now would be the best time to do that. I know that you were in love with Daniel, and still miss him. But there is a special place in my heart for you and I have been in love with you for some time now. When you suggested that I move to Alaska, I thought you felt the same about me. I was hoping we could take our relationship to another level?"

"You just told me to prepare for the worst in this investigation, and now you are saying you hope we can take our relationship to another level. I don't understand how you can say all that in the same conversation. I am not in love with you. However, I do like you as a friend, as a matter of fact, I consider you my only male best friend. That is why I suggested you move to Alaska."

"Madison, you appear to be upset, that was not my intention. I guess I was hoping for too much."

"Right now, Elliott I want to end this conversation about a relationship between you and I but, we need to be talking about what we are going to do and say if we are approached about this case again. Law enforcement officers have interviewed both of us. What do we need to tell our lawyers?"

"We cannot allow them to think we have a romantic relationship, because that is a motive. Law enforcement and lawyers would think the same thing."

"What do we tell them about how we met and the circumstances, and how we became friends. It does not look good that a police officer is good friends with a woman who worked for a company such as AllTuck. A company under investigation for software development fraud whether it was intentional or not," said Elliott.

"This investigator Alphonso from Soco & Soco could connect my brother and me to Sergeant Major Rick. He was the military point of contact for the company I work for."

"Our alibi's have to line up with this case. We could lose everything we have both worked for all our lives," said Elliott.

"How did I allow myself to get caught up in this mess with Matthew, my boss, and he has not even called me."

"I am going to call him when we get off the phone."

"When you talk to him, and if you find out anything new, please give me a call. Madison, do you know if Matthew got a copy of the report that Daniel had compiled for his company?"

"No, I don't, but that will be one of my questions to ask him. Well, I need to make that phone call to Matthew and get back to my parents."

"They may think I have abandoned them and thank you for calling." As soon as their call ended Madison dialed Matthew's number.

Joseph, Matthews's Executive assistant, had just completed budget briefing presentation for Matthew's briefing on tomorrow and his desk phone rang.

"This is Mr. Matthew's office; how can I help you?" "Hello, Joseph this is Madison."

"Madison it has been a long time since we talked. We all miss you around here. How is your mother?"

"She is doing much better. I missed each of you as well and thank you for asking about my mother. Is the boss in?"

"Yes, he is, hold on, will let him know you are on the line. Mr. Matthew, Madison is on the line."

"Okay, Joseph I will pick up. Madison, hello, I was thinking about you yesterday and was going to give you a call this week. How is your mother?"

"She is much better, considering she has had two strokes."

"Well, I am glad to hear that she is doing better. What can I do for you on this wonderful day?"

"First I was surprised that you and Joseph were in the office on a Sunday."

"Yes, we are finalizing a budget briefing I have to give tomorrow. We've only been here a couple of hours, as a matter of fact, we were discussing going home in the next thirty minutes."

"Matthew, what have you heard about the reopening of the case for Daniel?"

"There was an investigator by the name of Alphonso that came and talked to me last week."

"Why is this case being reopened?"

"It has been reopened, because of some new evidence that he did not share with me," said Matthew.

"Why was he here to talk to you?"

"He asked me questions about the software we developed for the military exchange stores, your brother and you. He thought it was a coincidence that your brother died right after he reported the problem to Major Rick."

"Well, I found that to be strange also."

"Madison did you have any involvement in your brother's death?" "Are you accusing me of killing my brother."

"Well you told me you, and he did not have a close relationship. I know that you have been a loyal employee of this company for over ten years and you have been loyal to me as well. So yes I wonder what extent you would go to, to protect this company?"

"Well, I could say the same thing about you, because if Daniel's report were to become public, you would lose your job."

"How dare you say I had something to do with Daniel's or Scott's death," said Matthew angrily.

"Well, we both have lied about this software, so we both could be viewed as suspects. So, neither of us should be throwing the blame gun around," said Madison.

"By the way, Madison, when you left, we allowed you to take one year of leave to take care of your mother. After that year is up, you signed papers also for early retirement. We have mailed those retirement papers to you effective the first of next month. If you have changed your mind, then you need to let me know today. So, we can cancel those documents that have been sent."

"I do have one question if something were to happen to me who would get my retirement?"

"You had designated your mother, and if something happens to her, it will go to your father."

"No, I don't want to change it, leave it as it is, and send me all that paperwork as soon as possible."

"Okay, so if you don't have any more questions, I need to finish up my presentation for tomorrow. You have a good evening."

"You too Matthew."

CHAPTER **26**

ARRESTS ARE IMMINENT

ALPHONSO awoke at 7 a.m. and turned on the TV. He had not been able to relax like this since he arrived in Washington. I have a meeting today with Landon at ten a.m. and a conference call with Soco brothers at one thirty both at Soco & Soco. Then tomorrow a meeting with Connie at her home, at ten a.m.

After about an hour of watching TV, he showered, got dressed and went downstairs for breakfast in the restaurant.

"Good morning Mr. Alphonso would you like coffee, juice or water?"

"Good morning, Gina, I would like coffee with crème and sugar, a glass of water, two eggs over easy, wheat toast and chicken sausage."

Within seven minutes she brought his coffee and meal. "Gina that was fast. I must be the only one eating breakfast this morning."

"No Sir, we have a chef that is really fast. We know our customers are busy or have a schedule when they come to our restaurant. Is there anything else I can get for you?"

"No that will be all. Everything was cooked exactly the way I liked it. I ate every bite off my plate and would have had seconds if there was more."

As soon as he finished, Gina came over and asked, "how was the food?"

"Everything was good as usual." He paid for his meal and gave her a tip. As he was walking away from his table, he passed Paul the DoubleTree security manager being seated. "Hello, Paul."

"Hello to you Alphonso. Did not know you were still here." "The management treat me so well, I decided to stay awhile."

"We try to please all our guest. I am glad you are enjoying your stay." "I am off to a meeting. It was good to see you again Paul."

"Same here Alphonso."

As Alphonso opens the door to his room he was thinking, I believe Paul knew more about those security cameras than he told me in the interview. I believe Paul and Elliott were friends something he failed to mention in his interview. Elliott had to have been informed by someone at the hotel to know a software upgrade was taking place for the security cameras the same day Daniel died. I will have to make sure Elliott is asked those questions by police when he is arrested in Alaska this week.

My investigation is about to end, and I have not met that special lady. You know Jocelyn the Delta ticket agent at the Fairbanks airport could be the one. I may have to give her a call when I get back.

Now I need to get my keys, laptop, and briefcase and get in this Washington traffic and drive to my interview with Landon. I am just going to jump on I-95 from the hotel. Surprisingly, fifteen minutes into his travel, there is not a lot of traffic this morning, even though it is a regular workday.

Once Alphonso arrived at the law firm he was greeted by Bethany, the executive assistant. "Good morning Alphonso, I am going to take you directly to the conference room where Darnell will join you in a few minutes."

"Thank you, and good to see you again Bethany."

"As you can see there is coffee and donuts if you have not had breakfast help yourself."

"I did have breakfast, but I may indulge in at least one."

"Help yourself. The more you eat, the less we have left."

Alphonso got his laptop signed on and did indulge with a donut. Halfway through eating, Darnell came into the conference room.

"Good morning Alphonso, just getting out of the firms morning meeting. I try to have one at least three times a week, to keep track of what everyone is doing."

"Darnell I am actually feeling good and relaxed this morning." "Glad you got some rest because as I told you last night, you have been kicking it. Landon will be here in a few minutes. He is sending out an email to a customer I needed him to communicate with. Alphonso, I still think you are wrong about Landon."

"I hope so. After speaking with Kathleen, his sister, it does not appear that he would do anything to his father."

"I have to clarify some things, and he has to give me honest, correct answers."

"Alphonso, I know that you are the best investigator this firm has and every case you investigate, justice is always done. I know it will be the same for this case."

"Thanks for your confidence Darnell it means a lot to me."

"Landon is here, I will leave you two. I will continue to do what this firm pays me to do, and that is work." Darnell closed the door behind him.

"Good morning Landon how are you today?" "I am doing okay. How about yourself?"

"I am doing good as well."

"Our interview today will not be as long as our first one. But some more evidence has come to my attention. I need you to clarify some of this evidence and identify some relationships you may or may not have had. Can we begin?" Asked Alphonso. "Yes, I am ready."

"When did you find out about your father's affair?" "About six months before his death."

"How did you find out about the affair?"

"I saw the two of them holding hands and kissing when they were walking into a restaurant. There were three other occasions I saw them together."

"How did that make you feel?"

"Initially I was angry and thinking about what this would do to my mother if she knew this was going on?"

"Why did you go to see him on the day he died?"

"I went to confront him about the affair and asked him not to do this to my mother."

"What was his reaction?"

"He knew I was upset and tried to explain to me he did not go looking for someone it just happened."

"It was evident he was not going to listen. I left his room and went back home. The next day I was notified he was found dead."

"Were you aware that he was a diabetic?"

"No, I was not aware."

"I guess I have to assume you did not see him give himself a shot of insulin or ask for something sweet because he was feeling weak."

"You would be right about both those issues."

"Was Connie your friend aware that your father was having an affair?"

"If she knows I did not relay that information to her." "Who else did you tell about the affair?"

"I told my sister."

"When we talked last week, you told me you did not tell anyone. Why did you lie about that?"

"It was not intentional. You made me nervous, and I couldn't remember if I answered any questions incorrectly. No matter how many more questions you ask me or what doubt you have, I did not kill my father. I wish you would go find out who really did," said Landon angrily.

"Why did you not tell me you had a gun stolen?"

"It was never found. I have been afraid that someone was going to hurt another individual with that gun and it was going to reflect back to me."

"Did you report that it was stolen?" "Yes, I did report it."

"By you reporting it stolen would that not cover you if it came up in some type crime? Your lying to me is the reason I had suspected you were involved in the death of your father. But I wanted to give you the opportunity to come clean about everything. I know you are a good lawyer and well respected by the Soco brothers."

"I did not want anything affecting my chances of becoming a partner in this firm because I have worked hard to get to that status."

"I have two more questions. Does Connie own a gun?" "She has not mentioned it to me, so I don't know."

"Did you tell her what time you were going to visit your father the day he was found dead?"

"Yes, I did tell Connie."

"Thank you for answering all my questions. I hope I did not interrupt your day too much."

"It is okay. Please put an end to this case so my family and I can get on with our lives."

"I will do my best. Will you let Darnell know we have finished, and I am going to remain in the conference room?"

Darnell walked into the conference room. "How did it go?"

"It went okay. Landon was a little upset with me. He emphasized that his family needs to get on with their lives. I understand how he feels. The only thing Landon is guilty of is loving his family and wants me to get this case solved."

"Alphonso, I know it is just twelve o'clock, and the conference call was supposed to be at one-thirty. Do you want to try to get my brothers in Alaska and Atlanta on the line now? Because of the time difference not sure if Jason and Jermaine are even in the office yet. It is eight a.m. there. I will call them first."

Darnell dialed Jason number. "Hello Jason, are you and Jermaine in the office?"

"Yes, we both were in a seven-a.m. meeting this morning."

"I love how hard my brothers are working for this company. Can you take the call now instead of later?"

"Actually, now would be better than later. We have a busy day today." "Hold on, I will call Jacoby and Karen in Atlanta."

Darnell dialed Jacoby's number. "Hello Jacoby, how are you doing this morning."

"I am doing okay."

"Can you and Karen get on the conference call now, instead of later or do we need to stick with the coordinated time?"

"No, as a matter of fact, Karen was sitting here in my office. We just finished another conference call. Now would be perfect."

"Can you call the conference number in five minutes?" "Yes, we can do that."

"I am going to hang up, talk to you in a few minutes. Jason are you still on the line?"

"Yes, we are."

"Can you call the conference number in five minutes?" "Yes, we will."

"Talk to you in five. Okay, Alphonso in five we will get this show on the road. I am going to take a bathroom break, I suggest you do the same. You know these brothers of mine can get long-winded?" Darnell and Alphonso arrived back at the conference room at the same time after a bathroom break.

"I let Bethany know we are not to be disturbed."

As soon as he finished his comment, Jason and Jermaine called into the conference call from Alaska, and right after Jacoby and Karen called. "Everyone is here. Good morning to Alaska and good afternoon to Atlanta," said Darnell.

"Thank all of you for adjusting your schedules and agreeing to help get this case solved. I want to applaud Alphonso for his diligence, dedication, patience, and the evidence he has gathered in bringing this case to almost a closure. I am thankful that this law firm has him as an investigator on our team." I ask him to give us some directions as to the next steps for this case."

"Thanks to Darnell and the entire firm for trusting me to find the evidence for our client Johnny. I have tried to keep each of you updated on every stone unturned in this case. I am surprised at all the evidence the local police and district attorney's missed or did not check to solve this case."

"However, so many people in the law enforcement community have really been helpful in Washington DC, Atlanta, and Alaska. These people made it possible for me to have access to information that maybe I would not usually have access to."

"I have eliminated Daniel's son Landon as a person of interest or suspect. A lot of things I thought he would have known he did not know or have knowledge of. But he had an excellent relationship with his father. All Landon wants now is for us to get this case solved so he and his family can get on with their lives."

"Thank you for that great news about Landon because he is one of the best lawyers in our firm here in the DC area. I would hate to lose him," noted Darnell.

"To continue I do know that Elliott who lives in Fairbanks is guilty of shooting Daniel, with Daniels own gun. This would be the second death. We call it the second death because according to the autopsy report Daniel was in a possible coma-like state or dead before Elliott entered his room and shot him." The coma-like state was the result of an administered overdose of insulin. This was the first death. I have not proved the early death yet. Madison the person Daniel was having an affair with may have given him that dosage in the wine in his room. We are hoping to get that information from Elliott.

"The autopsy report reveals that Elliott did not get any response from Daniel upon entering the room. He did not go all the way into the room initially. Elliott turned his back and shot Daniel in the forehead by pointing the gun over his own head. The first shot missed. It went into the wall beside the bed. Daniel did not move in the bed from the sound of the first shot, so Elliott walked in the room and found the victim's gun and turned his back and shot Daniel in the head with his own gun."

"I believe that Madison made Elliott aware that Daniel was authorized to travel with a gun from his company and he was bonded. Elliott left the room in a hurry and left the door slightly ajar."

311

"I believe Paul the DoubleTree security manager was Elliott's friend. In conversation and not intentional I think Paul told Elliott about the software upgrade of the security cameras."

"Therefore no one was caught on camera going in and out of Daniel's room."

"If we get Elliott's phone records for the last two weeks, I believe we will find a phone call from Paul. I don't think Paul was in on this murder."

"The firearm that was recovered by the Atlanta police department had Elliott's fingerprints on it, but somehow he had erased the serial number inside it. The Atlanta forensic folks used a beta software they had been selected to use for testing, allowed them to reconstruct the serial number, and it revealed the owner of the gun to be Daniel. The bullet that was removed from Daniel's head was from this same gun."

"Atlanta police found the victim's gun buried in the backyard of the home Madison sold to the current owners, who have been cleared of any involvement, and I don't think Madison knew the gun was buried there."

"Darnell, we need to get a warrant to look at Paul's cellphone." Based on all this evidence, it tells us that Daniel did not commit suicide. The first arrest we can make is Elliott, and that will be for Jason and Jermaine to handle."

"We can book him on first-degree murder," said Jermaine.

"My question is do we have to extradite Elliott to Washington DC?" Asked Alphonso.

"No, we do not have to, because this case was reopened in Alaska court. If he confesses, there will not be a trial, but there will be sentencing by a judge. We will get on that warrant with the police department as soon as we get off the phone," said Jason.

"We will need Jacoby and Karen to get the Atlanta police department to ship the gun to Fairbanks police department. They may not allow you to ship the gun unless there is a trial."

"We may only be able to get a picture of the gun, which should be satisfactory," noted Jacoby.

"Since we don't have all the information on the first murder, let's keep this out of the news media because we don't want anyone fleeing to another country," said Darnell.

"That's a good point," said Alphonso. "What's next Alphonso?" Said Karen.

"I have an interview tomorrow with Connie who is Landon's girlfriend. I believe she and Madison are key persons of interest for the first murder."

"However, I think Elliott, Madison, and Sergeant Major Rick were involved in Scott's death. An investigation of Scott's death would be out of our jurisdiction," said Darnell.

"I believe that Sergeant Major Rick was able to get Scott's gun to Elliott and he triggered it to fire when Scott was cleaning it accidentally."

"I have already drafted a letter for the military commander. I just need to plug in what Alphonso just revealed so they can make an arrest. As an attachment to the letter, we will need to get permission from Q'UP to give the commander a copy of Daniels report. This may get Sergeant Major Rick indicted and possibly Matthew of AllTuck. I do believe Major Rick was getting kickbacks based on the evidence Alphonso has presented," said Darnell.

"Alphonso, we will all standby to see what happens with your interview tomorrow, and the arrest of Elliott and possibly Madison. Again, I congratulate Alphonso on the investigative work he has done on this case. We have all did what our client Johnny asked us, and I say let's wrap up the rest of this case. If nothing else, we all must get back to work, make some more money for Soco, and please have a nice rest of the day," Darnell said laughing.

"Alphonso, man all this hard work has made me hungry let's grab some lunch."

"That's a winner for me."

"There is a deli about two blocks from the office that is good. Let's go there," suggested Darnell. I will get my keys, and we can head out." Darnell returned with his keys." I told Bethany we would be out the rest of the afternoon."

"Alphonso, I am so full of evidence, I think I might explode when I take my first bite of food. But it is good evidence."

"After we finish lunch, we need to make a stop at the Washington police precinct that investigated this case to request a warrant for the cell phone of Paul at the DoubleTree. We need to find out if he called Elliott in the last couple of weeks."

"Darnell, right now I just want to relax for about an hour or two."

The two of them walked to the car, got in and drove to the deli for lunch. After lunch, Darnell and Alphonso drove to the Washington Precinct.

Alphonso had been communicating with Captain Royster since he arrived in the city. Darnell parked the car, and they went inside and asked for the Captain. The officer at the dispatcher desk placed a phone call to the Captain, and he came right down to take them to his office.

"Good afternoon, Alphonso."

"Hello, Captain how are you doing? This is Attorney Darnell, my boss from Soco & Soco law firm."

"Good to meet you, Darnell. Have a seat, I will close the door, and we can have privacy. What can I do for you?"

"We will be arresting one of the people involved in Daniels murder on tomorrow in Alaska. We need a personal property warrant in the form of a cell phone from Paul, the security manager at the DoubleTree," requested Darnell.

"I remember Paul, he was questioned, about the cameras three years ago, and he was cleared."

"Captain, we don't think he had any involvement in the case, but we do believe he was Elliott's friend who used to be a police officer in this department."

"Yes, I know Elliott very well."

"We have proof that he murdered the deceased, and we are not yet ready for this to be in the news media, because we have a second suspect in this case, that we cannot reveal yet. We need this warrant to go out tomorrow," expressed Darnell.

"I don't know if I can get a judge to sign a warrant today, but maybe first thing in the morning. That would be fine."

"I am glad you are getting him off the street he was a bad cop here in the Washington and Atlanta departments. Some would say he is getting what's coming to him," said Royster smiling.

"When you get the phone and find the information, would you give me call?" Said Darnell.

"I will do that," said Royster.

"What happened to the captain that worked this case three years ago?"

"We don't really know, but he retired right after the case was solved. He left Washington, and no one has heard from him since then. I worked on parts of the case under him, and I was selected as the Captain after he left."

"That is all we needed for right now. Thank you," said Darnell. "Let us know if we can be of further assistance. Darnell and Alphonso, it looks like we missed a lot on this case."

"I will walk you guys out and look forward to talking with you on tomorrow." The captain walked them back to the dispatcher desk where they exited the building and went back to the car.

"Darnell, Elliott was someone that nobody liked."

"That may be why it was easy for him to shoot Daniel. If everything goes well Alphonso, he will be off the streets and behind bars tomorrow."

"You are absolutely right Darnell."

"I am going to drop you off at your car at the office, pick up my briefcase and go home and relax with my family."

"And I am going to the hotel and look over my notes for my interview with Connie tomorrow. I will come by the office after my interview," Darnell was now pulling up next to Alphonso car."

"Thank you for everything, and I will see you tomorrow."

CHAPTER 27

WRAPPING UP

JASON and Jermaine left the law office with evidence documentation for the police at the thirty-ninth precinct in Fairbanks. This documentation will be the justification for the detectives to get the judge to sign a warrant to arrest Elliott. They entered the police department where they asked to speak with Detective Jones. He was familiar with the case and was one of the officers who brought Elliott in for initial questioning.

Jones walked to the visitor's reception area to meet the two attorneys. "Hello, Detective Jones, you remember me, this is my brother Attorney Jermaine. We would like to talk to you about an arrest. Can we speak privately?"

"Good to see you again Jason and nice to meet you, Jermaine. If you just follow me, we will go to Captain Monty's office."

As they approached the captain's office, his door was closed. Jones knocked on the door, and the Captain asked them to come in. "Good afternoon gentleman. Captain Monty this is Attorneys Jason and Jermaine from Soco & Soco law firm."

"What can I do for you?"

"Sir we need your department to move forward with an arrest warrant for Mr. Elliott for the murder of Mr. Daniel. We have all the documentation that you can review before taking this action. There will be more arrest, so we don't want this arrest in the media if possible," said Jason.

"You will also need a search warrant for his condo in Fairbanks to take possession of his cell phone and for a report that references the investigation into a company called AllTuck. This report was put together by the victim for a company named Q'UP."

"As for as his cell phone, we need to know if he received any calls in the last two weeks from the security manager at the DoubleTree hotel in DC. by the name of Paul."

"This is where we are with this case, and we need your assistance." "Jones had already started to develop the document to get the warrant signed by the judge. He will just have to do additional paperwork for a search warrant for items you requested. We will make this arrest tomorrow," stated Captain Monty.

"Our firm thanks your department for everything," said Jermaine. "This is what we do, bring criminals in for justice."

"We will get out of your way, so you can do what you do each and every day to protect and serve the people of Fairbanks."

"Jones will walk you out."

"You guys have really been working hard on this case. Looks like the police did not do a good job of investigating this case three years ago," said Jones.

"We agree, and hope that we've covered everything in bringing this case to an end," said Jermaine.

"We are at the reception area, so will be in contact," said Jones. Jason and Jermaine walked to the visitors parking area for their car and back to the office.

Jacoby and Karen left the law office to go to the Atlanta downtown main precinct of the police department. Upon arrival, they asked for detective Shelia. She was the detective that Alphonso had been in contact with for this case.

Detective Shelia came to the reception desk where they were waiting for her.

"Hello, I am Detective Shelia."

"We are Attorneys Jacoby and Karen from Soco & Soco," said Jacoby. "You talked with our investigator Alphonso last week from our Soco office in Alaska."

"Yes, I did, he is very good at what he does. How can I help you?" "Can we talk somewhere in private?"

"Of course, we can go to my office. If you would just follow me." As they reached Shelia's office, she asked them to have a seat.

"You were about to tell me how I can help you."

"Because of the evidence your precinct provided Alphonso, we can now make our first arrest. We are doing all we can to keep this arrest out of the news media until we make a second arrest."

"This office discovered the gun that was used in this crime. We need the gun transported, or a picture of the firearm sent to the police department in Fairbanks," said Jacoby.

"The standard procedure is to take a picture of the gun and not transport the firearm unless the police department personnel transport that evidence in person," said Shelia.

"We would also transport the gun if there is a trial."

"We have the contact information in Fairbanks that you will need to transport that information," said Karen.

"I would like to get my Captain in on this process. If you would wait here a minute and let me see if he is in his office." Shelia walked to Captain Ray's office and knocked on the door. "It is Shelia, Captain Ray." "Come on in." He was just finishing up a phone call.

"I have two attorneys in my office from Soco & Soco, and they want us to coordinate with Fairbanks, Alaska police to either send a picture or the actual gun we found in the Daniel case. I would like to bring them to your office."

"Why don't we just walk back to your office," said Ray.

They walked back to Shelia's office. "Attorney's Jason and Karen this is Captain Ray."

"Nice to meet you both. Shelia has explained to me your request, and we will be more than happy to comply. So, Elliott is the person who killed this guy Daniel," said Ray.

"All the evidence we have to include the gun you found points to him," replied Jacoby.

"I knew it was something not right about him when he was working here with us, but we could never catch him in the act. Whatever we can do to help to put away this bad officer we will gladly assist."

"The procedure as Shelia has already told you is to take a picture of the gun and send it to the requesting police department. I am thinking about taking that evidence myself, just to laugh in Elliott's face. I guess that would not be right. I am going back to my office. Shelia knows what to do. It was nice meeting you both."

"Captain, Alphonso wanted me to relay to you and the entire law firm of Soco & Soco, what an excellent staff you have here, especially Detective Shelia and Forensic Specialist Kenneth. If it had not been for these two outstanding officers and your precinct, this case would not have been solved so quickly."

"Thank you for those kind words we do our best here. If we don't, it could cost someone their life," replied Ray. "If you give me the information of where to send the evidence, we will get it their today," said Shelia.

"Elliott will not be arrested until tomorrow and as I said we need to keep this out of the news media until all arrest have been made. We don't want anyone fleeing the country," said Jacoby. "Again, we appreciate all the help this precinct has provided in helping to solve this case."

"Just as the Captain said we are glad to see Elliott is getting what is coming to him for all the dirt he did while working in this precinct and this community. What else can I do for you?"

"That is all. I will walk you both back to the reception area."

Alphonso was now resting comfortably in his room after a nice lunch with Darnell. He has a meeting with Connie tomorrow, so he was reviewing the police, autopsy and Q'UP reports again to see if he missed anything. There were papers laid out all over the bed. A call was incoming to his cell phone, and he had to search for it under those papers. Once found he recognized it as an Alaskan number, but not one, he calls on a regular basis.

"Hello this is Alphonso; how can I help you?"

"Well hello, Mr. Alphonso this is Jocelyn. I thought I would give you a call and see how your trip is going."

"Wow, what a surprise did not expect you to call. My trip is going well, as a matter of fact, I am hoping to return home in a few days."

"How are things going with you?"

"Today is a slow day at the airport, so I thought I would give you a call to see if you would like to have lunch or dinner sometime when you return."

"Yes, I would love to."

"Give me a call at this number when you get back to Fairbanks. I must get back to work. Will talk to you soon. Goodbye."

That was a surprise, and I will call Jocelyn when I get back home Alphonso said out loud.

CHAPTER 28

WHO WOULD HAVE THOUGHT

I am so thankful this case is almost over. Looks like I am going to have a social life when I get back to Fairbanks, after the phone call I received from Jocelyn. Today is my last interview which is with Connie. She lives in Falls Church Virginia. It would generally take about twenty minutes to drive there. But everyone I talk to has told me it will probably take an hour because of the traffic. I will take a shower and get breakfast so that I can leave the hotel early.

I am going to miss this hotel and the excellent food they serve in the restaurant. My favorite meal is breakfast. "Good morning Ms. Gina." "Good morning Mr. Alphonso. How has your stay been here at the hotel?" "This has been the best hotel I have ever stayed in. And to top it off the food and service has been superb."

"Thank you for those gracious comments. What can I get you this morning?"

"I would like some coffee, a bagel with cream cheese, and a side of turkey bacon."

"I will be right back with your order and coffee."

"Thank you." Within minutes Gina brought my coffee with the bagel and bacon.

"Can I get you anything else, Mr. Alphonso?" "No, that will be all."

He sat for about twenty minutes enjoying his breakfast. Gina, the waitress, came back to his table to see how he was doing.

"How is everything and can I get you anything else?" "Food and coffee are always excellent. You can bring the check."

"I have the check right here if you are ready to check out." Alphonso paid the bill in cash, and gave the waitress a tip, then went back to his room. It is now eight-thirty a.m. I will brush my teeth, get my jacket, laptop and be on my way to the interview.

Alphonso left his room, stopped to get a cup of the fusion water on the first floor and then went out to his car.

While riding in the car, he was thinking about the conversation he had with Connie on the phone yesterday. She did not ask for a lawyer to be present or even question why I wanted to talk to her. I found that strange. Alphonso cell phone is now ringing.

"Hello, Alphonso, this is Jermaine."

"Good morning Jermaine why are you up so early. I know it is around four-thirty a.m. in Fairbanks. Are you calling to fire me or are you calling to tell me Soco is giving me a raise and an all-expense paid honeymoon?" "Alphonso, it is too early for jokes."

"It must be important if you are calling me."

"You are absolutely right this is an important phone call. I went with the police at three-forty-five this morning to arrest Elliott. This time was an assurance the news media would not be around."

"You know there is always someone around with a phone camera," said Alphonso.

"We did not see anyone. The cell phone and Q'UP report were confiscated. He did not resist, and It appears he was expecting us. It is hard to believe he kept that report all this time."

"That is excellent news, Jermaine. The question I would ask is how did he get a copy of that report?"

"Alphonso, I believe before the day is over, we will know the answer to that question and many more."

"Jason will go down to the police department later this morning and sit in on the interrogation of Elliott to ensure we get all the answers we need. Hopefully, he will confess."

"I salute you and Fairbanks finest for doing such a great job, and I am confident this case will be solved this week."

"Jermaine thank you for the update, but I have another call coming in. Talk to you later."

"Hello, Alphonso this is Captain Royster. How are you doing this morning?"

"Doing great, and you must be doing great as well because you are up early."

"A normal day for me starts at seven a.m. I just call to let you know we got the warrant signed by the judge, and we just exercised it by seizing Paul's cell phone. We are taking It back to the office to find that information you requested," said Royster.

"How did Paul react when you served him the warrant." "He was surprised, but appeared to be innocent."

"I do think he is innocent, but I believe he is friends with Elliott who is not so innocent. Another piece of the puzzle solved for this case."

"It has really been great working with you on this case. I must admit we missed obvious clues during the initial investigation of this case." "Captain, that's the one thing about this business we live and learn each, and everyday. We win some and lose some. Thank you again for the information, and you have a great rest of the day."

Alphonso reached the exit for Connie's condo, and it was now ten minutes before his appointment. I will take five minutes in the car to digest all the news I just received. Alphonso exited his vehicle and went to knock on Connie's door. She did not come to the door right away, as a matter of fact, I stood there for a few minutes before she opens the door. "Hello, Mr. Alphonso come on in. I received a call before you arrived about one of my patients. Did not mean to keep you waiting." "No problem and how are you doing," said Alphonso.

"I am doing wonderful, just glad to have a day off from work. Let's go into the living room where we can be comfortable."

"Before we get started with questions, there are a few administrative things we have to do. First I must identify myself by showing you my identification." Alphonso displayed his identification to Connie. "Second, I need to make a statement about my employer and the purpose of my visit for the record. My name is Alphonso, I work for Soco & Soco law firm out of Alaska. We were retained to reopen the three-year-old case of Daniel's suicide. You are being interviewed because you are a person of interest."

"Third you must sign this document that you refuse to have a lawyer present, you did not want to go to the police department to talk, you wanted to have this interview in your home and you agreed that I can record our conversation. Is all that true?" Asked Alphonso.

"Yes, I agree," said Connie.

Connie signed the document and Alphonso signed under her name. "Now we can begin with the questions. Have I stated to you my purpose for interviewing you clearly?"

"Yes, you have."

"Is this your current residence and if so, state the address for the record."

"Yes, this is my current address and it is 679 Long St Falls Church, Virginia."

"Who is your current employer and how long have you been employed there?"

"I am currently a family physician at Washington Medical Center, and I have been employed there for five years."

"How long have you known Landon and how did you meet?"

"I have known him about three years, and we met at an Italian restaurant downtown called Le'Diplomate."

"Would you say that the two of you are in love?"

"I am deeply in love with Landon, but not sure if he loves me."
"So, you can't be sure that he feels the same as you."

"That is true, I guess." Connie hesitated with giving her answer.

"Did you ever meet Landon's sister and what type relationship do you have with her?"

"Yes, I have seen her on several occasions. We don't really have a relationship. I like her, and I think she likes me."

"Have you met Landon's mother and what was your impression of her?"

"Yes, I met her for the first time since she is now visiting Landon. She is a sweet, concerned mother about her children. I like her a lot. Daniel was a lucky man to have had such a wonderful wife."

"How does she feel about you?"

"Her actions and vibes say she likes me, but she wants Landon to get married so she can have some grandchildren sooner than later."

"How well did you know Landon's father?"

"I did not know him that well, but Landon and I had lunch and dinner with him on several occasions."

"What did he think about you?"

"The first time I met him, he made me feel very nervous."
"Why was that?"

"He and Landon were very close, and he asked me a lot of questions as though he was investigating me. I did not like it."

"Landon had to make him stop. But after that first meeting, and subsequent other times he was cordial toward me."

"Is there anything you would say that you learned about Daniel that other people may not know?"

"He loved wine, and I assumed Pinot Noir was his favorite because he would order it each time Landon and I were out with him for dinner." "Do you drink wine?"

"Yes, I do, occasionally, but I don't have a favorite, I just like almost any type of white wine."

"Where do you normally purchase your wine?"

"There is a neighborhood wine store about three blocks from my condo." "Did you know that Daniel was having an affair?"

"Yes, I saw him on several occasions with another woman acting in a way that people who are in love would act."

"Did you tell Landon about the affair if not do you think he knew?" "No, I didn't tell him, but on several occasions, he had called me after visiting with his father, and he would be upset with him."

"Did you talk to Landon on the day before his father was found dead and if so, what was it about?"

"Yes, I did. Landon was going to confront him about something for the last time, but he did not say what."

"Have you ever talked to Landon's father without him being present?" She hesitated. "Yes, I have called Daniel on several occasions even though I don't think he liked me. It was just to see how he was doing since he was away from home more than most people."

"In any of those conversations did he ever mention he was a diabetic?"

Connie hesitated again." Is there something wrong Connie?" "No, nothing is wrong. Yes, Daniel did mention it to me." "Did you let Landon know he was a diabetic?"

"No, because he asked me not to mention it to him. He thought Landon would tell his sister Kathleen, and they both would worry."

"Do you have any diabetic patients?"

"There are diabetic patients at the hospital that I do treat." "Have you ever had to administer insulin to any of them?" "Yes, I have on several occasions."

"What could happen to a patient if they exceeded the recommended medical dosage of insulin?"

"They could go into shock or even die if medical care is not quickly given."

"When you say shock, do you mean a coma-like state?" "I guess you could call it that."

"Have you ever been in the DoubleTree hotel?"

"Yes, I had lunch and dinner there with Landon and his father on multiple occasions."

"Do you know if the DoubleTree has security cameras?"

"I would think so because most hotels I have stayed in have them."

"Do you know, or have you ever treated any of the staff at the DoubleTree?"

"I don't know him personally, but Paul, the security manager is a friend of my father, and they play golf together. I have been at my father's home a couple of times when he was visiting. I have never treated any patients at the DoubleTree."

"Would you say that part of Paul's job is to monitor security cameras?" "I guess if he is the security manager that would be one of his duties."

"Do you think that sometimes when one person loves another, that they will go to any lengths to protect them?"

"I guess in the case of trying to save someone's life, people do things without thinking."

"Do you think people do things for people they love for their acceptance?" "I am not sure what you mean."

"Did you not want to be accepted by Landon's father, when you knew or felt he did not like you."

"From some of the comments you have made today, it appears Daniel thought you were not the one for his son. He could have been turning Landon against you?"

"No, that is not true," Connie said frantically.

"We know from Daniel's phone records on the day he was found dead he called you."

Connie was angry and quiet at this point and hesitated to answer. "Yes, he did call me."

"And what was the purpose of this call?"

"His blood glucose level was lower than it had ever been. He was out of insulin and asked if I could bring him some until he could get to the doctor. He did not think he would make it through the night."

"What did you do?"

"I told him that I would bring it to him."

"What did you think about this man who did not like you and now he was calling on you for help?"

"I did not like it, and he did not want me to inform Landon. He knew I had access to insulin at the hospital. I went to the location where we stored it and got the insulin for him."

"What could have happened to him if you did not get the insulin?"

"He could have gone into a coma or died."

"Did you make the hospital pharmacy aware that you were taking insulin offsite for someone who was not your patient?"

"No, I did not think about it at the time. I was thinking about Landon and did not want anything to happen to his father."

"Did you do anything else before you went to the hotel with the insulin?" "No, I did not."

"Earlier you told me there was a wine store three blocks from your condo, but there is also a wine store two blocks from the hospital where you work. Your credit card records show that you purchased a bottle of Daniel's favorite wine at the wine store near the hospital the day he died." "Did you think by bringing him the insulin and his favorite wine that he would accept you as a good person for his son?"

"Connie was now in tears and trembling."

"I did everything I could to show Daniel I was a good person, even being a doctor was not good enough for his son. There was nothing he could say about being a good person. Look at how he cheated on his own wife."

"When I went to his hotel room with the insulin, he went into the bathroom to give himself a shot to bring his glucose level up. I injected a massive dosage of insulin in the wine that would cause his glucose level to reach so high he would go into a coma."

"When he opened the bottle of wine and had a drink, right away he would have coma-like symptoms such as dry mouth, increased thirst, stomach pain, and some other symptoms before going into a coma. I thought that since he been a diabetic for a while that he would know to call 911, but he must have drunk at least half of the wine and went into a coma right away." Connie said in an angry tone.

"Stop talking, you have just admitted that you intended to murder Daniel. I have to make a phone call and get some advice." Alphonso called Darnell and let him know what just happen. Darnell called Captain Royster at the police department and made him aware of what had just happened. Darnell called Alphonso back.

"Alphonso, Captain Royster was in the area when I called him and he will be there in five minutes to arrest Connie. Stay there until he arrives and let her know what is about to happen. Ask her if she would like to call her lawyer?"

"Thanks, will do," said Alphonso.

"Connie this might be a good time to call your lawyer. The police are on their way here to arrest you."

Connie starts crying uncontrollably. "I don't have a lawyer. The only lawyer I know is Landon, and I can't call him."

"I know what I did was wrong, and I thought I had gotten away with it. I hope Landon and his family can find in their hearts to forgive me and not hate me. I just wanted to be accepted by his father." Connie is still crying.

"Is there someone you need to call?"

"Yes, I need to call my parents, they will get me a lawyer." Connie retrieved her cell phone and called her parents. Her dad answered the phone. "Hello, Connie how are you doing?" Said Robert. Connie immediately started crying again.

"Dad, I am sorry I've disappointed you and mom, but I have done something terrible. Can you meet me at the seventeenth police precinct downtown?"

"Connie, why are you crying honey and why do we need to meet you at the precinct?"

"Dad, I can't talk right now, but just meet me there. Goodbye." Connie continues to cry.

"Connie, you have to pull yourself together," said Alphonso.

"Why should I stop crying. I have ruined my entire life and all that my parents have sacrificed for me. All because I wanted to be accepted by someone, who was never going to accept me. I will lose the one and only man I have ever loved, and that is Landon. All I did was prove Daniel to be right about me."

As Connie continued to cry, there was a knock at the door. Alphonso, open the door. It was Captain Royster and one other officer. Captain Royster came in and read Connie the Miranda rights and asked her if she understood.

"Yes, I understand." Before we go, can someone get the keys to my condo, so I can give them to my parents."

The Captain retrieved her keys and cell phone. The detective handcuffed her, and they all walked outside to the police car. Connie was put in the back seat of the police car, and they all headed to the police department.

After Alphonso got into his car and was following the Captain, his phone rang, and it was Darnell.

"How did it go."

"Connie is now in custody and in route to the police department. She was terribly emotional and does not have a lawyer, but she did call her parents and asked them to meet her at the station. Can you also come down to the station Darnell?"

"I am already in the car headed that way. By the way, I got a call from Jason from the precinct in Alaska."

"Jason said after they got into the middle of interrogating Elliott, he confessed to everything. He told the detectives that Paul, and he was friends and that sometimes they went out for drinks.

In one of their conversations Paul mentioned the software upgrade, and he knew the cameras would be down. It made it easy to get in and out Daniel's room. He did not know that Daniel was in a coma when he shot him. Daniel had the AllTuck report pulled up on his laptop, so Elliott sent himself a copy to his cellphone and then deleted it from Daniel's laptop." "Elliott did not know Daniel had already emailed the report to his boss at Q'UP, and It was his idea to kill Daniel. Somehow in the mix of things Madison fell in love with Daniel."

"I found out from Captain Royster that Paul had called Elliott soon after he finished his interview with you. Elliott also confessed that it was Madison's idea to kill her own brother Sergeant Scott, to protect her boss Matthew and to keep her job. Elliott and Sergeant Major Rick were in on tampering with Scott's military issued firearm so it would look like an accident when he was cleaning it."

"Rick was getting a financial kickback from Matthew at AllTuck, for not reporting the bad barcode software."

"That is bribery for Matthew and Sergeant Major Rick. Getting rid of Daniel would stop him from reporting the findings of the software." "Madison has also been arrested and pleaded guilty," said Darnell. I had a conference call with the commander and deputy commander at the military base. They are in the process of arresting Sergeant Major Rick. We need to finish the draft letter I started for the commander and attach all the evidence to it, as soon as we get back to the office."

"The Commander said they are going to do some type medal of valor and compensation for Scott's parents, which I think is great."

"I suggest we get on a conference call with Johnny, Landon, Violet, and Kathleen before all this hit the news media, Alphonso."

"I did promise Peter, Daniel's boss and Narvell at the Pentagon I would inform them when this case comes to a closure and before it is reported to the media."

"We can make individual calls to them after the conference call with Daniel's family," noted Darnell.

"Alphonso this was a massive cover-up of a company love of money. They could not do the right thing for soldiers who put their lives on the line for the country each, and every day. I want to thank you again for all the hard work you did to bring justice to this case. You need to take some time off when you get back to Alaska."

"That is already in my plans. Darnell, you know I usually feel good when we solve a case. But this time I am sad. So many people's lives have been affected by this crime, and it was all for the love of money, power, and acceptance."

"You would not be human if you did not have some sympathetic feelings. Justice sometimes hurts more people than it helps. If we feel like we have done the right thing to bring justice, then we are okay."

Darnell and Alphonso pulled up at the police department at the same time as the Captain, and they all entered the precinct together. The detective carried Connie to the interrogation room to take her statement. Captain Royster, Darnell, and Alphonso went to his office. Sitting outside the Captains' office waiting was Connie's parents Robert and Sharon and their lawyer Jay. Robert got up when he saw the Captain.

"Where is my daughter?"

"Will everyone come into my office. Please sit down. My name is Captain Royster, and this is Attorney Darnell and investigator Alphonso from Soco & Soco law firm. Connie is in the interrogation room giving her confession."

"Why is she giving a confession without her lawyer present?" asked Jay. "She did not want a lawyer present when she confessed to investigator Alphonso in an interview."

"What has she confessed to doing?" Asked Sharon.

"Connie has been charged with giving a fatal dosage of insulin to a victim who died three years ago at the DoubleTree hotel. Attorney Darnell and investigator Alphonso have been working on this case for several weeks at the request of the deceased family."

"Sharon and I remember that case, and this department ruled it a suicide." "It has been proven that we were wrong at the time the incident happened. Your daughter confessed today that she thought she had gotten away with the murder."

"Why would she do that?" Said Sharon.

"She was dating the victim son Landon, and according to Connie, Landon's father never accepted her to be good enough for his son."

"We met Landon, the lawyer, he is such a nice man. We thought they might get married and we would have grandchildren. I guess that won't happen now?" Expressed Sharon.

"Darnell if you and Alphonso will wait here in the office, I will take Connie's parents and their lawyer to speak with her." The Captain led Robert, Sharon, and Jay to see Connie.

"I am going to call Jason while we are waiting," said Darnell. Jason was sitting in his office thinking about what they should do next when his phone rang.

"Hello, Darnell. What's going on in Washington DC."

"Alphonso and I are at the police precinct. As I told you earlier, Connie confessed, and we have already notified the military commander of our findings."

"They have made their arrest of Sergeant Major Rick. What we need you to do is contact Johnny, Landon, Violet, and Kathleen and see if we can have a conference call at four p.m. We want to notify them before this gets in the news. If you don't call me back, I know, it's a go."

"Darnell this is a good idea. Talk to you guys later," said Jason. "Alphonso you know this has been the most straightforward case as for as suspects confessing. There is no trial, and all the judge must do is give sentencing."

"You are absolutely right Darnell. I wish all our cases were like this one."

Captain Royster, Attorney Jay, and Connie's parents Robert and Sharon entered the interrogation room where Connie was being held.

"Connie honey how are you doing?" Asked Sharon.

Sharon and Robert were allowed to give Connie a hug. "Mother and Daddy, I am doing okay. Everyone has treated me nice."

"This is a three-year-old case reopen by the victim's family. The victims' death was ruled a suicide. We found out today that was not the truth. The second person involved in this case shot the victim in the head not knowing he was already dead from the over dosage of insulin administered by Connie," said Royster.

"How can two people kill one person?" Said Jay.

"I just explained to you what happened. Both Connie and the other accuser had intent."

"Connie is the Captain telling the truth?"

"Yes. I did confess, and I signed a statement. There is no need for a lawyer. I intended to kill Daniel. He would not accept me as a person good enough to date his son."

"Connie honey you did not have to kill someone for acceptance. You are a wonderful person of whom any father or mother would be proud to have as a daughter-in-law. I wish you had talked to me," said Sharon.

"Mother, I know now I should have talked to you." "What happens next?" Asked Jay.

"We have provided the judge with all the information, and there will be no trial. Connie will go before the judge tomorrow for a sentencing hearing. The second accuser will also go before a judge in Alaska tomorrow."

"Connie will be in lockup so there will be no bail. If everyone would just follow me back to my office."

"Connie, I love you baby."

"Mom, I love you too." Connie's parents were allowed to hug her one last time. Everyone followed Royster back to his office.

They were all now back, seated in the captain's office. "Darnell now that your law firm has solved this case what is your next step?" Asked Attorney Jay.

"We have a conference call with the family of the deceased at four p.m. today at our office. A press conference will be held at six p.m. today to let the public know this case has been solved. At that time, we will have to reveal the names of the accusers."

"Everyone in the country will know that our daughter a medical doctor killed someone. I don't know how to handle this. What are our friends and neighbors going to think about us?" Said Sharon.

"I don't care about the neighbors and friends. I am thinking about how my daughter will survive in jail. She could possibly be there the rest of her life," said Robert.

"Jay, you and Connie's parents can attend the sentencing if you wish."

"If there is nothing else we can do here, myself and Connie's parents will leave," said Jay.

"I am truly sorry for what has happened to your daughter. If we can answer any other questions, please feel free to call. I gave each of you my card which is my direct number," said Captain Royster.

"Alphonso and I will be going to the office for our conference call and we will see you later today for the press conference."

Darnell and Alphonso left the precinct in their separate cars. They both arrived at Soco office around three-thirty p.m. As they walked into Soco building, Bethany approached them.

"Everything is set up for the conference call." They went directly to the conference room, and Landon was sitting waiting for them.

"Hello, Landon. I am sorry we have to notify your family members this way about the case, but we wanted you all to know before it hit the news this afternoon," said Darnell.

"Alphonso has done an awesome job in investigating this case and finding all the evidence we need to bring this case to closure. There is probably going to be some surprises on this call Landon, so be prepared."

"All of the Soco brothers will be on the call today, Johnny your uncle, and of course your mother and sister. Are you ready?"

"Yes, I am," said Landon. The first callers on the conference line were Jacoby and Karen. The last to call in was Kathleen and Violet.

"Hello everyone, I am Darnell and will be the spokesperson for the call. I want to thank each of the family members of Daniel for consenting to have a conference call today with the firm of Soco & Soco. It has been an honor that you chose our firm to bring resolution to Daniel's case after three years."

"We would like to explain everything to you first, and then answer questions afterward."

"There will be a press conference today at six p.m. to disclose our findings and the closure of this case, which will include the names of the accusers. Landon, you are welcome to attend. I will start the disclosure by stating that Johnny who is Daniel's brother came to our Alaska office and asked the firm to reopen the case."

"At that time, we told him that the only way to completely solve this case was to have an autopsy done. That consent to exhume Daniel's body and perform an autopsy came from Violet. We put Alphonso, the best investigator this firm has on the case. During this investigation, a lot of people have willingly helped us."

"Those include Atlanta Police department, Soco Atlanta, Soco Washington, Soco Alaska, Delta Junction police department, police departments from Fairbanks, Washington DC and Atlanta, AllTuck Company, Q'UP Daniel's employer, and the military."

349

"To ease everyone's mind, we found that Daniel did not commit suicide. It turns out there were five people involved in his death. Some of them you know and others you may not."

"Daniel was investigating a company called AllTuck. The military awarded them a billion-dollar contract to develop barcode pricing software for military exchange stores. Daniel found out that every other time a military soldier or their family member purchased an item at the exchange store the price of the item, automatically increased. AllTuck CEO Michael and Madison who was one of their Software Engineering Managers was responsible for the development and implementation of this software."

"A smart and very observant Sergeant Scott who was Madison's brother discovered there was a glitch with the software. Scott reported this problem to his superior Sergeant Major Rick. You Would Have Thought that Rick would have reported this problem to his superior, but he did not."

"Instead, Michael made a financial deal with Sergeant Major Rick better known as a bribe to allow AllTuck enough time to fix the problem."

"Madison and Michael figured out that AllTuck would lose billions if this story were to get out to the news media. Madison as you may now know Violet is your best friend who lives in Delta Junction with her mother. She met a police officer by the name of Elliott and befriended him in Atlanta. Madison became romantically involved with

Daniel. Violet this is something we did not want to tell you, but it is part of an equation that has led to your husband's death."

"Scott shared information he knew about AllTuck with Daniel. Madison found out about this and shared it with Elliott. Madison and Elliott worked with Sergeant Major Rick and rigged Scott's military weapon to fire when he cleaned it. This made it look like Scott accidentally killed himself."

"Madison and Elliott were also responsible for Daniel's death. By killing him, the report would not get filed about the software glitch, but Daniel submitted his report before he was killed."

"The last person involved in this case is Connie, whom Landon is currently dating. She is indeed more in love with you than you know Landon. Connie believed that Daniel thought, she was not suitable enough to be involved with you. Connie was very protective of Landon and had seen Daniel with Madison on several occasions. She thought the relationship Daniel was having with Madison was really upsetting Landon, so she felt she must protect him."

"Connie found out that Daniel was a diabetic through one of their phone conversations and knew that he was taking insulin. She also knew that Daniel did not want his family to know he was diabetic. On the evening that Landon visited his father, Daniel called Connie to get some insulin, because he had run out. Connie consented to bring it to him at the DoubleTree several hours before Landon visited with him.

351

Connie also knew what favorite wine that Daniel liked, so on that same day she purchased his favorite."

"When she arrived in his room, she presented the wine to him. Connie also pleaded with Daniel to not turn Landon against her, but he would not listen."

"Daniel went to the bathroom to give himself a shot of the insulin that would normalize his glucose level. While in the bathroom, Connie used a syringe and put a lethal dosage of insulin in the wine that would put Daniel in a coma or kill him. Being a doctor, she knew the exact amount to give him."

"Daniel did not drink the wine until after the visit with Landon was over. So, Daniel was dead from the insulin and just lying on the bed like he was sleep. Then Elliott came to his room after Landon left and shot Daniel in the forehead, not knowing he was already dead. So, Daniel was actually killed twice."

"We have informed the military of Madison, Elliott, and Sergeant Major Rick involvement in the death of Scott. Elliott, Connie, Madison, and Matthew are already in custody of the police. All five of these people pleaded guilty to murder and bribery. Neither of them will get bail, nor will they have a trial, but they all will go before a judge for a sentencing hearing except Major Rick."

"Sergeant Major Rick will go before a military court because we have no jurisdiction. In summary, there were five people involved in

Daniel's death. I thank each of you for listening to all the evidence and circumstances behind this case."

"We will notify Daniels manager after this call because we promised him, we would. I am so sorry that Daniels family had to go through this investigation twice. I hope that some closure will come for each of you after today, and are there any questions or comments?"

"I would like to thank Soco & Soco law firm and all those who worked with you to prove that my brother did not commit suicide. I felt in my heart all these years, the Daniel I knew would not bring harm to himself. Violet, I am sorry we had to have Daniel's body exhumed, but it was necessary to get the outcome we have heard today.

Landon and Kathleen, I know that both of you loved your father as much or more as I did. I am so sorry you will not be able to enjoy your adult years with him. But you both have already made him, your mother and me proud, by how you have handled this entire situation. Both of you are successful in your individual careers. I also hope that you can find in your heart to forgive me for taking you through this again," said Johnny. "I want to also thank Soco & Soco law firm for bringing my husband's case to closure. Johnny thank you for having faith and wanting resolution. I believe we can all get on with our lives now," stated Violet. "Alphonso, I ask you to forgive me for my actions, for I know now that you were doing all you could to bring justice to my father's case. I thank my Soco family for putting the best resources we have in this firm to solve this case. I am proud to be one of your lawyers," expressed Landon.

"If there are no more questions or comments. I thank everyone again and have a nice day." Everyone hung up from the call.

"Landon are you okay?" Said Darnell.

"No, I am not. 'WHO WOULD HAVE THOUGHT' Connie would kill my father just because she thought he did not like or accept her," said Landon.

"Landon the last thing Connie said to us, she hopes you and your family would forgive and not hate her," stated Alphonso.

"Landon, you coming to the press conference?" Said Darnell.

"No, I am going to skip it. I need to process all this. My mother's best friend help to plot and kill my father and her own brother. What kind of person is that? Darnell, I need to take some time off maybe a couple of weeks. I am going to fly down to Atlanta this evening. I hope my sister and I can talk mother into moving closer to where we are."

"Take all the time you need," said Darnell.

"Alphonso thank you for all the investigating you did, and I did not intend to give you such a hard time."

"If it were my father, I would have done the same thing maybe worst." "I am going to shut things down in my office, go home pack a bag and get a flight to Atlanta."

"We will see you when you are ready to come back. Keep in touch," said Darnell in a fatherly voice.

"Alphonso why don't you make those last two phone calls. I need to run to the bathroom and to my office for a minute."

Alphonso decided he was going to make one call to Peter and Narvell via a three-way call. He flipped through his phone and found Peter number and then Narvell. He dialed Peter first, and he picked up on the first ring.

"Hello, Alphonso."

"Hello, Peter, can you talk for a minute?" "Yes, now is a good time."

"Can you hold on one second, I am going to get Narvell from the Pentagon on the line with us. What I have to say is the same for both of you."

He dialed Narvell and got him on the first ring as well. "Hello Narvell, this is Alphonso, I am going to put you on a three-way with Peter from Q'UP. Are both of you their Peter and Narvell." Peter and Narvell said yes in unison.

"I just call to give both of you the update on the case. Today Elliott the police officer, Michael from AllTuck, Madison who was Daniel's mistress, Connie who was Landon's girlfriend, and Sergeant Major Rick were arrested for Daniel and Sergeant Scott deaths."

"There will be a press conference today at six p.m., and you will see all the details. Like I told you both earlier, I would brief you concerning the closure of this case before it hits the news."

"Alphonso, thank you and your firm for working so diligently on behalf of Daniel and his family," said Peter.

"Thank both of you for all the input you provided for this case as well." "If you are ever in the area again, give me a call," said Narvell.

"Will do. I have to get to that press conference, so I am going to say goodbye to both of you."

Darnell was now back in the conference room." Are you ready to head down to the precinct for the news conference," said Darnell.

"Yes, I am ready. Glad this is almost over."

"Alphonso since you have gotten so familiar with this city why don't you drive."

Landon went out to the parking lot, got in his car and headed for home. While he was driving, he started thinking about Connie. I really did care a lot about her, and I see now that I did not show her how much. If she had known that it did not matter what my father thought about her. But it is too late now. I feel sorry for her parents because she was an only child.

He arrived home in record time. As soon as he parked the car in the garage and walked inside the house his phone was ringing.

"Hello, Kathleen, I was just walking in the house. How are you and mother doing?"

"We are okay. I am sorry about Connie. Mother and I had a talk after we got off the conference call. She has decided that she is going to move to Atlanta with me."

"That is the best news I have heard in weeks."

"After she heard what Madison did, and she was supposed to be her best friend, she decided it is time to leave Alaska. I have decided that I am going to take two weeks off work, go back to Delta Junction with her and help her get some things packed and put the house up for sale."

"I am going with you, to help her get her affairs in order. I just told Darnell I was going to take two weeks off work and he told me to take all the time I needed. I also want to spend some time with uncle Johnny when we get there."

"I want to do that as well. Johnny is the only uncle we have."

"I am going to fly down to Atlanta tomorrow morning, and we can all fly to Alaska together."

"Mother is sleeping right now. I will let her know when she wakes up. I know she will be happy we are all flying back to Alaska together. See you tomorrow. Love you, Landon."

"Love you too sis."

A Dream Come True: Who Would Have Thought?

Webster's definition of a dream is a series of thoughts, images, and sensations occurring in a person's mind during sleep. To me, a dream is an accomplishment you reach after a journey of (1) highs and lows, (2) life's curves, hills, and mountains. Sometimes that accomplishment is reachable in days, and sometimes it's not reachable for years. Often, we blame others, but ultimately a dream is something that we have carved out to be the one thing in life I am doing for me. And then we sometimes reach to accomplish a dream no matter what the cost. The two things we forget which are the most important are wisdom and knowledge. Without these, our dreams and accomplishments fail every time. After many years of trying to write this book, I finally figured it out, and I am thankful. "Who Would Have Thought" is my dream come true. I hope everyone who purchase this book enjoys reading it as much as I have enjoyed writing it.

Made in the USA
Columbia, SC
31 March 2019